To Dom,

for all the
years of
friendship
conviviality

Gary

# THE TWOWEEKS

# THE TWOWEEKS

*a novel*

## LARRY DUBERSTEIN

THE PERMANENT PRESS
*Sag Harbor, NY 11963*

For information, address:
    The Permanent Press
    4170 Noyac Road
    Sag Harbor, NY 11963
    www.thepermanentpress.com

*Library of Congress Cataloging-in-Publication Data*

Duberstein, Larry–
    The twoweeks : a novel / Larry Duberstein.
        p. cm.
    ISBN 978-1-57962-224-4 (alk. paper)
    1. Love stories. gsafd  I. Title.

PS3554.U253T96 2012
813'.54—dc23                              2011034626

Printed in the United States of America.

for Lee

# 1

## Snowing in Passumpsic

### (December 26, 2008)

"I gotta pee," said the boy, recently turned four, to his mother.

"You have to hold it till the sign changes. See the picture of a buckle?"

"*Mama.*"

"We're on an airplane, baby. They have different rules."

"I'll take him," said Jake, the boy's father.

"It's not that I wouldn't take him, big guy. It's the seat belt thing."

"Come on, Al," said Jake, hoisting him. "Don't worry, Cissy, I'll get special dispensation from the nice flight attendant."

"I'll bet you will."

"Hon, the kid's gotta go."

"Life can be rough," said Cicely, lightly sarcastic yet delighted in truth to be rid of them both for a few minutes. They scared her sometimes, they were so much alike. Big guy and little guy, 180 pounds and 40 pounds, otherwise identical. And neither could hold his water for five minutes.

She spread her arms, closed her eyes, and listened to the reassuring drone of their passage through the air above America. The flight had been so smooth it made her wonder why the seat belt sign was on. Not that she much cared; sometimes it was easier to accept such things, and pointless to question it all, as Jake did. His sister Hetty was the lawyer in the family but it was

Jake who, in Hetty's words, "ceaselessly and incessantly cross-examines the world." (Indeed, he cross-examined her when she said it: "Ceaseless *and* incessant, Hetto?")

On the ground, inside the terminal at LaGuardia, Jake took the boy again while Cicely waited at the carousel. Jake needed to keep moving, to get it done, whatever it was. Soon enough she would be letting him drive the rental car, because there was nothing worse than allowing him into the passenger seat. Might just as well sign up for the waterboarding as undergo his running account of her every failure of muscle memory at the wheel. It wasn't so much that he was wrong, or even obnoxious, as that he was so *relentless*.

"What's a throg?" said Al.

Twenty minutes earlier, they had crossed the Throgs Neck Bridge, heading toward Connecticut, and since that time the boy had been trying to work this problem through on his own.

"A throg," said Jake, "is a frog with a speech defect."

"Jake," said Cicely.

"What's a speech defect?" said Al.

"Thatsh when you can't shpeak normal."

"Normally," said Cicely, correcting his grammar, before chiding his political incorrectness as well.

"But I *can* speak normally," said Al, enunciating carefully.

"So there you are, bud. You're not a throg."

They were passing through Fairfield, half an hour later, before he spoke again. "Mama, he didn't ever tell me what's a throg. He just kidded me."

"He doesn't know, baby."

"*You* tell me, then."

"I don't know either. It's kind of a mystery, actually."

"Does Grandpa know?"

She laughed. "Your grandpa knows the same way your daddy knows. He will answer the question, it just won't be a real answer. But we can ask him, if you want, when we get there."

"Will Aunt Hetty know? She's the smart one, right?"

"We'll ask everyone we see until we get to the bottom of the mystery, okay?"

The boy was doing well. They had left Oregon in the pre-dawn dark, flown six hours, and now were driving another five, with stops in Rhode Island and New Hampshire. Long before they reached their destination in Vermont it would again be dark.

They would wait to eat, though, as Grandpa Cal was making his special spaghetti and a banana cream pie for his "favorite grandson." Al was crazy for the banana pie, and he had reveled in the favorite grandson status until the day last summer when he realized he was the only grandson. He demanded a new title then (Favorite Grandkid) to make clear that his cousin Lorna did not compare in importance.

"Absolutely," Grandpa Cal readily conceded. "You are my favorite—you and Lorna, tied for the gold."

With that he had scooped them both up and raced downhill to the pond, where he stood them up on the splintery old table and raised their right arms in triumph. "The gold!" he declared, and Al was appeased, even if the definitions were not as precise as they might be. The truth was he liked Cousin Lorna so much he almost didn't mind that Grandpa liked her too.

They made good time to Providence, where Jake's sister Hetty, cousin Lorna's mother, lived with her husband Carlos. Carlos wasn't coming with them, though, which seemed highly suspicious to Al. "*Brazil?*" he shouted, as though the very word was a joke. How could Uncle Carlos be in Brazil at Christmas time? And if that wasn't bad enough, Lorna was bringing two suitcases, instead of the one-each allowed on airplanes.

"Our child needs to eat something," said Cicely.

It was her standard prescription and generally it worked. This time, after an apple, some peanuts, and a juice-box, Al had new issues: "I'm cold," he said, "and I gotta pee."

They peed him, as Jake put it, at a rest stop on 93, after which his mother said, "Al, sweetie, if it's okay with you, we're going to ignore you now for a while."

Ten minutes later, he and Lorna were sound asleep, jumbled together like puppies in the far backseat.

"Peace in the valley," said Cicely, with an involuntary sigh.

"And to maintain that peace," said Jake, "cell phones . . . off."

"I'm not expecting any calls," said Hetty, by way of ignoring his edict. Jake and Cicely disdained cell phones, so the order pertained only to hers.

"You are never *expecting* any calls, they just come, unexpectedly. What time is it in Sao Pãulo?"

"I don't know. Why?"

"Because if Carlos is awake, he is about to call. Unexpectedly."

"Oh, shut up," said Hetty. A lawyer who trafficked in ornate and formal language at times, she was sometimes reduced to more direct expression by her big brother.

"You two stop it," said Cicely. "If they wake up, they wake up. They're not such terrible company."

"Not terrible," said Jake. "Just relentless."

"Oh my, look who's talking," said Cicely softly, amazed (yet not surprised) to hear the very word.

Then quiet; no one talking; the landscape rolling by like film footage.

Winter had come late this year. Asked about the weather back east, Hetty had reported, "It's probably the same as yours—damp, gray, in the forties. Oregon weather." But then it had snowed, enough to submerge the yards, enough to settle on pine boughs along the highway like a million white sleeves. So it was New England weather now, the weather they were all hoping for, white Christmas and all, sledding with Grandpa, snow cones with maple syrup. . . .

Jake and Cicely traveled east fairly often, considering the distance, and they did aim for the calendar photo moments—lilacs in May, lush summer, autumn glory, white Christmas. For Cicely this was storybook stuff, literally. She was an Oregon native, from a "pioneer family," her grandparents liked to say. The phrase had real heft out west, though their claim was slightly divergent:

they were among the first black families in Clackamas County. Some serious pioneering there.

Jake had grown up in New England, had even stayed around for college, and though he knew all about dreary March and damp drizzly November and mud season and black flies, he wanted it to be storybook stuff too, wanted his son to see Vermont at its best. Jake, who had struggled with the idea of bringing a child into a world so badly warped by its addiction to debilitating technology, hoped Al would somehow be drawn to the natural world as powerfully as he had been.

"It's snowing," said Cicely, though the snow looked phony, like TV sitcom snow, with great spaces between the floating snowflakes.

"Not really," said Hetty. "A few flurries, they said."

"Look north, Hetto," said Jake. "Looks real enough to me. And it might be very real in Vermont."

"It isn't even sticking," she pointed out, for it was melting on the windshield and on the heavily traveled highway. But it did start collecting on the roadside and in the woods, and it was sticking everywhere by the time they hit Interstate 89 and started the northwesterly vector toward White River Junction. Farther north, on the two-lane into Hanover, it would be slow, slippery going. The worst, in a way, because it was not yet enough snow to bring the ploughs out. Hoarding their budgets against the long winter to come, hopeful road agents in each small town would be clinging to the weather report Hetty heard the night before: light accumulations, no major concerns.

"We should wake the kids," said Jake.

"I thought your plan was to drug them into a submissive slumber," said Hetty.

"Not drug them, *club* them. But that was then. They'll want to see the snow."

"Oh, I think they'll be seeing it," said Cicely, as they pulled onto the parking patch outside Iris' rented condo in Hanover. "I believe they will see it plenty in the Northeast Kingdom."

"You love to say that, don't you?" said Hetty.

"It is just funny, sister-in-law. This itty bitty place calling itself a *kingdom*? You could put the whole of New England out west somewhere and never find it again."

"Yeah, yeah."

Iris had not finished packing, of course, but she did not want them coming inside with snowy feet. "Give me one minute," she called out from the vestibule, and in his gentlest tone Jake sought clarification ("Clock minute or Iris minute?") just to see her make the face.

Iris astonished each of them, for different reasons. Hetty could not believe that her younger half-sister, who had been a child to her even more so than she herself had been a child to Jake (the good old pecking order), was about to be a doctor. A full-fledged grown-up professional.

To Jake the astonishing aspect was that this particular doctor was going, in six months, to be a Doctor Without Borders. Who needed borders more than Iris Byerly? Borders, boundaries, lines, lists, categories: whatever organized the world, Iris required. They dared not enter her house with wet shoes, knowing the trauma it would engender, and yet she was going off to Namibia or Bolivia, someplace at any rate where she would have no protection from muddy water, contaminated food, tsetse flies for all they knew. From chaos, the opposite of order.

"A doctor without borders?" Jake had said in disbelief, when this plan was unveiled. "Does that mean you get shot at by every faction in every insane conflict everywhere?"

"It means you get protected by every faction, dummy. You're the doctor."

"Well, be sure and wear your blue hospital scrubs at all times, so they *know* you're the doctor."

Cicely's puzzlement had nothing to do with Iris' chosen profession. She simply could not believe that a girl as gorgeous (and as likable) as Iris could be single. Iris' explanation, the first time they spoke about it, was that all the boys she knew were doctors, hence all kings of the world in their own minds, hence no thanks. To which Cicely had responded, "No problem. Come west, girl, we will find you a nice logger, or a fisherman. We've got all kinds. Even some women loggers," she added, just in case, for though there had been no such indications, you had to allow for the possibility.

It had become a joke since then, back and forth long distance, and so the first thing out of Iris' mouth as she slid in next to Cicely in the middle seat was "Where's my logger? I thought you were bringing me a logger."

"Here he comes," said Cicely, as Al dove recklessly over their heads and scrambled down onto Iris' lap.

"Kind of a *little* logger," said Iris, ruffling the boy's shaggy black curls, "but I guess I'll take him."

"Back!" said Cicely, as though taming animals, "back where you came from, you two," and Al and Lorna climbed over and buckled themselves in again.

"We're off," said Jake.

"I gotta pee, Daddy," said Al, unbuckling.

"At least he's house-trained," said Hetty, as Cicely rolled her eyes.

"I'll take him," said Iris.

She took them both, removing their shoes in the small foyer, disappearing inside, and reappearing after a noticeable number of Iris minutes, to begin shoeing them, as Jake put it.

"Warning, captain," said Hetty, while they waited. "Short cell call coming up."

"Carlos is awake?"

"Wrong, bro, not who I'm calling." Then she shushed him, as their father came on the line and she said, "It's us. Or it's me."

"Are you here yet?" said her father.

"Not quite. We are almost being allowed to leave Iris' house. So there's that. But also the storm is slowing us down."

"Storm?"

"Snowstorm, Pop. It's been getting worse by the mile. It's not snowing there?"

"Of course it's snowing here. It's always snowing in Passumpsic. Snow is general over Passumpsic."

"James Joyce?"

"Good for you, kid. Want to try for sixty-four thousand?"

"Sixty-four thousand what?" said Hetty. "Do you want to talk to Jake?"

"I haven't talked to you yet, but no, no more phone. Just get your backsides up here and we can talk all week."

"Sounds a little scary, Pop. We might want to turn back. Just kidding, just kidding."

"You do have Iris?"

"We do. Or she has us. But she is shutting the door behind her as we speak. She is approaching the vehicle. We should be departing Hanover in approximately one minute."

"Clock minute or Iris minute?"

"Clock, I think. Yes: she is now inside the vehicle, she's buckling up, and . . . we're off!"

## 2

# The Backstory

Lara had found the pages she had written shortly after The Twoweeks ended—or not found them so much as excavated them from a folder in a carton in a trunk in the barn. "Who knows why" was what she said (why she had written them, why she had so stored them, why she had extracted them now) but then who-knows-why was more or less Lara's take on life. It was not as if she ever expected an answer to the question.

So they had this unearthed journal, they had the evening at their disposal, and she guessed it would take a couple of hours to read it through, and that had become the plan. Cal had never seen it—never even knew it existed—and Lara, who had not seen it in decades, felt ready to revisit those days in detail. The Twoweeks, after all. It had been a pretty big deal.

He made the fire, she walked the dogs to Hollenbeck's and back, they scrounged up three unfinished bottles of bourbon (yielding perhaps a pint in all) and settled down to start. Lara did start, and managed to get halfway through a sentence before Cal lodged his first objection.

But this was not trial testimony, subject to objection, she was obliged to point out, nor was it a piece of writing subject to correction. It was a journal. "It says whatever it says and there's an end on it."

"That's fine," said Cal. "I wasn't concerned with the end on it, I was concerned with the beginning. You did say you would begin at the beginning."

"I was hoping to. Where else, really?"

As it happened, Cal wanted to begin *before* the beginning, before The Twoweeks. The "backstory," as he kept calling it, would give shades of meaning to the journal itself.

"You haven't read it, Calvert. For all you know, it might already have more shades of meaning than the King James Bible."

Before he spoke, Lara knew exactly what he would say in response, and he did: "We aren't *in* the King James Bible."

He didn't know that either, she nearly countered. Countering would be counter-productive, though, if she wanted to get on with the reading. So she held her tongue.

"Just give me five minutes," he pleaded, tapping her hand-written heading (Day 1) with his index finger and insisting they revisit briefly "the real Day One," the day they met, and perhaps devote another minute or two to the handful of encounters which, taken as a whole, constituted the "genesis" of The Twoweeks.

"Otherwise it's like saying the Civil War began in 1861. Forget about the Missouri Compromise, forget the Dred Scott Decision."

"Cal, the Dred Scott Decision does not come into play here. The Twoweeks is a small matter of insignificant personal history, which happens to have begun on June 22 of that year."

"At the very least, it began on February 22 of that year—a night I recall very clearly, by the way, even if I don't have a little *journal* to prove it."

"This isn't about what we remember, though. It's these pages," she said, riffling them. "Just a dry, factual account of those fourteen days as they unfolded."

"Written words are hardly the same as facts, Lara. And even if they were, facts have no meaning without a context. Context is what gives meaning."

She had fallen partway into the trap; she had started taking him up point for point and was in clear danger of going on with it ad infinitum. "That's nonsense," she wanted badly to say. "Nothing gives meaning, there is no bloody meaning," she had to restrain herself from arguing. But she succeeded. She held her tongue. The only way out is through, someone said in a song. The way up is the way down, T. S. Eliot said in a poem.

"Five minutes," she said. "And I'm holding you to it."

"Five should do it," said Cal.

~

THE FIRST time we actually stood face to face and spoke was on Church Street, near the old Radcliffe Yard. I almost knew your name, you did know mine. You knew a lot about me from Winnie, who would inevitably slip into talking about me and even more so about the kids. Socially we were her default position: Calvert, Jake, and Hetty. She could bore you to death with our exploits.

That was a weekday, a quiet afternoon in the Square, which back then was still a university village, with none of the teeming artificial life it has now—the tourists, suburban kids, spare change guys. The occasional busload of Asians with cameras. None of that back then. It was a student town. Now you only realize that when the hour chimes and herds of students cross Mass. Ave. carrying their Starbucks and chewing on their cell phones.

Elsie's, Tommy's, Buddy's. Hayes-Bickford, the U.R., the S.S. Tasty. There wasn't a single chain store, only one-of-a-kind businesses, each one an institution unto itself. Cronin's, Mr. Bartley's. At least a dozen book stores, half a dozen record stores. The college was at the heart of it all, but none of us were connected to the college anymore, except for your husband—except for Ian. Winnie and I just hadn't left town yet, hadn't figured out a better place to be.

For me it was still a pretty good place just because there was so much theatre, with more opportunities than anywhere outside New York. You and I had that in common: you were writing poems no one read and I was acting in plays no one came to see.

"Hey, I know you," I said, and you said, "Either that or you are being a bit forward."

Which was perfect, it was just like you, with your outmoded genteel airs. Like it's rude to open a conversation without first handing the servant your card in the vestibule and waiting patiently by the cast-iron boot-scraper for a reply. Miss Fiddlestick will see you now.

"Forward or backward, you are still Winnifred's friend Laura. Aren't you?"

"Close enough. And you are Winnifred's husband Calvert. So we've got that all straightened out."

I remember the late afternoon sunshine pouring through the horse chestnut trees behind you, thinking what a splendid day it was, watching your smile become part of that splendor.

"Which way are you headed," I asked, harmlessly, and you said "Paris!" Said it with a sassy top-*that* tone.

"*Well*, then."

"Sorry. Couldn't resist. We aren't actually leaving for a month. Though I did just buy this hugely expensive map," you said, brandishing it.

"So many *arrondissements* to master," I said, giving you the needle. But you didn't deflate. Didn't feel the needle.

"I've yet to set foot in a single *arrondissement*. Have you been there?"

"I was there a few years ago, at a very bad time. 1969, when the gendarmes were extremely hostile toward anyone carrying a guitar or a book. Or who needed a haircut, in their view. The policy was more or less, Eh, François, why not whack these kids upside the heads with our nifty billy clubs."

"You could use one now, actually. A haircut, that is."

"Who is being forward this time?"

"Sorry. Couldn't resist. So how long were you there?"

"Too long. We had made the mistake of assuming we'd love it. Have a blast and want to stay as long as we could."

I was beginning to register your face, to get a bead on the offbeat beauty, how it worked. Beautiful would not have been the word, if you had pressed me on the spot. Interesting, maybe. *Original* could easily be the word. I wasn't felled like a tree or anything, I just found myself enjoying the occasion because of this wonderful original sunny face and the slightly challenging comic spirit that came with the face.

It crossed my mind to suggest a cup of coffee, but that felt like the wrong thing. A shift of venues, from sunshine to shadow, or a shift in the pace we had fallen into would not have worked out. And there were parameters: neither of us was eager to leave, yet we both sensed it was time. We had hit the outer limit of the occasion, a chance encounter between acquaintances. Anything more would have constituted flirtation. So I went home, you went to Paris, and we didn't meet again for quite some time.

⁓

LARA HAD been restraining herself on a couple of counts this time, the most obvious being that he had it all wrong. What he had taken for flirtation on her part was nothing more than simple joy. She was high that day, sailing. He had caught her at a point of perfect freedom: leaving her job behind without losing it, going to France where Ian would be working while she would be free to do as she pleased. It was like getting a giant poetry grant for which she had never even applied.

She spent that summer roaming, mastering quite a few *arrondissements* in the process. She explored the river for miles, mined the bookstalls along its banks, met all sorts of people. Her French improved so much she was sometimes mistaken for a native speaker. At Ian's last lecture, the one in Lyons, they pretended Lara was Ian's interpreter, not his wife.

Anyway, what Cal experienced that day on Church Street was nothing more than her exhilaration at the footloose summer to come. He was just breathing the secondhand smoke.

But he was also wrong in pegging Church Street as their first encounter. They had met a month earlier, when she and Winnie stopped by the apartment and found Cal at home. At home and in a very bad mood—so bad that Lara had taken against him, which was hardly what she would have expected. Given the picture Winnie had painted, Lara assumed she would find him at the very least appealing.

Winnie was a very pretty woman. By the criteria of the times she was ideal, with the long blonde hair, the lovely smiling eyes, and a figure (as they used to call it) not a bit compromised by the bearing of two children and which no accumulation of faux hippie rag trade drapery could entirely disguise. In today's parlance, she was hot. But she was also sweet. Pure.

Sometimes a woman like that will ally herself with an outwardly homely guy. Not so much the beauty and the beast thing as beauty joined to intellect, or to power. It happens a lot, because to a woman looks aren't everything. And male model looks, movie man looks, are not the ideal in any case. Belmondo's messed-up mug was a lot more interesting to Lara than a pretty face like Alain Delon's.

So she had allowed for the possibility that, all of Winnie's testimonials aside, the guy might look like Edward G. Robinson, or Sartre. A frog face. Which he did not. So far as looks went, he came as advertised. He was reputed to be this cool dude, though, the All-American boy and the Bohemian rebel rolled up into one, and instead he behaved like a pinch-faced middle-aged accountant.

Winnie had brought him a present that day, a hat or a scarf, nothing of significance. And he was all over her about the money: couldn't afford it, didn't need it, had one already, whatever it was. He was not joking, not smiling, not remotely pleasant. For all Lara knew he was about to haul off and slug her. Plenty of women who talk about how great their husbands are, or their

20

boyfriends, those are women who get pushed around. It's real, that whole syndrome, and for all she knew that was exactly what she was seeing.

Far from feeling harmless envy of Winnie, as she half antici-pated, Lara ended up feeling badly for her. Afterwards, Winnie was at pains to convince her this had been a baffling departure, Cal was *never* like that. And he wasn't, of course. It really was an aberration. Still, if it was *backstory* Cal wanted, she felt obliged to mention it.

"Actually, that wasn't the first time we met. We met at your apartment, a month or so earlier. Which is why you 'almost' knew my name."

⁊

I was talking about our first one-on-one, our first conversation, if you will. And in case you don't remember where we had our second conversation, I'll tell you.

You were walking down Mt. Auburn, coming up from the Square, and I was walking the other way—with Winnie's mother. Who almost never came to visit us. She was there that day, though, fated to glimpse the woman she would come to hate. And apart from Nazi war criminals and a few right-wing pols, Priscilla never hated *anyone*. So you came to occupy a unique position in her iconography.

To give you your due, or her hers, I will add that she felt no such way at the time. "That was an awfully charming young lady," was what she said to me as we walked on. And she gave me her knowing look, accompanied by her famous ironic chuckle, meaning Oh yes, don't think for a minute I didn't see you drinking her in.

You were dressed as follows: blue jeans, blue sneakers, small leather jacket of faded forest green over a faded pink oxford cloth shirt. The jacket looked a size small, probably a hand-me-down or a Dollar-Dealer, and that may have been the first sign of trouble. That this ill-fitting jacket looked so right on you. I know

⌒ 21 ⌒

our third meeting held such a portent, an "insignificant detail" that later proved not quite so insignificant. But I'll get to that.

You told us you had just returned from California, from a poetry symposium in Big Sur. You had met Gary Snyder and Ferlinghetti, and you had helped run a seminar with someone else whose name I recognized. You were really getting around.

"You do look more mature," I said.

"You mean I look older?" you said.

"You look just fine, dear," said Priscilla, "whatever Calvert means."

"I meant that all these worldly endeavors have added a soupçon of sophistication to your resumé."

"He is such a bull-slinger," said Priscilla, cackling at her familiar no-nonsense line, a line she had aimed at so many of the men in her life, foremost among them myself and her husband Johnny. Then she patted me affectionately and added, "But he's really a wonderful man. One in a million, I always say."

"Right, and then Winnie always says, Let's hope so. It's a little vaudeville routine they have worked out."

You laughed, Priscilla laughed, and then I promulgated for the first time the notion that we ought to get together soon, "we" being the two couples, you and Ian, myself and Winnifred. More than anything else this was a parting mechanism. Even as I said it I was thinking it didn't sound promising, or likely. I had never even met Ian, and with the kids we didn't have much time for that kind of social life anyway, couples getting together. As I say, it was just a way of rounding off the occasion.

Then you were gone and Priscilla made her remark about how charming you were and when I said nothing in response, she pushed it a square farther across the chess board: "Pretty too, don't you think?"

"I didn't notice," I told her, with a disarming smile she would take to mean I was kidding, of course I noticed, and it could not matter less. We went on to the Square, bought whatever it was she had wanted to buy there, and then went back to the apartment, where Winnie and the kids were just waking from a nap.

"Our turn now," Priscilla said, with the cackle, and that's what we did. We each took a nap. It was a good transition, too, because I was still slightly focused on you. Mildly distracted. I attributed it to the blue sneakers and the green leather jacket.

∽

"That was all very interesting, and now I see your five minutes have expired."

"And we are almost done. But there was that third encounter. The one featuring the insignificant detail which would later prove to be not so insignificant?"

∽

Given the nature of this detail, I can see why you might not have as clear a memory of the occasion, but I can tell you precisely where we were standing at the time. Who knows, our DNA may linger there to this day, as proof positive.

There were four of us in front of (and reflected in) the plate glass window of the Empty Café on Holyoke Street. Do you remember that much? It was one of those eateries which fail no matter how many times they get a new owner and a new name. Which is why everyone called it the Empty Café. Because it was always empty.

That's how the conversation began. You were with some guy and I asked in confusion and wonderment if the two of you had just partaken at the Empty Café. You both laughed, in on the joke and clearly kind of tight with each other, though he wasn't Ian, he was introduced as "my friend Keith" or whatever.

I was with my friend Fitz, who would not have had much to say. He would have mostly exuded, and let his twinkling blue eyes imply the great good fortune of having such clear skies, such excellent marijuana, and yes, of finding himself in the presence of such a lovely lady. I would have done all the talking.

And you, by the way. Admit it, deny it, or pretend to have forgotten the day altogether; it remains the truth that we hit it off. We had the verbal spark from jumpstart.

Still, it was the pants that marked that occasion. They were characteristic of the times, certainly, not at all characteristic of you, as I would later learn. To me you had been the girl in the green jacket, now you were the girl in the Carnaby Street trousers. Circus pants, colorful bellbottoms, hence flared absurdly at the calf, yet also very snug in the seat, let us say. Those pants informed the world that Lara Cleary was in firm possession, let us say, of a world class—what? Ass, would have been the word back then, hence the egregious phrase that descends therefrom, a piece of ass.

You always said *bottom*, another of your genteel word choices. Jewish moms say tushy, spankers say backside, nowadays people say butt. In the '70s one had a lovely ass, or didn't, of course. You did.

This was out of keeping with the rest of you, or one's perception of the rest. There was no sense of roundness, or protuberance about you. You had registered as a lean, fine-boned, modest-breasted lass, and fetching in your green jacket. Now you were the same girl, with the same attractive features, plus the new "insignificant" detail, a frankly astonishing *bottom*. Which changed the equation. Though I say this retrospectively, it seems that sex, or sexual appeal, had become a factor.

∽

"I HATED those pants," said Lara. "They were a mistake and I never wore them again. I had no idea what the back of me looked like in them, all I knew was that the front of me looked ridiculous and that they were uncomfortable. I couldn't wait to take them off. Though I gather you couldn't either."

"It wasn't exactly like that. All of this coalesced gradually in my mind. I do remember being disappointed to see you in a dress a few weeks later, on the occasion of—let's see—must have been our fourth meeting. At the Turtle Café."

"We never met there."

"Not us. You and Ian. Me and Winnie. It really was still a small town in those days. You would always bump into friends on the street, always take two hours executing a simple errand. So it was either that aspect or it was fate, but the pace at which our paths crossed by accident was accelerating. The backstory was building."

Perhaps registering her clear impatience with the whole backstory idea, Cal held a palm up, then reduced it to an index finger: bear with me, one more minute. Surely she could not be so petty as to refuse him a single minute?

"And the attraction, I might add, was obviously building too. It was hard not locking in on one another that night. Pretending to listen to Ian's wine recommendations or participating in Winnie's soup versus salad conundrum . . ."

↶↷

HE HAD it wrong again, one hundred percent wrong. Memory was surely a curious business. She did wear a dress (her angel dress, Ian called it, who knows why) and they both liked the dress a lot. Who really liked it was her father, probably because it reminded him of the '40s or something. But he was with them that night at the Turtle.

Her mother was not there, so undoubtedly it was during one of her parents' 57 varieties of separation, though the truth was that Lara had not a single memory of sitting in a restaurant with both her parents. Maybe it never happened. Maybe if you strung together the 57 separations (ranging in duration from one night to three years, before the actual divorce), there were scarcely any occasions when it would even have been a possibility.

In any event, they had just been fielding The Dad that night. He and Ian got along fine. When it came to "making conversation," the two of them were championship material. So it was their show, with Lara as moderator. Seeing Winnie come in did brighten her evening and surely it was a treat seeing Jake and Hetty. But whatever Cal thought of her, or the circus pants, or the angel dress, he occupied very little space in her consciousness on that occasion.

The funny thing, given what Cal relayed about Winnie's mother, was that her father had a similar reaction, only more extreme. He was absolutely floored by Winnie. The Dad struck most people as this dry stick figure. "Buttoned-up" is an expression that might have been invented just for him. No one would readily connect him to the idea of human sexuality, whereas in truth he was always a sucker for a pretty girl.

When her friends were fourteen, when they were in college, later at the wedding, The Dad reliably fell for the pretty ones. He could be charming, always prepared to trot out his courtly persona, but he tended to be very low wattage around women who struck him as homely, and something else entirely, *beaming*, upon the ones he judged to be "lookers."

Had this ever become overtly sexual, he would have made a fool of himself for sure, like the character in the Marlene Dietrich film, *The Blue Angel*. Brilliant and yet utterly helpless before the force of female beauty. Professor Unrat? In any case, The Dad was safe there. He kept it in bounds, buttoned-up, and her friends felt flattered, not assaulted.

Lara, who knew all his tricks and disguises, was mostly amused as she watched it unfold that night with Winnie; as she watched Winnie knock him arse-over-teakettle. He would bring her up out of the blue months later. ("By the way, how is your friend Winnifred doing?") That night at the Turtle did it for him.

So for Lara, there was The Dad, there was Winnie, and there was Hetty. That little girl was the one who bowled Lara over, and maybe she did envy Winnie her children. Winnie had changed all those diapers and now here she was, out the other side, with a quiet thoughtful little boy and a charming little girl who spoke in complete but very funny sentences.

✌

"You know something, Lara? I may have two separate occasions confused, or conflated," said Cal.

All through Lara's disciplined silence, he too had been silent. Pensive, as though groping after some missing fragment, an unreclaimed detail. Now it had come back to him, or so he declared.

"We didn't have one accidental small-world encounter at the Turtle, we had two. There was that time before The Twoweeks, when Winnie and I did bring the kids, and there was another time when it was just Winnie and myself. And the second time was not only after The Twoweeks, it was literally the *day* of the Two Hours."

✌

He had this one right. It had been the night of the day of the second Two Hours, actually, which made it an absolutely brutal occasion. They had been together in bed that afternoon and then, too soon after, found themselves in the world's tiniest restaurant, with their respective spouses.

How many tables did the Turtle have? Six? Seven tables, tops, plus the row of seats at the counter, because it used to be a diner. It was impossible not to make constant eye contact, impossible not to make conversation. Officially the smoke had cleared, outwardly there was peace in the valley, but nobody had bargained on dinner-for-four.

It was a scene right out of a French marriage farce, one of those excruciating situations where the audience takes satisfaction from knowing *they* weren't the ones who had done this to themselves. Oddly, what made it slightly less unbearable was The Dad. He was there that time too, to provide some comic relief.

He liked the Turtle, it was that simple. Given how persnickety he was, this was a great gift. In most restaurants, The Dad would study his menu, sigh extravagantly, order a cup of soup reluctantly—then leave it untouched. But he liked the pork chop at the Turtle. Sliced thin, well done, with grilled onions. It was almost like a dish from the children's menu; you cut it up for him. But he would order it without a list of special requirements ("the asterisks," Lara's brother called them), and damned if he didn't eat it. So the Turtle was how they did him.

Nonetheless, Lara experienced ninety minutes of soft-core torture that evening. Never in her life had she felt so utterly stuck, or so wrong in so many ways toward so many people. Jake and Hetty may not have been at the restaurant, but they always ranked first on her guilt list. They were always present. Winnie was her friend, Ian was her husband. There was even Cal, by then; she could hurt him too. The Dad, for once, was not a problem. He had his pork chop and he had Winnie's face to stare at. Hog heaven for him.

Lara kept her head down and picked at her salad with great concentration (really getting after the *radishes*) for what must have seemed an uncommonly long time. She tried leaving her body altogether, hopping onto some freight train of the imagination. Or a plane. She took a shot at picturing Paris, traveling back to Paris in her mind. Just get me *outta* here, man.

Of course, Paris had been spoiled too, in the late days of that magical summer, when she fell in step briefly with Guillaume. In the end, Guillaume was just someone else she had disappointed. You will come back, he had said, you must come back. "I will be checking every flight from Boston, waiting until I see your name."

Which was nonsense, obviously, or perhaps (to give Guillaume the benefit of the doubt) metaphorical. He would not be poring over any passenger manifests. He was not another heart-shrunk existentialism-bleating Gauloise-gobbling Frenchman waiting for American lightning to strike him in a café. He was human, and quite sweet. When she boarded that plane, however, when she tried to escape from the Turtle Café on that imagined night flight, Guillaume blocked her way. In her mind's eye, he was waiting on the ground at Orly, gazing up from the wet tarmac like Bogart knowing he had just lost Ingrid Bergman.

Like Bergman in Casablanca, though, Lara had the letters of transit. At the moment she might be stuck in a tiny restaurant where everyone present had reason to despise her, but it was in her power to change this and she resolved right then to do so. It was over with Cal. She would never sleep with him again and that was flat. End of story.

Winnie (closely monitored by The Dad) was eating her flan and Ian was sipping coffee, as Lara arrived at the one outcome she could control. It was the easiest outcome as well, since it was what everyone believed to be the status quo: Ian and Lara, Cal and Winnie, period. The Two Hours was never a program, or a decision, it was an accident that happened and now it was *over* forever.

"You're right," she said, "about the two Turtle dinners. There were two."

No need to walk him through the trivial agonies of that French marriage farce, and no need for further delay. Cal had introduced into evidence the green jacket, the silly pants, and the two Turtle dinners. Now end-of-story could translate into end of backstory. Decanting more bourbon into their glasses, she threw a meaningful glance up at the clock. "Are we all set now?"

"Except for the business of February 22, we are. Though the story of that night does involve my coming to work at Gallery Allison. You got me hired."

Lara shrugged. It was true, just not the truth. And certainly not grounds for an extension, when his "five minutes" were already closer to an hour.

"I am not claiming you campaigned for the idea," said Cal, as though to deflect the qualification he read on her face. "I realize it was mostly Winnie's doing. She was constantly job-hunting on my behalf, something to bring in a little money until Broadway came calling. When you mentioned that the handyman got canned for showing up soused, Winnie said, Aha, they must need a new handyman, Calvert is handy."

⌀

Winnie insisted it was a perfect fit and you explained it was pretty much a janitorial gig, maybe not so perfect. But you did get me an interview with Allison. You even assured her I was honest and hardworking! Of course, I wasn't half as handy as she wanted me to be. I could tighten the odd screw, maybe change a lock. What she wanted was a full-time plumber/janitor/carpenter/electrician. She only hired me because of your recommendation and the fact I would work for three bucks an hour.

I did like the job. I liked the place and I liked being around you, but it was good clean fun, nothing more. You were Winnie's friend, not mine, and beyond that you seemed approachable but not available. A flirt yet, in spite of your playfulness, proper. *Moral*, if that's still a word one can use. It never crossed my mind to look at you differently until after I'd been hijacked by Sasha Blackburn. It was that lapse, somehow, which opened a window on the world of possibility.

Believe this or not, I was in no way looking for anything like that to happen. An affair. I did not instigate it and I did nothing to encourage it. On the contrary, I resisted to the point where it became a sort of joke between us, where Sasha was Why-not and I was Why. She was Gather-ye-rosebuds and I was Love-the-one-you're-with. She just wore me down.

The joke progressed to "Check back with me in a week," which to me was just a way to conclude the discussion and to her was a promissory note. Every Monday night after rehearsal she would sidle up and say, "I'm checking back, Calvert, is this the week that was?" Until finally it was. I was walking her home, there was a light November snow, the streetlights had a certain frosty charm, she said her Why-not and somehow I was fallen.

I'm not saying I did it simply to get her off my back. Maybe I was your typical harried married man, something had gone out of my life, blah blah; maybe it was all perfectly sad and trite that way. But let's face it, Sasha Blackburn was damned attractive. She made it onto the screen in Hollywood while I was still scrounging parts in Providence repertory. So if the devil made me do it the first time, the second time I done it on my own. And the third.

At some point, though, I had begun to fall under your spell. You and I were taking those long coffee breaks in the alley, with Gerald and Debra, and Myra, and Sid. Henry and June. Sometimes Allison even deigned to sit with us. It may have been to enforce the clock, or snoop on us, but I think we were all having such fun she felt left out.

And it wasn't like anyone was breaking down the gallery doors at ten A.M. That's why the fifteen-minute breaks were always at least half an hour. Work-wise, it hardly mattered. But you and I would be out in the alley first, and stay out there longest. We couldn't stop talking, or didn't want to. We could have talked all day. Something had started happening.

☙

No POINT arguing otherwise. They did enjoy hanging out, they did become close friends. They each looked forward to the workday a bit too eagerly and they were increasingly incautious about it. All true, yet not the truth.

Then he opened his big mouth and changed everything, so they could no longer be friends. Or to put it in his terms, Cal became Why-not and Lara remained solidly Why. Really, she was just plain *No*. They had so much to lose, so much they were capable of destroying. Her life was fine, his life was fine, above all his *kids* were fine. If they did what he suggested ("simply because we want to"), there was a damned good chance nothing would be so fine afterward. Which made it not merely wrong but mighty stupid.

๛ 31 ๛

So naturally they went ahead and did it. Not right away, certainly. Again, to frame it as Cal had with regard to the spectacular Ms. Blackburn, they were walking home together, it was a fine frosty February afternoon, he said Why-not, and she was fallen.

She could have said no (as she had again and again) but she didn't—who knows why. Sure, she was powerfully attracted, maybe more so than ever before. But Lara had always believed you got no credit for being moral if you faced no temptation to be immoral. Once a Catholic always a Catholic. It had to *cost* you dearly, before you earned grace.

There was something else at work back then. They were living at a time, and in a place, where such behavior could seem almost right. Their so-called generation had fought the good fights, for civil rights and peace and women's rights, and along with those principled stands came a natural backlash against all restrictions. Maybe this was a crock, history as sound byte, yet it did contain a few grains of truth. The notion of fidelity was at the very least called into question.

To Lara, it could be confusing. She believed in fidelity, yet at the same time fidelity could be made to seem almost silly. Small-minded, outmoded. Cal made it seem that way. So many songs and movies made it seem that way. There were forces in the air, in the culture (vibes, so called, ideas without words) which made it *feel* that way. You could lose track of who you were, or who you meant to be.

At times her confusion made Lara unsure to what extent she was resisting sin and to what extent she was simply being timid. She understood she could be reluctant to step over lines simply because the lines were there—more Catholicism, perhaps. And knowing she had that tendency, she would occasionally choose heedlessness as a kind of counterweight. Lara was sure this was precisely what happened the day she fell in step with Guillaume.

So there was a sense in which she would not have been calling Cal's bluff so much as calling her own. She knew she possessed this power—to remain the angel or let herself run with the devil—and she enjoyed having it. Every now and then, she could let herself be a bad girl. The choice was in her control.

"And it was," she said, "until I let it happen. After that, no one was in control."

"Pardon? Control?"

"Sorry. I guess I was thinking out loud, about how I let the devil rule me that night. Your famous February 22."

"The devil? I would not have said you were particularly hell-bent that night! At best I'd say you had staked out a street corner in purgatory. Technically yes, you permitted the removal of clothing, permitted the interlocking of previously private parts. What you held back was any sense that there might be a reason for doing so."

"Come on, Cal. Even you know there were better reasons for *not* doing so."

"Were there? One day, as we were squeezing past each other at the back door of the gallery, we kissed. It was totally unpremeditated—we were too close, too proximate physically that is, and our hands were fending off, hence hands on shoulders, hands on hips, I forget exactly how it was choreographed. It wasn't a brush on the cheek, though, it was a genuine kiss. It lasted a while. That kiss, which we more or less pretended had never even occurred, was far more erotic than what took place on February 22, when you 'surrendered.' "

∽

Which is precisely what you did. You said nothing negative, did nothing positive. You needed it to be a notch or two above rape; you would not participate, merely abide. Which, incidentally, is not how the devil fucks.

In my overheated goal-oriented state, I set that aspect aside. I knew you were ambivalent, I knew we both had to be nervous, plus there is bound to be some awkwardness between unfamiliar partners. Even Fred Astaire and Ginger Rogers couldn't have been perfect the first time they danced. I figured we would do it again sometime soon, in a day or two, and do it better.

We did it again much sooner than that, actually, almost at once. You did touch me as we lay side by side, your hand strayed to my hip, and I took it as an invitation to try again. You were ready now. And the odd thing is that physiologically you were extremely ready both times, but your mind or your heart still forbade any real involvement.

Once again you lay back and permitted it. No attempt to reverse positions, or go adventuring after pleasure. It was more like, *This* again? I couldn't keep myself from enjoying it, couldn't slow the body's motor with good old delirium on the way. But I could, even in the moment, notice that you were subject to no such transports. Not so much rollicking as resigned. Counting sheep or goats.

It threw me. I never dreamed we could choose to go ahead and yet remain so distant. To me, the folly lay in denying ourselves, to you the folly lay permitting it to happen, so clearly this difference was being reflected. Still I was sure we would be closer once we crossed our little Rubicon. The act would make us lovers, after all, and not just technically. Lovers in a sense involving some aspect, some fragment of whatever "love" is.

Because even at that age I was not a frivolous person. Certainly you weren't. If we did this, surely we did it to gain some small portion of a love we both suspected we could have had, would have had, and did not have simply because of other prior loves. And fair enough. But that was the rule we chose to break. The rule saying one is all you get. In breaking it, I assumed we were saying no, we get two. In some partial, painful, temporary fashion, we will be taking two. We will not miss out altogether.

And you were saying, guess again. You wanted it to fail, to prove meaningless. You wanted it to go away. Afterward, you didn't even bother telling me you feared you were pregnant. You didn't tell me anything. You know the Bob Dylan line, Just act like you never have met? Well, that was you.

And that, old girl, is the backstory. I'm sorry it took so long, but you did interrupt a number of times.

∽

"WELL, I don't know if this constitutes an interruption or a post-script, Cal, especially as I have nothing to say. Certainly I will not be discussing my sex life one bit. I won't discuss the pregnancy scare either, other than to say I was a complete idiot to assume you knew what you were doing. I mean, you *had* children. Somehow I assumed that meant you knew how *not* to have them."

"Wouldn't it be more logical to say *you* were the one who knew how not to have them? And how not to have them was birth control pills, which I happened to know you were taking. So if I was an idiot, I wasn't the only one."

"I was on the Pill. I was proof it wasn't foolproof. The one-tenth of one percent, or whatever. Anyway, I had no good way of telling you anything at the time. The gallery was closed that week, your telephone was also Winnie's telephone, what was I supposed to do? I wanted to tell you. We already had secrets, which I hated. We already had complications, which I hated. And now we had this—or I had it."

"And dealt with it."

"I hated that too. This morning-after pill they have now, whatever it consists of, is apparently reliable. Safe. What they had back then was experimental, sort of off the grid, as I recall. The woman told me it 'usually' works and then listed about four hundred charming side effects."

"None of which you had."

"That's because she didn't list the two biggest. Catholic guilt and female regret. The two got rolled in together at the time. Anyway, I did manage to tell you that I had taken care of the problem."

"That you had it and that you had taken care of it, yes. In twenty-five words or less."

"I was at a pay phone, you were home with Winnie. I guessed you would tell her it was a wrong number, or another hang-up call. Because I'd hung up three times already, waiting for you to be the one who answered."

"Twenty-five seconds or less. Which is more than I got from you after the gallery reopened. No eye contact. Maybe a few grunts. You basically drove me out of the job."

"I tried to, certainly."

"Oh, you succeeded. And I did not see you again, not even for twenty-five seconds, until the day you came to deliver The Sentence . . ."

# 3

## The Sentence

"I have two weeks," she said, "maybe late June."

That was The Sentence. Lara spoke it and was gone. Yet I remember that moment the way people are said to remember where they were standing when the Bombs were dropped on Japan, or when Kennedy was shot in Texas. When the Towers came down in lower Manhattan.

It's absurd to place our insignificant personal history (as Lara liked to call it) alongside those momentously struck notes of epochal history. Nevertheless, it had three things in common with them: it came as a bolt from the blue, it was something I never imagined much less anticipated, and yet it had the capacity to change the way everything to follow was experienced. Looking back over the decades of my (admittedly insignificant) life, The Sentence is the solitary instance that even comes close to fulfilling these three prerequisites.

I was sitting in the children's park on Hancock Street with my new friend Sydney—Female Sydney, as we called her—on that lovely spring day, the last day of April and the nicest in a long time. Everyone was taking lunch outside, heading for the parks or down to the river.

Sydney worked, as I did now, at Uncle Bunny's Incredible Edibles, on Mass. Ave. This was my second get-a-paycheck-any-paycheck job since leaving Gallery Allison under duress. I had been fired from the first job (tending bar at The People's Republic) for pouring too generous a glass; I was about to be fired from this one for packing too full a quart of ice cream.

Female Sydney was just someone who made the job more pleasant. Cute, impulsive, and always entertainingly dressed, Syd was a trip. She was fun and I wondered why I felt so certain she could not be more. I was curious about the difference between Syd and Lara Cleary, who had likewise "made the job more pleasant" at Gallery Allison. And the incredibly simple answer, according to my analysis, was that I could never love Sydney. In that regard she was like every appealing woman I had met in the last ten years—except Lara Cleary.

The same Lara Cleary whom I had not seen in two months and yet who (as I looked up from my chicken salad sandwich, no doubt with some of that chicken salad lingering on my chin) I now saw motioning to me from over by the swing-set. She had materialized out of thin air, as in a dream, or possibly a hallucination.

She was also the same Lara Cleary whom I not only could love but had: we had become lovers, finally. To me, at any rate, we were lovers. To her we were two people who happened to have sex. We had sex and then she shut me out, completely. Not because the sex was bad (though it was), but because however it had gone for us she knew it meant trouble.

We both knew that. It happened because we could not quite step around it and Lara hoped that by doing it (and dismissing it as done) she could step around it now. Or so I assumed. As for knowing, I knew nothing. In the total news blackout since our one rash hour in bed, I had spent my best energies trying to shake free of the strange web we had woven together. But the worm of it had crawled inside me.

Even in the many and even predominant moments of happiness at home, I found myself profoundly distracted. As wonderful as my children were, as much as I adored and enjoyed them, I often felt a sense of relief when they were safely asleep. Then I could get back to the essential business of being miserable. In some bizarre way I needed to be miserable, as though Fate was saying to me, Deal with this or I will never let go of your soul.

Now at the arched cast-iron portal to the playground, where our slow two-shot drift toward one another concluded, Lara (in the flesh, not a hallucination) placed both palms against my chest. This was affectionate, a sort of caress, but it was also a stop sign: no embraces, it declared, nothing beyond this one gesture.

She looked absurdly beautiful to me, not so much tanned as lightly toasted in a way that glorified her gray-green eyes and streaky chestnut hair. She seemed to have thrived during our time apart, seemed to have been anything but distracted or miserable. Only the words she spoke hinted otherwise. "I have two weeks, maybe late June."

At first I had no idea what to make of this, no background against which to place her declaration. Lara's palms were still pressed against my chest and now she pushed off, launching herself backward like a swimmer kick-turning at the end of the pool. Dumbfounded, I watched her recede down Hancock Street and then turned to field a glance from Female Sydney that was more like a dart, all of her "And-what-have-we-*here*" irony focused into a sly accusatory smile.

"What was *that?*" she said. "And do not tell me you don't know."

It was, of course, the only true answer I might have summoned. I didn't know.

"Just a friend," I offered to Syd, who wildly mugged her disbelief.

Lara Cleary had her principles, God knows, and apparently those principles dictated she utter not one word more than she had. Presumably this had mostly to do with her husband Ian, to whom she had owed fidelity and now owed loyalty in some skewed form. It also had something to do with her approach to risk.

Her approach was that she would never take a risk if she could identify it as such. While the long unsettling tug of love and war between us (leading up to February 22 and now to The Playground Statement) may have seemed fraught as hell with risk, it wasn't, exactly. Lara understood how far she could push a situation without harming Ian irreparably (or losing him), and she was forever reckoning how far she could push herself without endangering either her marriage or her mortal soul. She may have been wrong—the calculus was intuitive—but it was there.

I was good at closing distances, Lara was good at maintaining them, sometimes even in times of intimacy. She was as charming as a woman can be; she could charm the pants right off you. After she had done so, however, it did not gain you any rights or privileges. Pants or no pants, you might find yourself at arm's length.

As I pondered her words later that afternoon (as I dipped and rolled the mile-high ice cream cones at Uncle's), the fog of mystery blew away from them. Lara's appearance was so melodramatic and her proposal so startling that initially I resisted its narrow clarity. But there was no other possible interpretation. She had managed, by whatever means, and for whatever reasons of her own, to obtain a fortnight of freedom from Ian, and if I could somehow arrange to do the same we might share that fortnight.

It was an invitation and, by her lights, a handsome one: confessing to interest, hinting at attraction. But one spare sentence, with no room for a reaction, much less a hug? The delivery was as strictly limited as the message itself. It was absolutely minimal and so I took it as literal. Just as we had never been permitted a past or a present in her iconography, we would be denied a future. Or any future beyond the two weeks on offer. Even as she tendered the invitation, Lara was reprising her refusal to acknowledge any real bond between us. Two weeks was what we might have. Up to me. All the same to her.

Had I declared it impossible, Lara was covered. No problem, she would say, sayonara Cisco. Clearly she had feelings; just as clearly those feelings were not to be granted primacy. It was a handsome invitation and at the same time it was a gauntlet laid down.

There was genius in it. If one could get away with such temporary arrangements—if one were a sophisticated European, in the mythology—many a sagging marriage might be propped up by it. Revival, survival, call it what you will. For the most part, the grass only *seems* greener on the other side of the hill. For the most part, we choose a spouse carefully and for sound reasons, so there are qualities to fall back on. There is, or presumptively has been, love.

Reviewing the handful of women I had been attracted by over the course of my marriage to Winnie (cute Shelley, funny Elke, undeniably sexy Lynn), I could see nothing that would have threatened us under the mythologic European format, the stray-and-return model. There is jealousy to consider. I am aware, from movies seen and books read, that there can be jealousy even in Europe. Sometimes in French films there can be *guns* brandished, in violent final scenes that cloud the credits with gun-smoke. So I suppose we are talking percentages here.

Meanwhile we are also talking about a couple, Winnie and myself, who had never bandied about (much less adopted) this European dream of personal freedom. I doubted it was any different with Lara and Ian. What had Lara told him? I was willing to bet she had not uttered any outright lies to him, yet precisely how much truth had she told? How much truth had she acknowledged to herself, for that matter? Because Lara did find it useful to keep herself in the dark regarding her own emotions.

And why would she shake Ian up that badly without first gaining some assurance that I was on board? My compliance with the odd proposition could hardly be taken for granted. Maybe she did want to stick her neck out, though. Maybe playing it safe, like lying, would have felt immoral to her. Lara would want to be punished (and by God, no less!) if she refused to accept the consequences of her sins. So here she was slipping a twisted thread of loyalty into the fabric of betrayal.

I was guessing at all this, flying by the seat of my intuition. Nor did my "analysis" matter a whit. I had not been placed in charge of her half of the plan; I was assigned to deal with my half. Did I or did I not wish to play a serious high-stakes game of relationship roulette, a dangerous game in which the goal might be to beat the house but the end result might be to raze it.

Even if I agreed this was a good idea (or more accurately an irresistible opportunity), even if I elected to grab those two weeks and squeeze the spice out of them, how in the world would I manage it?

Lying was the obvious first option for me to weigh. I was never the moralist Lara was, I was a pragmatist and lying was pragmatic. But a good lie can be hard to find. The best one I conjured up was to say I had been offered a part in a play running two weeks in Cincinnati, or farther west if necessary. Winnie would not doubt it (indeed, she would applaud it) and she would not be free to accompany me.

I got as far as considering the specifics (would this play be a Shaw, an Ibsen, or something new and experimental?) before reality erupted and blew up the inchoate plot. Winnie might not come along to the nation's midsection, but she could certainly telephone me there, a detail not easily finessed. Likewise the problem of fabricating contracts, publicity photos, reviews. And while she could not get away from work for two weeks in Ohio, she might insist on being there for opening night.

Long before that, she would expect to be my sounding board. Expect to help me rehearse my role. Ah yes, my *role* . . .

I did consider telling the truth. The truth had one obvious advantage, namely that the guilt of infidelity would not be accelerated by the guilt of dishonesty. When people insist they prefer to be told the truth, though, what they really mean is that they prefer the truth to be different than it is. Would Winnie really feel better hearing of this tidy little scheme? And why should she be asked to countenance such treason? Winnifred is an extraordinarily fair person, liberated and flexible, and would have forgiven an infidelity more sensibly than most. She wouldn't forgive me in *advance*, though. Why should she do that?

For a time I weakened (or had I strengthened?) and fell to thinking I would just say no. Thanks much, but as it happens I do not "have two weeks." What simple relief it would provide from the tricky calculus I was mired in. Where the other choices were fraught and stressful, this one seemed weightless. It whisked the problem away like a TV cleansing agent.

Except, of course, that it did no such thing. Letting go of Lara (especially when she was, for once, not proposing to let go of me) was way past counter-intuitive. It was impossible, emotionally. I knew that already and now it seemed Lara knew it too. If not, there would be no such prospect as these two weeks, however stingy or limited in scope.

So it seemed reasonable to wonder if she might sign on for a less apocalyptic arrangement. Why did it have to be this deal or no deal? Lara had rendered her terms, why couldn't I render mine?

That phase of my deliberations lasted about a minute. Somehow I knew that her offer was writ in black ink, that it was more an ultimatum than an initial chip. She had parsed the terms of the contract, bargained back and forth with her "better self" (and possibly her husband) on the fine points, and this was her best offer.

I went back to just-say-no and stayed with it for a solid week. To prop up my wobbling willpower, I took on extra shifts at Uncle Bunny's. At home, I took over all the cleaning, shopping, laundry, and cooking. I took over the kids completely: pick-up and delivery, meals and snacks, games and baths, songs and stories. They were such lovely children, who could ask for anything better than taking them over? Who would dare ask? Was I not as fortunate as a soul could be?

Truly, I was. All my life I had been blessed, from the genetics on up. Unless you counted money (and I did not), I lacked for nothing that mattered. The "rest of the story" was that now I did lack Lara Cleary. And though I could and did reply "So what?"

to this purported hardship, something inside me kept laughing off the so-what defense. My normally sturdy psyche was being undermined, collapsed by unseen tunnels. I could never quite extricate Lara's image or voice from my mind, could not dislodge her essence from my corpuscles.

Who knows from effing *corpuscles,* you say. Who has ever seen a corpuscle? It's an absurd conceit, an extreme one, yet mine had become an extreme state of mind. Lara had become so deeply embedded that I felt as if I twisted left and she twisted with me; I bent and she bent. As with the sharp pain from a kidney stone, I could achieve no posture that provided a haven from the pain.

So what, I told myself again. Even if the pain is real, even if it *counts* the way a dislocated shoulder counts, it can always be endured. I could choose suffering—not for two weeks or a year, but forever, if necessary. People suffer terribly, in so many ways. In a case of such minor (and elective) suffering, I *should* choose it and, moreover, not dare call it by that name.

All through this time, I kept expecting my boy Jake to say, Papa where *are* you? What are you *thinking* about, as I had said so many times to him, in his own abstracted moments. I was that absent, that inadequate. Jake is the most alert, yet how could any of them fail to notice? Especially when I began to lose my temper. . . .

The phrase is wrong. You lose your cool, you find your temper; it's just that you didn't want to find it. My policy was never to rush Hetty at bedtime. If you rushed her, it would not only end up taking longer, it would provide a joyless experience for all concerned. One night, nevertheless, I could not manage to keep it together.

I had been faking it for hours, going through the motions of engagement with both of them. Their need was for routine and for the love that lay at the foundation of our family routines. My need was to be released from the rare gift of familial happiness into a murky pool of confusion, a private facility where I could wrestle undetected with the trivial misery I almost, in an odd way, cherished.

Generally I could use the hour before Winnie came home to process the confusion, cram it back in its box, so I could be composed for her. Be "normal," or at least appear normal. To the eternal spousal question ("What's wrong?") the eternal answer ("Nothing") can never be rendered convincingly—and mind you, I say this as a trained actor. If the question must be asked, then "Nothing" is simply not among the plausible answers.

That night, in any case, I refused to read the one-more-story Hetty invariably requested. The one-more was like the encore at a concert, it was part of the set list, planned in advance as the real final number. Instead of reading the one-more, I tucked Hetty in almost forcibly, right up to her cool sweet chin, which I kissed, as I kissed her forehead and sweet soft cheeks and her nose. I adored her, after all. But I fled the room almost angrily and refused to return for the curtain call. When finally I did return, I was still stern-faced and pinch-voiced, a complete stranger to my darling child.

"Why are you being mean, Papa?" said Hetty, another sentence, by the way, bound to stay with me all my life.

Inevitably I was mean to Winnie as well. Hetty was still awake, still squalling, when her mother got home. It was her late night at work and she was rag tired. We were all tired and short-tempered. (We were "not ourselves," or such would become the explanation.) I cited charges that were utterly baseless, or misplaced. Winnie was stunned to hear these charges, that she had been neglecting Jake, neglecting me, never had the energy for sex. Has there ever been a purer example of what the therapists call projection?

We went to bed in a jangle and rose the next morning feeling as though the house had been shattered by a storm overnight, a tree had come crashing through the roof. Weary and reeling, we looked around and began picking up the pieces, groping our way toward breakfast like shipwrecked survivors rearranging the island.

It was awful, it was entirely my fault, and somehow it ended up being my ticket to ride. Inadvertently, it set the seed of a notion that would sprout into two weeks of liberty, a way to eat my cake and have it, without apocalypse and without even asking. I'll explain.

We put the family back together that Saturday. In the afternoon, I loved the kids to heaven and the Henry Bear toy store, and in the evening we all went for tacos and enchiladas verdes at El Phoenix Room, where Jake drank two fingers of my beer and Hetty conducted a lengthy conversation with their plastic donkey. In the midnight hour Winnie and I had tearful (her) guilty (me) sex, and on Sunday morning, at my insistence, she slept in. I brought her coffee in bed, made the kids blueberry pancakes, and labored to erase all memory of the monster they had glimpsed the night before. Order was restored. We were "ourselves" again.

Nevertheless, not surprisingly, hints and bits of trouble persisted, poking up at unpredictable moments. It seems I was not hearing everything they said to me (all three reported this separately, lending credence) and when I did hear, I was apt to respond in odd ways. I made toast for Hetty, after she had declared for cereal. I ran a bath for Jake, though he always took showers. Like any amateur criminal, I was drawing attention to myself.

I stayed in control, though, striving to remain outwardly blameless, and so could seem blameless to my wife when eventually she gave voice to the obvious, that I was not quite myself after all. I seemed distracted, possibly even depressed? My reputation went so far in the other direction (irrepressible, undepressible) that this was alarming.

If I assured her that I was fine, she would just smile and kiss my forehead. When I forgot things (though I never forgot to pick up the kids) she would joke that I was "not firing on all cylinders." Her trust and caring shamed me to the core. How could I fail to love this person absolutely? And when she steered the conversation toward the suggestion I might benefit from some time alone, how could I fail to steer it clear of what I knew to be a ruinous rocky coast?

Not only did I allow this proposition to be aired, I labored to shape it. Some time alone? Maybe that was something we *each* deserved. Two kids, two jobs, tight budgets, tight schedules: we would be foolish to deny there were strains involved. Surely it made sense to take a break from it all, if the details could be managed. . . .

Somehow my slump, as she had come to call it, got folded into a hypothetical plan whereby each of us would be rewarded with "a week or two off," what nowadays is called personal time. We called it a retreat, as though we would be bound away for the tranquil monastery in Paxton, whose grounds we used to stroll.

First Winnie would go, then I would, and finally both of us, as a child-free couple. Part Three, she called it. We would dump the kids on parents, on sisters and brothers, and get away together. We could camp out in the Berkshires, hike around, rent a canoe—or maybe just stay home (sneak right back to the empty apartment) and go to bars, to movies, to bed. Be the way we were in our carefree romantic days. It would serve as a reminder, act as a restorative.

This sounded so wise and so promising that I almost forgot it was all an elaborate trick, a selfish device designed to liberate me so I could betray my wife and abandon my family. Winnie did not really want to go anywhere alone. She went for a single night, stayed over Saturday with Jess Merriman in Northampton, and was back by dinnertime on Sunday.

"Mama," Hetty cried out, flying into her arms. They have antennae; they feel everything.

"I missed you too, rabbit," said Winnie, hugging her daughter, shrugging at me with her eyes. "I did have a nice time," she assured me.

It was my turn. I would hold off, I said, and see how it went. Maybe things would lighten up, maybe I could just skip it. And I could always go later, maybe toward the end of June . . . I might just hole up at the monastery and read my way through all of Shakespeare's plays.

"That sounds like a *lot* of fun," Winnie joked, pained no doubt but pretending for my sake. Not understanding (how could she?) yet *being* understanding.

"It's a crazy idea, isn't it?" I said.

"The kids would miss you. So would I."

"I'd miss you too. Maybe I'd end up coming back in twenty-four hours, like you did. Though," I added, carrying along my Machiavellian deception, "I have always been more disciplined than you."

It was a perfectly hideous act of stagecraft. Of cruelty and betrayal. Of evil, I suppose I should admit. By the time all my tacit lies had tumbled into place, I might barely be able to face myself. But I could say to Lara Cleary (however and whenever I found a way to do so) that yes, I had two weeks too, toward the end of June.

# 4

## *The Twoweeks*

$D$ay 1, Wednesday, June 19. As arranged, we met in the alley behind the gallery and the instant I saw him I realized the whole proposition was a mistake. Not only would it be pointless (and likely painful), it would be incredibly awkward. It would be weird.

There had been moments when I thought two weeks with C. would seem unbearably brief. Now as we stood on the street unable to decide the simplest stupidest aspects (Do we kiss hello? Theoretically yes, but standing there I felt a total absence of affection), two weeks seemed unbearably *long*.

To make matters worse, I learned he had not told Winnie what we were doing. So we would be hiding and skulking, the exact situation I had tried so hard to avoid. It wasn't as if we were being whisked away to sunny Marseilles; we would be right here. We had no plan and no money. How could we make ourselves invisible for one hour in this town, much less two weeks?

C. had been this irresistible force. Making something happen between us had seemed imperative, to use a word I don't believe I have ever used before. Now, though, I felt no force fields pulling me, I felt only the strangeness of the occasion. Who *are* you? I thought. What are we doing here?

"This could be a long two weeks," were the first words I managed to speak.

C. looked surprised. Not because he disagreed (or agreed), but because he had not thought ahead two minutes, much less two weeks. "Why don't we just take it one day at a time," he said, as if this calm trite utterance represented a workable approach.

"In fact," he added, "let's take it one hour at a time," and that helped. An hour? An hour seemed workable. I am an acknowledged problem solver. If I greeted each arriving hour as a brand new problem, I might downright flourish. While this bright breakthrough did strike me as a little batty, the whole deal, The Twoweeks, was perfectly batty, and it was all about coping.

The truth is that solving that first hour actually did solve the entire first day. We just started walking, randomly. Walked all the way to North Station, which in itself took an hour, and as a bonus provided us with topics as we marched across Boston. Then we boarded a train for Gloucester. Our criterion? Gloucester was where the next train happened to be going.

It also happened to be a perfect destination. Where better to go on a gorgeous June morning than Cape Ann, and what better way to get there than by train? Trains free you up; I don't know why, they just do. We did not even feel a need to talk as we rattled along. It was enough to let the passing landscape (faded signs and loading docks, salmon-colored bricks leached by sunlight, emerald green lawns and pale green fields, white clapboards and acres of silvered shingles) speak for itself. The process of moving through such scenery together carried us clear of the city, both physically and psychically.

It restored us to being the people we were, a pair of drooling morons who had stepped into terra incognita without roadmap or compass. Strangers to one another still, yet by now recognizable. We walked again, over the rippled rumpled strand. Sea air, wet sand, the long horizon, blue vault of sky. We had brought no blankets, of course (no bathing suits, no packed lunches, nothing), yet it was wonderful. It was like looking at a blank page and knowing I had a poem there somewhere. Knowing that something was happening without caring exactly what it would turn out to be.

This was the same emotion I felt that spectacular afternoon in France, riding the Deauville train without Ian, off on my own. Though it began with a jangly anxiety, it quickly switched to wild exhilaration as the bright world whirled past and I came to realize it was mine. It was all for me, as soon as I managed to get out of my own way. I could step outside myself, like a body leaving its ghostly host in a movie. Like Cosmo Topper, slipping his transparent aura, free to do the unexpected.

Gloucester was a tame enough adventure, to be sure. No special effects there. No ghosts or explosions, no riderless white horse careening down from the hills. What we had was a clam shack, a six-pack of Black Label beer, and lots of waves breaking around our knees. Two kids in the water challenging each other in rapid-fire Spanish. A sky so uniformly blue it seemed painted, custom-blended to Cerulean Blue.

Two sailboats looped around the point and, though the sailors remained unaware, we entered them in a serious high-stakes race to a bright red buoy. (My boat won easily.) But we were just hanging out together. Suddenly comfortable with it; somehow relaxed. C. suggested we stay overnight, sleep on the beach.

"I didn't bring a toothbrush," I laughed.

"I bet they sell toothbrushes here," he said, and that's when it hit me he was serious. He wasn't simply a bad planner, he was utterly clueless. He didn't know Ian was gone, didn't realize we had a place to stay. Which in a way was my fault—how would he know if I didn't tell him? Still, did he really expect us to sleep under the stars everywhere we went, like Frost's two tramps in springtime?

I pulled him into a hug. Touched by his innocence, flattered by his faith. I had called and he came, no questions asked. All along I had allowed for the basics: one, that he was male and therefore wanted sex; two, that he was married and wanted nothing *more* than sex. Now I had to concede it might be a little different than that.

It did feel weird again at Miller Road. I had cleared the decks there, changed what I could change (shoved the bed under the window, turned the kitchen table ninety degrees), but it was still our house, mine and Ian's. Ian had been *in* the bed two nights earlier and he would be back in it come July. So it got tricky for me there; it fritzed my brain for a while, like intermittent static.

C. did not appear to experience the weirdness. He had set foot inside the apartment just once, so it held no particular significance for him. To him it represented shelter, a hole we could crawl into at night that was a few steps up from a hollow log. He truly had imagined a hobo existence, sleeping on beaches, in parks, on trains, maybe splurge on a motel here and there. If that constitutes a plan (as he alleged with a straight face), he had one.

I was glad we weren't virgins together. That chilly occasion in his friend's bedroom? It counted. That room in all its appalling filth and ratty disorder, and the out-of-body experience during which I tried to see and feel nothing? It nonetheless counted as sex. We had done it before and now we were going to do it again, which made it so much easier. Plus of course I had bargained for it. Might as well face that one, lady.

We did set guilt aside; it simply wasn't present. And C. was so sweet, I could accept his tenderness—could move with him beneath the flannel sheet and hold him close without feeling threatened by what we were doing. Which was crazy, of course. I was never so threatened in my life. But at least it was my own damn fault.

⚭

"I DON'T remember you writing anything down. What did you do, hide out in the bathroom with a yellow pad?"

"No, you're right, I didn't do it then. Ian and I went to Maine later that month and I had a few hours each morning in a cottage, at a desk. Where supposedly poems were being written."

"So you're saying this entire account is based on mere memory."

"Very fresh memory. And I did have a calendar marked. You saw me do that."

"No."

"I went by the calendar for the raw data. Which day was which. That on Wednesday the Umpteenth we did such-and-so. The rest was easy enough—emotion recollected in tranquility."

"Wordsworth?"

"Good for you, Calvert. I'm impressed."

✐

Day 2. We had yet to begin calling it our water-park theme, but it was already tending that way. And given those late June days, what better way for it to tend?

My first thought upon waking that morning was . . . I am waking. Profundity thy name is Lara! But this was "I am waking, therefore I have slept" and how was it possible to sleep in that bed, in that house, on that night? There was a different man on my husband's side of the bed and yet I slept like the concrete block chained to a disposable mafioso. Something had to be seriously wrong with me.

I made coffee. Made it and then sat on the back stairs drinking it . . . with C. instead of Ian. How could I? What kind of a heartless freak was I? Firing his dishwasher and hiring a new one, a restaurant owner might feel more remorse.

Mrs. Ridley frowned in confusion at the lineup change, though she did do her queenly little wave. Possibly she mistrusted her eyesight. ("My Ian" looks different today, she maybe thought?) I leaned toward chickening out and introducing C. as my brother from out of town. I mean, why not lie to spare Mrs. Ridley? Even Father Chastain might approve. But the moment was defused, the sin deflected, when she ducked back inside her apartment—most likely to check us out more closely through the curtains.

What next, was the question. (It would frequently be the question.) I suggested Walden Pond, C. ruled it out. Too many friends could float up, so to speak. Not to mention Winnie and the kids. I pointed out that there was privacy, a jungle really, on the far end where the train tracks run by. He said fine, if they'll copter us in. Otherwise you have to start from the tiny public beach, where every face is visible and you are visible to every face.

I was expected to sign on for this cheerful paranoia. We are being watched! The *federales* are coming after us with pistols drawn! Instinctively, I resented it. Let Winnie be there, I thought. I didn't make it any easier for Ian. I didn't lie to him. Why should I be forced to lie now, for someone else?

On the other hand, I had zero interest in being confronted by Winnie, or in tackling the whole big issue of what anything *meant*. I did not care to defend myself, or explain myself, or even just be hated. Above all, I did not want those beautiful children impacted in any full frontal way. Thus did moral relativism stare me in the eye.

I have always despised it. Always believed an act was moral or it was not, however one might try to fudge it. Now I was buying in (I'll have a hundred shares of fudge futures, please) and telling myself it was "for the best." Famous last words before fording the River Styx.

We boarded the Concord train at Porter Square. Got off in Concord and hitchhiked to a bridge where they rent canoes. This was distinctly not the River Styx. It was a sweet throwback scene featuring unpainted wooden shed, iconic red Coke machine, and green canoes strewn like pickup sticks on a sloping grassy riverbank.

This time we came with provisions, strawberries and tuna fish sandwiches and a bottle of wine. C. asked if the river water was drinkable and the owner hit us with an are-you-serious smile, so we bought two Cokes from his machine. Didn't want to declare the wine, for fear it might be confiscated by the river police.

"There's a pair of great blue herons nesting half a mile downstream," the owner cued us. "If you head that way you'll likely see them."

So we headed that way, downstream, though we never did see them. There was no shortage of birds, just nothing as dramatic as a great blue heron. ("What's so great about them, anyway?" asked C., predictably.) We did see dozens of turtles, basking on flat rocks and fallen trees. Saw a hundred hyperactive dragonflies.

With the gentle current and a breeze at our backs, we glided effortlessly down the twisting river, concluding we must be complete naturals, seriously talented paddlers. Oh how we praised ourselves for timing, synchronicity. Recalling the canoe trip, at good old Camp Cornish, when Andrew Eagerman declared me a hopeless klutz, I suddenly understood the problem had been Andrew, not me. A Concord River epiphany.

Because C. and I were a team, weren't we? Beyond the simple act of teaming up (traveling, boating, bed) you have to function well together. You have to mesh and we were meshing, weren't we?

It helped that we did our meshing in a paradise: lush sun-threaded forest, meadows and marsh, no houses or cars. We never even encountered another canoe.

"Let us pray," said C., "that these folks do better on the weekends, or they will starve to death running this business."

"Let us assume," I prayed, "that they run it as a tax shelter and could care less how many canoes they rent."

The riverscape became our world in the same way the weedy gravel patch by the Gal Al dumpster had been ours. There was never any hint of our real lives back there, no suggestion of Ian or Winnie. Apart from any obvious metaphors involving garbage, it was a place defined by our presence, our connection. Likewise on this pretty river: it was easy to forget we were a couple of cheaters, easy to feel entitled to the freedom we had so ruthlessly seized. And the further we glided, the freer I felt.

We parked on a tiny island, not much larger than a sub-urban yard. Jumped out and dragged the canoe to where rocks and gravel gave way to grass. When my jeans got soaked in the process, I simply removed them and hung them on a tree in the sun. This was paradise, after all. The island smelled wonderfully of sun-dried earth, of grass and water mingled. Mountain laurel was in full bloom along the south-facing bank.

The red wine (dollar and a half at Libby's) tasted fine and we went right through it. "Pass the bottle!" we kept saying—the refrain from a Russian song C. knew, possibly from a Chekhov play? I would take a swig, he would exclaim "Pass The Bottle!" and then vice versa until we started to lose the rest of our clothing. It was like strip poker without the poker.

After we had sinned deliciously, we sank down into an even more delicious sleep. I did suffer one brief pang, one small wave of guilt that rolled over my soul as I was drifting off. It was a vision of Ian's face, looking so disappointed, sorrowful, as he had the night he left. He wouldn't let me take him to the airport, which if designed to make me feel terrible was well designed indeed. Now it cheered me to feel terrible. It allowed me to think I might be human after all; that I might have "a shred of decency" in me.

Then I was out like a light. It may have been ten minutes, it may have been two hours. (We shared an aversion to wearing watches.) However long a time, we woke to a radically changed day. Paradise Revised! The sun had vanished, the sky had turned a nacreous gray. A chill wind made it feel like late October.

An occluded front, said C., whatever that meant. "Is that a weather joke?" I said. "Is there such a genre?"

The joke was on us, in any case. Everything had changed. That imperceptible current was mighty perceptible as we pad-dled back upstream and into cold swirling gusts. As we battled our way back, it began to dawn on us just how far we had glided.

(Too far, by miles.) Weakened by wine, sex, and sleep, we were no longer claiming to be championship paddlers.

"We're fucked," said C., in his inimitable low-spoken way. "Though hopefully it was worth being so?"

Perhaps, at the time. But now the rain began, and as cold as it was, I suppose we could be grateful it didn't *snow*. Conditions were so freakishly awful it was almost funny, like a bad road movie. Or a good river movie, *The African Queen*, where Bogart and Hepburn (squabbling and seedy and falling into love) tow the damaged tugboat through leach-infested waters.

No cameras on us, and no soundtrack except the seething rain and tubercular wind. We pushed and the river pushed back. Time and again, the wind spun us off course. October gave way to November.

We were shivering and soaked, and it was all such an obvious stacking of the deck against us that at one point we both started laughing and couldn't stop. Mild hysteria, of the contagious sort. Finally C. managed to speak, and reminded me that even after we made it back to the rental shed, we would be miles from the train depot. We would have to hitchhike there (and who would pick up two wet strays?), then take the train, then the T, and then walk again, another mile to the house. "It could take years."

It did take years. By the time we got back to Miller Road, we were wiped out. Frozen, hungry, and *poor*, because we messed up that nice man's tax shelter by owing him an extra fourteen dollars for going past our time limit. Yet somehow we did not hate each other. Somehow we were happy to share the blame. We were a team of fools, a lot less effective than a team of mules, but a team after all.

We sprinted for the shower, jostling for position, and C. cranked it to maximum heat (Scalding or *Flaying* maybe— whatever it had said before the words wore off the valve) and stood under the stream thawing. The cure for being wet, it seems, is being wetter.

Eventually we soaped one another's backs, and bottoms, and unmentionables, until such shenanigans led us straight to bed, all for the sake of warmth, to be sure. The amazing aspect is that later—*later*—when we were clean and dry and dressed, it was not only still light out, it was summer again. The storm had passed and the sun came back in time to set in standard dramatic fashion at the end of Western Avenue. The world-class pollution over St. Johnsbury Trucking yielded a Biblical sunset so grand that one was tempted to begin walking toward it, like a pilgrim.

"May we?" I asked. I probably sounded like a teenager asking her homeroom teacher for a permission slip.

"You don't think we've walked enough today?"

"We have. But I want to walk too much."

"Well, Winnie should be home at this point," he said, clearing what was, by his lights, the first hurdle.

But a strange new flutter passed through me. I was not deluded. I knew the deal; I had *made* the deal. Still, after the day we had just shared, cautionary thoughts of Winnie seemed inappropriate. Which could only mean that it was time to install a few cautionary thoughts of my own; to slap myself upside the head for making fine distinctions within the mea culpa.

"Which leaves only two hundred other people who might see us together?"

"We are friends," he said, approaching the next hurdle. "We did work together. If someone could bump into us, why couldn't we have bumped into each other?"

"That's our story?"

It was, and I would be simultaneously relieved and disappointed that no one bumped into us en route to the House of Florence, or during the hour we sat inside sharing a pizza and a pitcher of beer that was as bad as it was cheap.

Cheap had begun to matter. C. had started with $150, was already under 100. I started with 75. "We could end up eating mushrooms in the woods," he said, "like Elvira Madigan."

"I always wondered whether those two were doomed lovers or just helpless fools?"

"Either way," said C. "Don't you think we qualify on both counts."

"Speak for yourself," I said, alluding to the many cans of tuna and many boxes of pasta in my pantry and the *job* I would be going back to, in less than two weeks. If I stooped for any wild mushrooms, it would be for the gastronomic pleasure.

C. liked hearing that about as much as I had liked his bringing Winnie into the frame. So there were these frissons, little electric shocks, already happening. It was still becoming less complicated for us at that point, easier to be together, yet looking back I see that the complications were massing just offstage, like the clouds that mustered while we were snoozing in Eden.

"Not bad."

"No complaints?"

"It's not my place to complain, dear Lara. Mine is merely to ruminate, and maybe elaborate here and there. I was ruminating on outdoor sex, and how it's kind of an ancient memory at this point. It's not something one does after a certain age, is it?"

"I would imagine that's circumstantial."

"The main circumstance being youth! But one does remember the instances of outdoor sex. There's always something memorable. The mud, the mosquitoes. Getting *caught*. Remember the guy with the camera in Ogunquit?"

"It's the very first occasion I plan to forget, as soon as my Alzheimer's sets in."

"The funniest part about that time on the island was that we were so into it, *really* into it, but in my mind's eye I kept seeing your shapely white bottom rising and dropping in the bold blaring sunlight. Thinking what a sight it must have been for someone slipping quietly past the island in a boat."

"Mercifully, apart from your mind's eye, it went unseen."

"Who knows? At the time, we wouldn't have noticed someone standing two feet away, making a lollygagging Maori face at us."

"We were such fools. I mean, really, what were we thinking?"

"Thinking?"

"Actually, I know what I was thinking. I was thinking God might be too busy to find us right away. Two weeks? With any luck we might be back in our rightful beds while He was still sorting out Angola, or Libya."

"That's where your head was at?"

"It was more like a little prayer I prayed. That He wouldn't strike me down. That I'd make it to confession before He cottoned on to me, and then He would have no choice but to forgive me."

"Did He?"

"I'll find that out at the pearly gates, wise guy."

✍

DAY 3. That next morning was so lovely (our little tong wars, our jousts and jests, somehow morphing into easy affection) that I had to fight off the illusion this was my life. Had to work at remembering that it was *not* my life.

I had not forgotten Ian—how could I?—but it seems I had compartmentalized him. He was my husband, who I dearly loved and with whom I would soon be reunited. That's who he was. Until the night of July 6, he was not so pertinent.

Not that this was conscious. Consciously, alas, I did not even need to push him aside. I was where I was, and glad of it. I might dislike being a woman who could shuttle Ian out the front door, bring C. in through the back, and be *okay* with it. And maybe I should have been bearing down, staging more of a struggle against this callous edition of myself. We were too far inside the storm at that point, though; the wind was pushing us too hard.

God knows I resisted any consideration the storm wouldn't blow over. If C. was right, that the "problem" was sexual, it was all the more likely to pass. For the moment, the deck was unfairly stacked in our favor. In effect we were taking a dream vacation—no work, all play—and taking it in the first beautiful flush of summer. Under such circumstances, I might have been happy running around with Godzilla.

We had taken flight and simply averted our gaze from the crash landing that lay ahead. C. was more and more relaxed. He must have compartmentalized Winnie, as I had done with Ian. Could he compartmentalize the children too? I didn't know how to ask, and didn't ask, just wondered. According to Marisa (she of the three boys, with a fourth on the way) you *always* compartmentalize the children. The trouble is that their compartment is so much larger than yours.

I did ask if he was keeping in touch with home. After all, what if there was some sort of emergency? Wasn't he having nightmares of ambulances and fire trucks gathered outside his house? It turned out he did have a system for putting his mind at ease. If anything like that came up, Winnie would contact Fitz and Fitz would "find a way" to contact C. So I had to assume Fitz knew the deal; that he was an unindicted co-conspirator.

Which did not surprise me. What surprised me was that C. actually had planned ahead, in this one way. But then I did know those children were more important to him than anything— important enough, it turned out, to activate his brain!

I got the car back from Pete that morning ("The clutch," he told me, "should be okay for a while") so we had new means of travel, even a cramped rolling hotel in a pinch. We didn't go far, though. Did not "flee the area," like a pair of escaped killers we heard about on the radio that morning. We began by driving west about twenty miles, stopping for a picnic at Nagog Pond.

The pond is surrounded by woods, though there is a road along the western edge and a few houses before the road dissolves into rocky shore. We jammed the car into a hole in the trees, then bushwhacked fifty yards or so to a minimal beachhead, a silky sandbar not much larger than a living room rug. A huge boulder squatted at the far edge, like emphatic punctuation.

The spot seemed so private, the clearing so intentional, that I assumed we were breaking the law.

"What law would that be?" said C. "We still have our clothes on."

"Well, trespassing is one obvious possibility. And adultery, come to think of it. That's against the law, you know."

"But we still have our clothes on."

"Ingestion of a controlled substance?" I offered next, as I saw him breaking out a joint.

"Worth going to jail for, I'm told. Chimichanga Red, or something—the crème de la cream."

"According to—?"

"Fitz. Who does know his dope."

"You don't?"

"I almost never touch the stuff."

We had discussed this, actually, at one of our dumpster symposiums, and had agreed the "correct" position on marijuana was to enjoy it if it proved enjoyable (for me, not very), but avoid heavy use (Fitz) or major expenditure (Ian's colleague Merrill Bauer).

"Fitz insisted on giving us a present."

"So he does know our sad little story."

"He is the only one, and he won't tell a soul. For a drug addict, Fitz is surprisingly reliable."

"All right, but I don't think I'm into the cream de la crème today."

"There's always tomorrow," said C., a phrase that was fated to become a comic routine between us. He would say there's always tomorrow and I would point out that for us there would *not* always be a tomorrow, and he would look at me as though Day 14 lay somewhere in the next century. The man is not exactly a visionary.

Then we had our little scare. We were in this hole-in-the-woods hideout (and had seen no sign of human life on Planet Nagog) when out of the silence a gravelly voice behind us went

"Howdy." Scalps tingling from the shock of it, we turned to see a gray-haired fellow decked out for fishing.

Damned if C. didn't say "Howdy" right back, even as he was smoothly palming and stowing the joint. You could have peeled the old gent right off a Norman Rockwell canvas: the flannel shirt and overalls, the rod and reel and creel.

"I'm afraid we've invaded your favorite spot," I said, once the shock had passed.

"No. This is Roger Sessions' land, not mine."

"It's a pretty place."

"And you are a pretty lady, so fair's fair. Oh yes, I can still tell by *looking*. No offense, I hope?"

Genuflecting to the feminist movement, I suppose. He was harmless enough and clearly he meant to be sociable. In fact, he seemed delighted to have company—so delighted he refused to let us leave. We tried hard, kept feeding him closeout lines, said sayonara in several languages, and the fellow just kept clutching at our ankles. (Metaphorically.)

"Here's to good fishing," said C., taking my hand, and starting away.

"Care for an apple, either of you?" was the reply.

It wasn't exactly a non sequitur and it wasn't a sequitur either. It was a device. He was binding us to him with an offering.

"I was pretty sure that was a poison apple," C. would later say.

"You've read too many children's books."

"I would bite into it and die, he would slide my body into the pond, then have the pretty lady all to himself."

I had a different paranoia going. In mine, this fellow was an emissary from Winnie, a bolt of reality therapy, a jolt of a reminder that the world is always with you. You can run but you can't hide, and "all that happy horseshit" as Ian would say.

We finally shook free, continued west, tried again for our picnic in a tame state park. The main trail was cordoned by a thousand flowering rhododendrons and featured more seating facilities than a cafeteria—bench and a barrel here, bench and a barrel there, that was the master plan. We ate the lunch I packed (and smoked the joint), then decided to head back to town. Everything on our agenda was going to be arbitrary, but somehow this super tidy slice of "wilderness" seemed to beg the question. It was still early afternoon when we got back to Miller Road, plenty of time for our next arbitrary move.

"So here we are," I said, "with nothing to do."

"Maybe we'll get lucky again," said C., tackling me onto the bed and starting to strip off my clothes, of which there were few. It might have been the Chimichanga Red that had us rolling around like puppies and laughing.

It was kind of brilliant, C's way of making sex a joke (or framing it as a playful game, which after all is what it is) because it had been so good the last time that it made me shy. Absurdly, I had felt some pressure to match or top it and now that felt ridiculous. C. eliminated the possibility of "failure." Had it been flat, or merely passable, we could just say, Oh well, not so lucky after all.

Which did not prove necessary, though we will have no specifics here from Sally Cleary's daughter. I thought of her actually, after the pyrotechnics. I remembered the phrase she had for men she found attractive, mostly movie stars from the '40s and '50s. "A fine physical specimen," she would say. Gary Cooper was her favorite, and later Robert Mitchum. Even back then, even without showing any sex in the movies, Hollywood expected people to see it and they did. My *mother* saw it, for goodness' sake, in her fine physical specimens.

It isn't C.'s looks, though. I might have thought that, but I am afraid he could be ordinary looking and still have presented a big problem. It isn't his other obvious attributes, either, that he is smart and funny (and fun, which is another matter entirely) and much nicer than I ever dreamed. He gets high marks all around. He was even a track star, I gather, should anyone care about such things.

The problem was more that he is so comfortable to be around. Comfortable with himself, comfortable in the world.

That we were so comfortable together. I was beginning to trust him even though from my point of view nothing could have been crazier. Trust what, exactly? Lower my defenses for what earthly reason? But it isn't like that. It's an emotion, and I was in danger of disappearing down into it.

∽

DAY 4, June 22, was a bad day for the simple reason that it was such a good day. Such were the paradoxes I found myself fielding. There was even a moment when the word "love" flashed across the sky of my childish mind. Just a word—and a word unspoken, to be sure. I never *said* love. Plus, as the song says, "a moment isn't very long." Hadn't there been a moment, the very first time I met C., when I actively disliked him? So that was not valid either.

I remember a quiet start to that day, sun blasting the bedroom early, coffee and toast (with Dundee's orange marmalade) and the newspaper parceled out like old marrieds. How did we manage to have this? Why did Ian and Winnie allow us to have it? I do understand we were selfish and we took it. Still, what were they thinking? I was almost angry with them for not stopping us.

Ian nearly did, of course. Walking home one day, he reported, his "liberalism faded, big time" and he decided to write me off. He was all set to walk in and say "Fuck you, go if you want, but you won't find me awaiting the verdict when you get back." Why didn't he stick to his guns? What would I have done if he had?

Honestly, I expected nothing less from him. I never dreamed he would say fine, get it out of your system, I need you to lay it to rest as much as you do. Yet that's what he said, before and after. That he loved me and he knew it; that he needed me and would take the chance. "It's a chance I get you for good, as much as a chance of losing you." As though I were a prize of some sort.

It's almost a joke that these two attractive men, men who could have their pick of the litter, would pick me. Ian, who broke up with Amanda Hooper for me, and C., who is married to the beautiful Winnifred. In a field which included Amanda and Winnie, I am somehow the prize?

Officially, I am "fun." That's always been said, even in high school—and why not, it's a high school sort of category, a year-book accolade, Most Fun to Be With. So I was maybe fourteenth most-fun-to-be-with. But no one ever called me beautiful. No one even found me attractive until I was eighteen. At which point I must have been a distinctly unusual attraction, at five feet six and about 99 pounds.

I may be a slightly stronger candidate now (at five feet six and 114), yet it remains bizarre, this intense attention. I don't think anyone is lying, exactly, I just can't trust it. I am no more immune to flattery than the next person, it's just that I was inoculated against its worst toxins early on. Any day, I caution myself, the bubble could burst and they will again see me as I really am.

Anyway, on Day 4 we shared an impulse to lay low, stay home all morning and be lazy, and we might have done that had C. chosen a different phrase. "Why don't we just stay home," is what he said, though, and the word sounded in my skull like a gong. This was *not* home, or not our home. We were sublessees and our lease was short.

The day was broiling hot by the time we headed out Route 2 again. The freshly hatched (and of course arbitrary) plan was to explore out by the Quabbin Reservoir, maybe find some place to swim, eat lunch in a diner somewhere. This was hardly a tightly wrapped itinerary, and it got a lot looser when we decided to hike down a blazed trail in search of the "splendid prospect of the central valley" that was promised on a faded bulletin board.

We never got the splendid prospect. Lost track of the yellow blazes, veered off the trail, and fell among mosquitoes and their smaller cousins, no-see-ums according to C. We didn't see 'em but we sure felt 'em, and we were also feeling the building heat of the day. There was a bit of shade on that forest track, but there was no breathable air and no breeze at all.

"Two expensive educations wasted," I said, as I murdered another mosquito. "Off we go into the woods to engage the enemy on his own turf."

"Her own turf. Or didn't you know that only the female mosquito bites?"

"To me, that is an insignificant detail, not an indictment of Germaine Greer."

"I wasn't indicting anyone, just correcting the possessive pronoun. As someone so expensively educated ought to do."

"Correct this," I said, bumping him with my backside.

"Impossible. The body part in question does not allow of correction."

"You can stop flattering me, Calvert. The seduction part is done. We're in the muck now."

This was not metaphorical. We had come into a marshy area (clearly a Mecca for insects) where our shoes made sucking sounds each time we lifted them. I was about to suggest we turn back, just make a run for it, when suddenly the woods opened out onto smoky blue sky and dead treetops, and we found ourselves at the edge of a small weedy pond.

"Water!" we cried, like desert rats spying an oasis. C. was out of his clothes and into the murky pool in ten seconds flat. My reaction was more cautious, as in No way, not I. Snakes occurred to me, and leeches. But I changed my mind after a minute spent watching C. splash around like a happy child, while I stood there providing a landing strip for every female mosquito in Massachusetts.

He had thrown off his clothes as though they were on fire. I removed my own a good deal more carefully, and even more carefully folded Gram's necklace into the neat pile I made. Then I went in, just as carefully, step by experimental step. This water, or *soup*, was totally opaque; you couldn't see a thing under the surface. It was cool and soothing, though, once I became submerged. Snakes were still on my mind, but for the moment no one was feasting on my flesh.

"Why do you suppose God even made mosquitoes?" I said. "Do they do something useful?"

Only our heads were above the waterline when C.'s head said, "God? Is that someone I should meet?"

We were both raised Catholic. C. now is as religious as a brick—it's utter nonsense to him—whereas I am unable to say that. I can see it *appears* to be nonsense, but I can't quite say that it *is* nonsense. (What I say instead is, Why do you suppose God made these bugs?)

We had not jumped into anyone's classic old swimmin' hole. That water was pretty gross. Any time your feet touched bottom, a swirl of disintegrating leaf matter was released upward. If you raised an arm, it came out coated with blackish bits of stuff. When you stood to your waist, your breasts were so heavily decorated with this subaqueous compost you felt *dressed*, albeit like a creature from a horror flick.

And when finally you waded out, the muck on your backside somehow clung to and revealed hairs that were "not really there—they're only there when the mud defines them as such," or so C. told me later, in the shower, as he leaned down to examine me closely (both visually and manually) and failed to locate these hairs.

We had debated what was worse, staying in or getting out. We were lost in the woods, I mentioned, but did that dictate staying in or getting out? C. assured me we could not be lost because he had a compass in his head. "Is this it?" I said, rubbing a sort of knob on his cranium.

Maybe it was (and maybe he was just lucky) because he did get us back to the skein of blazed triangles and then quite briskly to the car. Soon enough we were pulling into a roadside hamburger stand shabby enough to serve people who looked the way we did—which is to say extremely marginal, like escaped criminals who hadn't had time to change clothes. There was one umbrella table on a gravel turnout and we sat there, dining al fresco, downing our cheeseburgers and Cokes like true-blue Americans. For some (unexamined) reason I felt ridiculously happy.

Then about twenty ridiculously happy miles to the east, I let loose a sudden bloodcurdling scream that, to C.'s credit, did not cause him to drive off the road. I never go anywhere without Gram's necklace and I never, ever, take it off. But I did take it off at that godforsaken pond to avoid losing it, and so I lost it. That chain was *always* around my neck, how could I not notice it was gone? How could I have been so distracted?

Even in my moment of stark panic, though, I did grasp that this was not war or cancer. It was a trivial, sentimental, bourgeois loss. Which only meant I had no justification for the *grief* that flooded my throat and chest. It was the same constriction I had felt there when Gram actually *died* and I had to walk myself through the fine art of breathing.

There was nothing for it. The necklace was an hour in the rearview mirror, a mile into the woods, and who knows how deep in the damp disintegrating leaf matter of that swamp. All I could do was to keep breathing and start adjusting. Grow up and start getting used to the fact Gram's necklace was gone.

Offer it up, as Mom would say. Because life was loss, end on end. Only by offering up your losses could you manage to absorb them. She never said *how*, and it did become something of a chuckle between us. What it boiled down to for her, I think, was a good trick for hanging on to your happiness. A way to keep loving life even when life did not love you.

"Offer it up?" said C. "Now there's one I haven't heard in a while. You must have known my Aunt Grace."

"My mother. Maybe it was their whole generation, or at least that generation of Catholics . . . Cal, what are you doing?"

(He was hanging a U-turn, was what.)

"It could have been worse," he was saying. "We could have got all the way to Cambridge before you realized it was gone. Hey, it won't even be dark for hours."

"Calvert, you don't have to do this. It's just a necklace. It isn't even real. I mean, the stones are paste."

"You should see your face. If you think you can convince me this isn't the most important object in the world to you, just take a look in the mirror."

"The point is we'll never find it. We'll never even find that place. Honestly, I will survive."

"We might not find it, but we have to try, don't we? If we fail, then it'll have to be okay. You can pay for the extra gas, if you feel that bad about it."

"I don't get it. Where is your famous temper? Where is your legendary impatience?"

"Bum raps, obviously. And I do like a challenge."

"You think you'll find it, don't you? A treasure hunt. Find the tiny necklace in the big messy bog."

"I'm just saying we give it a shot. Why not take advantage of the compass in my head?"

I gave his head a vigorous rub (for luck) and joked about the compass, but my emotions were all over the map—a big messy bog. I was sad about Gram, ashamed of myself, grateful to C. for his determination to cheer me up a bit before admitting that needles in haystacks are not really findable.

Sometimes they are, though. He had no trouble getting us back to the pond and to the clump of brush where I had piled my clothes ("It wasn't likely anyone had erased our footprints," he said) and no hesitation in fishing the necklace from a handful of shallow soil. He gave it a quick rinse and placed it around my neck and that was that, as if nothing could be more ordinary. As if he had not just performed a miracle.

And though I could not/would not say so, at that moment I truly did believe in God. All appearances favored Him.

The ride back was sweet and quiet, listening to WCOP on the radio and sort of musing. How could C. have been so considerate, I mused? How (I mused) could he have performed this little miracle so gently? Was this the same man who had snarled at Winnie that day?

That man might well have said, If a stupid piece of jewelry was that important to you, why didn't you take better care of it? And he would have been right to say so. Instead he gave my hand a squeeze, wheeled the car around, and retrieved Gram's necklace for me—a needle in a swamp. I am wearing it now and I don't doubt it will stay right where it is every second from now until the day I die.

I just wonder if every time I touch it, I will think of C. first and not Gram. Because so far (not very far, admittedly, not yet a month) that has proved to be the case.

∽

"I LIKE it. I don't like the part where you expected me to be a shit, but I like the outcome, where I cure cancer and walk on the moon. There is one minor correction—"

"It can't be *corrected*, Calvert. It's a historical document. A primary source."

"One major omission, then. You left out the whole quicksand panic."

"Quicksand?"

"Come on, Lara. You went on and on about it. How you had no fear of anything in nature. Lightning, avalanches, crocodiles— there was a long impressive list of everything that had never alarmed you in the slightest. And quicksand was the sole exception. You had watched a movie when you were eight. The safari starts to ford a jungle river and only too late they realize it's . . . *quicksand*. They start sinking, their rifles and backpacks go under, their mouths, their hats—and then they're gone."

"Quicksand is really scary."

"You were convinced the floor of that pond was quicksand. You were dead set against going in."

"I had a shred of common sense, if that's what you mean. Face it, Cal, you would jump into any old water. So I had you test it the way paranoid tyrants have food-tasters. If you sank from sight, I would pass it up. If you didn't, I would take a refreshing dip."

"So you do remember."

"Here's what I remember: that when we were driving home the second time (we had retrieved the necklace, you had cured cancer) and we were quiet and happy and extremely tired, I watched the landscape going by and realized quicksand was the perfect metaphor for what we had stepped into. Muck and mire you wash off and go on with your life. Quicksand you sink, helplessly."

⟋

DAY 4 had taken some of the starch out of us. It wasn't the miles we walked, or the miles we drove. It was the bugs, the heat, the being lost, the whole necklace fiasco. It was doing everything twice, backtracking, under pressure. Something else Mom once said came back to me: when you get past fifty, the morning can be stronger than you are. So I guess we were fifty-four that morning.

We took our toast and coffee back to bed and just lay there talking as sunlight poured into the room. Did not budge, except to get ourselves more coffee at "break time," as Ian calls it. The only job he ever had where they did a regular workingman's coffee break was one summer in college, as a laborer on the Alaska pipeline. He was there about two months and yet ten A.M. will forever be "break time" to him.

We were just bumping feet, massaging legs with toes, talking. About C.'s parents, an engineer and a nurse, and about his Uncle Lew, who played minor league baseball and then became a sportswriter for the Albany paper—the *Times-Union,* maybe? About high school. I was surprised to learn he didn't have a girlfriend until he was seventeen, then had a pregnancy scare that warned him off serious sex until college.

I remember feeling self-conscious when I went back to the kitchen, and considered how odd that was when we had been naked together for the last ten hours. I reached for my robe, though, and C. said, "Please don't, I'm watching you." (Maybe that's why I felt self-conscious. Watched!) "In fact, I'm taking pictures of you in the nude."

"I *hope* not," I laughed, and he assured me his pictures were "not pornographic, not even erotic, just beautiful. Plus of course there is no actual camera."

I leaned over, kissed him on the nose, and put on my robe. Only to take it off again a minute later. Clearly, not everything makes sense. Who knows why I wanted to cover up when I was standing ten feet away, and didn't care at all when we were close enough to sin.

Afterward we put together the water leitmotif. How each day, willynilly, we had wended our way to sea, river, or pond. This was logical enough ("It is 'late June,'" said C.) and I wasn't complaining, just identifying a pattern. Then, because C. likes a challenge, I challenged him to come up with a land-locked destination for the day at hand.

"I know a place we can get to without driving, that has no recreational water, and where there will be twenty thousand complete strangers. Care to guess?"

"State prison? Army barracks? M.I.T.?"

"Close. Fenway Park. What do you say? A dollar apiece, if we sit in the bleachers."

"Won't we be bleached?"

"Broiled. But they have beer for that."

"Twenty thousand people from around here might not all be strangers, Cal."

"We'll go in disguise. Sunglasses and hats, for starters. Maybe I'll walk with crutches."

"Why stop there? Why not rent a wheelchair and have me push you. Why not wigs?"

"Wigs, for sure! I know a place that rents them."

Over the phone, C. told the saleslady we needed one Harpo Marx and one Elsa Lanchester ("her *Bride of Frankenstein* look") and was encouraged to pleasehold while she checked. In the end we settled for the sunglasses and hats (she had those in stock) and altered hairstyles. I put mine up and pinned it inside a scarf (with the sunglasses, I was Garbo) and C. slicked his straight back, greaser style. To us, at least, we did not look like us.

The ballpark turned out to be a pretty neat place to spend an afternoon. I loved how the green green grass seemed both warm and cool, the way the stands felt both crowded and roomy. Maybe there really were twenty thousand people, but there are over thirty thousand seats. The bleachers were so sparsely populated that we became fast friends with the beer man and the hot dog man. Hot Dogs even sat with us for an inning. Unstrapped his hamper, lit a cigar, and took in the game.

I must say that baseball is an awfully casual sport. It unfolds almost in slow motion, or slow motion punctuated by absolute stillness. All those terrific athletes with nothing much to *do*. Bernie the right fielder was sufficiently bored to engage with the fans, frequently waving and smiling. Before each inning he and another outfielder would heave a ball back and forth, then he would look for a kid in the stands and toss the ball to him.

Nice as Bernie seemed, one beer-swilling beer-spilling leather-lung kept riding him, screaming what a bum he was, what a dog. Bernie was cool. He would just turn and smile. After he made a good catch, kind of casually over his shoulder, he gave the guy a quizzical shrug as if to say, How am I doing now?

Oddly, no one appeared to care a lot about winning or losing. Like us, Bernie seemed content to be stationed out there in the sunshine, on that lovely grass, though C. suggested he might also like the fat paycheck. A couple several rows behind us heard him say this and came down to discuss it. "Do you mind?" we heard someone say, and before we could mind or not mind we had new friends, Sol and Abby.

Sol, who was very serious and clearly political, felt a need to inform us that Bernie made more money standing still two hours a day than he, Sol, would earn from working hard all year. I saw Abby touch his arm gently—it was clear Sol had gone on about this before—and speculate that Bernie gave a lot of it to charity.

"Ask him," said C., only half joking, since Bernie seemed perfectly willing to join in any conversation.

It struck me that to Sol and Abby we must appear to be a relaxed, sociable couple from Cambridge. We did not explain that each of us represented fifty percent of a different, legitimate couple and that we were therefore blackguards, archvillains. They had come down from Maine for their "annual baseball-junkie junket" and they seemed as uncomplicated as Midwesterners—though I did recall the one subtle gesture, Abby restraining Sol's political tirade.

Much later, back at Miller Road, C. would point out to me that they might be plenty complicated. That for all we knew they were just like us: escapees, cheaters, *swine*. We could not even corroborate their claim to be from Maine. "Sol sounded more like New Jersey to me."

"You don't suppose those were wigs they were wearing?"

"I wouldn't bet against it. Things are not always as they seem."

"Maybe things are never as they seem."

"Discouraging, isn't it. Trying to figure anything out."

"Such as?"

"Us?"

"That one is easy. There is no Us, Calvert."

"Oops, I forgot. Though it's interesting that, as you say, to Sol and Abby there did seem to be an Us. Or do we deny that too?"

"No, we admit that."

"Just as to us—lower case us, of course—there did seem to be a Sol and Abby."

"Fair enough."

"Okay, now we're getting somewhere. Would you admit there was a 'we' sitting in the bleachers this afternoon—the very same 'we' that is lying here now? And, if so, would you admit that 'we' are about to be fucking?"

"Get away from there," I said, but he didn't and so we were (fucking, though I do not care for the word) and I will not discuss it except to say it was not a lower case F—.

Here's the thing with sex: it's what matters. Nobody cares what two people do together, so long as it isn't sex. They could be incredibly close, totally interdependent. They could meet for coffee, take long walks in the arboretum, go to the movies. Provided with a magical mystical guarantee there would be no sex, their spouses wouldn't much mind the rest of it.

It's sex they mind, just as it's sex we wanted the freedom to have. Otherwise we would not have needed The Twoweeks. Why didn't I know this, when it was so obvious? Normal people probably learn it in junior high school: that the only dangerous attraction is sexual, the deep desperate jealousy is sexual.

After the ball game we went for tacos and beer at a place near Fenway Park—went, that is, with our dear friends Sol and Abby! We talked baseball, jobs, and politics with them for over an hour. We even covered read-any-good-books-lately. By the end, we were *exchanging phone numbers* with them, and let's see how *that* works out.

I couldn't help thinking we were playing at "couple life," as Ian calls it, the same way we were sort of playing house. There is a loneliness to cheating. You are out there on a two-man raft, bobbing on an open sea, and it's an awfully circumscribed sort of freedom. Sitting in an arbitrary bar with an arbitrary couple somehow pushed back that lonely-making aspect. We weren't cheating, we were just having this tiny little two-week-long marriage.

I am sure it's why we started talking about a get-together with Gerald and Debra. Or I did. C. could take it or leave it.

"Couple life, you say?"

"Social life," I revised, so as to leave Ian out of it. "At its most basic level. Four friends at a dinner table. I was also thinking it might lighten the load to tell someone."

"To tell what we're doing? Fitz knows."

"Someone besides Fitz. Someone who knows us."

"Us, did I hear you say?"

"us, is what I said."

He heard the distinction. And he shared a sense that after all the hours we had spent with them at Gallery Allison, we probably were something of a couple to Gerald and Debra. They knew of Ian's existence, and Winnie's, but we were the ones they connected with. We were there at Gal Al, and we always came as a pair.

"Let's decide tomorrow," said C., for whom (I have figured out) "tomorrow" is nothing more than a storage bin for unwelcome questions.

"Sure. Or never. It's just an idea. But—further incentive?—they do have that house on Plum Island for the summer. We could resume our water leitmotif in style."

"We'll do it. One of these days."

As if we had days to burn, an endless skein of days. Clearly, C. would not see the finish line until he tripped over it. At times, I shared his delusion. At other times, I wondered if we should move the finish line up, end it sooner if we hoped to get out intact. It was increasingly obvious that to hoard these days, to treasure each hour, was to invite real trouble. We were barely five days into our little fake marriage and already it felt too much like a life.

A warped and narrow life, to be sure, yet the situation did create a ferocious focus that bestowed upon that handful of days the illusion of a long-term relationship. With everything so compressed, so accelerated, we knew each other on a level we might have expected after progressing for months at a normal pace. And the closer we grew, the more I wondered whether we were lucky (as we had all along presumed) or very unlucky to have this time together.

When I doubted out loud that we would ever know the answer to that question, C. replied without the slightest hesitation (or the tiniest scrap of reflection) yet with the utmost authority, "Oh, very lucky. Blessed, entirely."

∽

"I NTERESTING."

"Acceptable, though? To your restless probing mind?"

"It's what you wrote down. What you saw and felt. Now as to what you omitted—"

"Not another quicksand moment? Something essential I forgot?"

"It seems unlikely you *forgot* it, so soon after. Omitted, is what I said. And for good reasons, I'm sure."

"All right, what was it, and what were the good reasons? Whatever I remembered at the time, I surely don't remember it now."

"It was a pimple, my sweet. And the reason—here I'm guessing—would be simple kindness. And possibly the fact that while it was important to me, it was superficial to you. Not worth mentioning."

"You took your shirt off. We discussed that, how unfair it was that men could take their shirts off on a hot day and women couldn't."

"You were tempted to take yours off just to make a point. Or two points . . ."

"But I didn't, of course. You did, and there was a bump on your back."

"A pimple, yes. So you do remember."

"I do now. You were very self-conscious about your bump. More self-conscious than I would have been with my breasts showing."

"Or so you said."

"You were vain."

"Not vain. Concerned. That you might be repulsed."

"I told you that bump had been there for days. Calvert, I had been in *bed* with you for days. I had even *touched* your terrible spot."

"Spot. Bump. So kind, my dear Lara. But bed was one thing, the cruel harsh sunlight of the bleachers might be another. So I worried."

"You needn't have."

"On the contrary. I was insecure because you made me insecure."

"You? Insecure?"

"I was madly in love with you and you kept counting down. Nine more days, eight more days, a deal's a deal . . ."

"That *was* the deal. It had nothing to do with pimples, it had to do with Jake and Hetty and Winnie. With Ian."

"You know what I had forgotten? To change the subject just slightly. Sol and Abby. I could have given you chapter and verse on the loud asshole who was hassling Bernie Carbo, but I completely forgot our friends from Down East."

"No one's perfect, I guess."

"I also forgot how easy it was to go to a game at Fenway back then. You could stroll up to the windows, buy a ticket for a couple of bucks, walk in and watch the game."

"That was the hard part. Watching the game."

"Like watching paint dry, you said at the time."

"Yes, though I also said I like watching paint dry, given a hammock and a pleasant summer day. And I remember liking the way you could see the hands of the men changing numbers on the scoreboard. From inside the Green Monster."

"They still do that. Everything else there has changed. It's such an institution now, it's like the Pops or the MFA, it's become big business."

"You sound like an old fuddy-duddy, Cal. Why back in *my* day . . ."

"I am an old fuddy-duddy."

"Young skin, though. Isn't that what you were told by some wench at a party? In fact, let's have a look at your back. Step into the light, you whippersnapper, and we'll check you for bumps."

"We could go upstairs and check? If you like."

"Another time, champ. Let's get on with this."

❧

D<small>AY</small> 6. That was the morning I called Debra, who was cool with the idea of a foursome, though I was assessed a verbal tax for calling it that. "It's not a *foursome*," C. insisted. "We won't be playing *bridge*."

He didn't much like the idea, or maybe the way I had got locked onto it. I guess he had less of a problem with the intensity—the unnatural intensity—of our days. Really, never in my life had I spent a hundred consecutive hours in the company of one person. Nor had I dreamed I was capable of such a thing without going bonkers.

Again, The Twoweeks "format" dictated this to a great extent. By allotting us a fixed reservoir of hours, it created a powerful drive to wring every drop from each hour. Add the sad truth that we were having a magical time, a *uniquely* happy time together, and you get to thinking (at least I got to thinking) we had better dilute this somehow or else end it ahead of schedule.

What had I expected from The Twoweeks? For that matter, what did I want? If I were honest with myself, I would say I wanted it to be a howling success—for maybe twelve days. Special but self-limiting. It would tail off, we would both become eager for the end, maybe bag it a couple of days early, and feel delighted to be going home.

I suppose I wanted C. to find me hard to get around, because who wants to be easy to get around? But I refused to work for that result. To the contrary. On principle, I paraded all my warts. Gave him every excuse to dismiss me out of hand. Nixon, for instance. C. was exactly like Ian, he had a pressing need for me to hate Nixon as much as he did. But Nixon was so pathetic, I couldn't hate him. How could you not feel a little sorry for such a sad slimy creep?

The Church was another instance. To C., the Catholic Church was worse than just the smoke and mirrors, it was corrupt and oppressive and a danger to children. So I assured him I still believed, in a way; and still attended Mass. Which I do, very occasionally. I refused to emphasize the occasionally, though I emphasized the attended.

Then there were my actual warts, all my physical shortcomings. Let him make what he would of my below-average breasts or the mole on my belly. Let him prospect for *cilia* on my muddy bottom. Far from luring him on, or seducing him, I would be the least appealing version of myself, the Plain Jane version—and positively riddled with uncool ideas. If I hoped he would find me irresistible in spite of it all, that would just be human nature.

Determined to be as honest with myself as well, I took to weighing out my emotions in milligrams, reckoning affection in fractions. Why couldn't one admit loving someone say nineteen percent if she loved her husband the other eighty-one percent? Or even forty-seven percent and fifty-three percent, which would seem a clear enough margin in any presidential election. Does anyone, *should* anyone, ever love a spouse with *all* her heart? It seemed so unlikely, so unrealistic.

Anyway, whatever I expected or wanted (or *got*), our twosome had two days to fill before our foursome on Plum Island.

"Let's fill them with hot air," said C., "and soar above this vale of tears."

"Cal, you're the bad actor. *I'm* supposed to be the bad poet."

"Can we afford to fill them on the Cape? The two days, I mean."

"The Cape? It's summer, Cal."

"Yes and no. It's Monday and it's still before high season. Plus, you wouldn't want to go down there when it's *not* summer."

"Would so."

I happen to prefer the Cape in October or November. I like walking on a deserted beach with my clothes on, my below-average breasts and my mole entirely private. But if we went to the Cape, C. might stop pretending his eyes weren't darting around like dragonflies, watching for Winnie any time we left the shelter of Miller Road. The odds of seeing her in Harvard Square might be 5 to 1, the odds on Cape Cod more like 5,000 to 1.

C. and I had very different memories of the Cape. Ian and I spent our honeymoon there, in Truro, in a sail-loft on the Pamet River. The tidal creek, the leaky rowboat, the creaky bed tucked under pitch-piney ceiling planks. (They sloped down in such a way that not hitting your head became an art.) I did love Ian one hundred percent that week. Given one year to spend anywhere on earth as the world was ending—this was more or less a party game—we agreed we would choose that cottage on the Pamet.

Meanwhile, Patti Page had not crooned so sweetly about Old Cape Cod to C. and Winnie. Taking up the offer of a free house in Woods Hole one summer, they got a solid week of rain. They tried it again the next year and both kids were sick the whole time.

So we scratched Woods Hole on grounds of bad vibes, scratched Truro on grounds of good vibes, and decided to try the ruined Cape, some no-longer-charming town where no one we knew would ever go. Dennisport was the lucky winner! The denizens of Dennisport were first in line for our tourist dollar.

It was just barely pre-season in terms of all the nasty variables (traffic coming and going, traffic there, July and August prices) and because it was a Monday, we got a decent one-night deal at the Horizon Motor Hotel. As of July 1, there would be a minimum three-day stay there, but on Monday, June 24, our hostess Mrs. Amirault was happy to have our twenty dollars while retaining the right to price-gouge someone else on the weekend.

All the rooms opened onto Nantucket Sound (the Horizon part) in back and onto the parking lot (the Motor part) in front. Each room had a minimal flagstone patio with two folding chairs and the general idea seemed to be you sat in the chairs, drank gin-and-tonics, and stared at the water.

"Keep going?" said C., when he caught me dutifully (and quite blissfully) staring out to sea. "Is that what you're thinking? We should keep going and hide out in the Azores?"

My smile was that of someone tolerating a naughty boy, affection mingled with playful disapproval. What I was thinking (which I kept to myself) was that it might be best to do the Cape Cod days, do the visit to Plum Island, and then bag it at nine days. That would allow some time to enjoy, enough time to give Cal notice, so to speak, and time to adjust.

We went to the beach for a couple of hours—I waded, he swam—then came back for a "nap" around three. Before dinner, we took a quart of cold Colt .45 and sat by the pool with it. This was part laziness on our part—packing up to go back to the beach seemed almost like work—and part research on mine. I have always wondered why beachfront motels even have swimming pools and the reason, it turns out, is that surprisingly few people swim in the ocean.

On the beach, people will wade, sunbathe, read (and *stare*, of course), but if they swim, they swim in the pool. And this is especially true of parents (such as Sherry) with small children (such as Bart).

C. adopted little jug-eared Bart on the spot. In fact, he so devoted himself to little jug-eared Bart (the swimming lesson, the floating basketball hoop, the ice cream treat) that Bart's mom started looking a bit nervous. For all she knew, C. was a molester and I was just his beard. There was no way to convey the utterly simplistic psychological truth to Sherry, that this man (the father of a boy he has temporarily abandoned, loves to distraction, feels sick with guilt over) was using her son as a surrogate.

"He loves kids," was all I said, smiling at Sherry and her well-above-average abundantly-displayed breasts, and then in a grotesquely us-girls moment I added, "He's really just a big kid himself."

Did I actually speak that sentence? How pathetic we can be, when confined by the shackles of sociability. It was true, though, about C. and children. When Gerald asked him, two days later on Plum Island, why he went and had two kids before the age of twenty-six, C's answer was perfectly unguarded, so innocent: "Why don't you have any? Hey man, you're past thirty."

I have never known a man who enjoyed his children as much, and it's a very appealing trait. How bad can he be if his heart belongs to them like that? Really, what better definition is there of a "good man"? A selfless jungle doctor, braving black mambas to cure malaria? Sure. But in everyday middle-class terms, you might have to go with the loving husband and father.

C. may fall short on the loving husband part, Ian on the fatherhood. "Not ready to share you with another man yet," he has said, a statement rendered ironic only through my own failings. He claims that, given a choice, most men would never have a child. "They cost money, get in the way, absorb the little woman's attention, and wreak havoc on her girlish figure." He was grinning as he ticked off these charming arguments, but I could hardly imagine Ian horsing around with little jug-eared Bart at the Horizon Motor Hotel.

We ate fish and chips (eight dollars total, which included horrible coffee in Styrofoam cups) sitting at a bench in another parking lot. Walking back from that fry shack, our ice cream cones rapidly melting, I felt strangely contented. I was the existentialist princess, safe inside the Cape Cod bubble, cut loose from past and future alike.

Then I noticed C. was on a different page. He had begun to seem uneasy, distracted. Guessing it was about Jake and Hetty (withdrawal symptoms, guilt?) I urged him to call home. He didn't have to tell them where he was, just say hello.

"I don't want to lie to them."

"Just to Winnie?"

"I don't want to lie to her, either. I *won't* lie to them."

"Tell them an obvious lie, the kind of lie that's more like a game. You're prospecting for diamonds in the Congo, something storybook that they'll just laugh at. Just so you can hear their voices, and they can hear yours."

He smiled absently (translation: No Sale) and I pretty much let it go at that, except to urge upon him that if his reluctance had anything to do with a sense of fairness to me, he should abandon it. I *wanted* him to call. When he did break down later and call, though, it made matters worse. No answer.

"Try again later," I shrugged.

"It's already late," he said, despondently. "It's past their bedtime."

This was a worry. If they were not home at bedtime, where were they? Even I knew Winnie could never resist picking up the phone. She is one of those people who hears it ring and constitutionally can't not answer.

"Maybe she was busy *putting* them to bed and didn't get to the phone in time."

"I dialed it twice," he said, despairingly.

Then it hit him, eureka eureka. They were going to the country for three days, to Winnie's parents in Bearsville. That's where they were, that was the explanation, and the bonus was knowing they would be having a great time. They would be happy.

Then we had one last flurry of worry: they would be fine "if the car went all right."

"Is there something wrong with the car?"

"Is there something *right* with it?" said C.

At that point, though, he was pretty much done worrying. I pretty much had him back. We could be lower-case-us again, at liberty in charmless Dennisport. Standing on the beach, we watched the ceaselessly arriving waves (each one different, like snowflakes) and noted the crescent moon. ("Dwindled and thinned," I had to quote Hopkins.) At a bar inevitably called the Boathouse, somewhat wearied by our efforts to be carefree, we toasted the ocean with frosted mugs of Tuborg.

Then home to the Horizon Motor Hotel. Now that C. had wrestled down his demons, he was ready to wrestle me again. Gloomy-guts was ready to be playful. Briefly, though. With all that sun and beer and worry, he fell asleep the instant we were done.

I was not so fortunate, though I might have been. I'd had the same long day. Sleep was indicated, no question, it simply wasn't going to happen. For one thing, cars kept pulling in and out. Every time I started drifting, another engine would clear its throat in the parking lot, another set of headlights would sweep our window like a searchlight.

Then a poem started pecking away at me. A shard here, a thread there, finally a shape of sorts—a sense of what it was trying to be about. As coherent lines began forming, I did feel responsible for at least moderating the process.

An hour later, I was off the poem and doing some basic math. According to my calculations, we were nearly halfway through The Twoweeks and would be nearly two-thirds of the way when we returned from our foray to Plum Island. If we were to shut it down after nine days, as I contemplated, we would be at the finish line after Plum Island! This was serious, even radical momentum.

When I tried going back to the poem for solace, I found it had flown. The sense of it escaped me. At a bright red 3:18 on the digital clock radio, I got out of bed and went outside and there (*right there*) was the white curling surf, the restless front paws of a worldwide tide that turned and returned twice each day from the shores of far continents. That such a vast global tub-tilting could reveal itself at the back door of the Horizon Motor Hotel somehow calmed me. Our precious days were once more rendered trivial. However many or few we had left to us—however happy or sad, however free or fraught—they were obviously trivial, and somehow this condition reassured me. Somehow, mercifully, it allowed me to sleep.

According to a placard atop our TV, we were "Entitled" (no less) "to the Sandbar Breakfast, served Free of Charge in the comfortable sunroom off the lobby."

The sunroom was comfortable enough, but the coffee was weak and burnt, and the pastries were dry as dust. Stale last week. I suggested a diner we had noticed half a mile up the highway, but C. wanted to stay and eat a few stale free-of-charge crullers. Getting our money's worth was his thing.

Which meant breakfast at the diner was on me. Which was fine. The who-pays-today game was just a joke, though perhaps the exchanges were indicative. I laughed when C. was stuffing that ghastly thing into his mouth, but would I have been laughing if we were married? If we were a real couple (traveling, foraging) and he reacted that way? Ian and I had always been nicely aligned on the money question, both willing to "waste" a little money when it is yielding zero enjoyment. C. would suffer through an awful movie because why waste a ticket he had paid for; Ian and I would make our escape, and gladly, because why waste the time?

It started out rainy that morning (Day 7) and people scattered like cockroaches when the kitchen lights come on. Off-season or not, all the roads were clogged with cars. Maybe stale crullers were the continental breakfast at every motel, because that diner was packed, no chance at a table. We grabbed the last two seats at the counter as a waiting line was forming. Hungry souls loomed over us as we ate.

"Pretend you're still chewing," I said, as the impatient horde pressed forward, looking ready for open revolt.

"I *am* still chewing," said C., chipmunking his cheeks to prove it. The refill lady just gave him a dirty look when he held out his coffee cup for a refill. Not today, bub.

Rain or no rain, we took a final stroll down the beach, where half a dozen intrepid couples were walking their dogs. (Although it did appear, as C. remarked, their dogs were walking *them*.) This was obviously a daily ritual, and carried an unspoken declaration: we are the year-rounders, the true proprietors of Cape Cod. The rain was their validation. The fly-by-nighters had flown.

Dogless and homeless, we were as far from permanent residency as you can get. We were impermanent non-residents. Still, we earned a few smiles for our willingness to accept the wet weather. We even forged a cheerful agreement with two of the year-rounders that a day was not erased, the Cape not cancelled, simply because it was raining.

Then either the rain ended or we outdistanced it. The sky brightened as we traveled back to Boston. To break up the drive, we made a few peculiar stops, most memorably the topiary zoo and a miniature golf course. Was there perhaps an air of desperation to our agenda that day, I asked, as we were teeing off with our putting irons.

Hardly, C. insisted. These were *perks*. These were the small luxuries of freedom. "Activities you would never find the time for."

"Activities you would never spend any time on," said I, though actually it was all a hoot. Lions and tigers carved out of (or into) boxwood hedges are impressive in their way, not to mention a boxwood monkey perched on a boxwood zebra's back.

And who knew that miniature golf still existed? That was a real trip back in time for me, to senior year and my first date, with Les Carney and his restless paws. We went on a "double date" that night. Is that sort of thing still done, or was it just a device from a more innocent time—guarding Our Virginity through peer oversight? If so, it didn't stay Les Carney's restless paws, or keep Bill Friedlander from practically raping Mary Burgundy in the backseat.

C. could do me one better. I had already heard the tale of his own miniature golf date and how it ended up on a cabin cruiser, where he surrendered his own virginity—not to his date but to the girl's sister, somehow. How he was so sick afterward (from the shock of sex? from the rolling seas?) that he threw up over the side for an hour.

These were stories we had shared at Gal Al and we did not retell them that day. Instead, we pretended it was real golf, where no conversation is tolerated. Where there falls a respectful hush. We hushed, and we frowned with appropriate high seriousness, until there on the last "fairway" (lining up his shot, mock-testing the breeze by flipping shorthaired grass into the air), C. suddenly burst out laughing. Soon enough I was laughing too and neither of us could stop. We laughed until my stomach ached.

When our hysterics finally subsided (out there on the fairway) C. hugged me and said, "You know, it would be crazy if we weren't confused right now." While this was a nugget, to be sure, it was hardly something we could fall back on for support. Confusion was not a solution, so we fell back on the respectful hush, and later a cup of coffee at the Howard Johnson's on Route 24.

That was just after our first bout of car trouble and just before the second. Both times the radiator boiled over and we were lucky to get going again. Wait fifteen minutes, pray, and turn the key—such was our approach. Hardly the stuff of auto-motive know-how, but it worked.

At the Sagamore Bridge, we had dared to gloat about how all the traffic was headed the other way. We were done gloating as we sat on the side of the highway wondering who in Heaven's name we could call for help. And speaking of Heaven, each time we got going (and *kept* going) C. proclaimed he could almost believe in God again.

"Why would He do us any favors?" I asked.

"Possibly because He moves in mysterious ways His wonders to perform?"

The next day Pete would replace a radiator hose he told me looked like the thousand-year-old man's artery. I did not ask to see his medical degree, not after he handed me the hose, parched and cracked and soft as pudding.

*⁊*

"Wʜᴀᴛ ɪꜱ that face supposed to mean?"

"I didn't care for the Bart part. The kid. You made that part up."

"That's a perfectly absurd thing to say, Calvert. The evidence is right here in black and white, recorded at the time. It's irrefutable."

"Inadmissable, you mean. And certainly uncorroborated. I am sure I was okay about Jake and Hetty at that point. I knew they were going to Bearsville. I knew there would be a house full of people, with lots going on."

"Think what you will."

"Plus, you garbled the story of Sarah Schilling's sister. The seduction took place in the little boathouse, an hour before we went on board—"

"Oh my, in the little *boat*house. And is that a tongue twister? Sarah Schilling's sister?"

"Is that an act of rhyme? Twister and sister?"

"I'll rhyme you. Sarah Schilling's sister had a blister on her keester."

"Anyway, I was feeling sick before we went out that night. The seasickness just finished me off."

"The way I heard the story, it was the older sister who finished you off. And by the way, shouldn't she have a name? Doesn't the woman who deflowered you deserve naming rights?"

"Linda, maybe? Lucille? Pretty sure it started with an L. I remember the person, not the name."

"The person or the person's creamy white bosom?"

"Her hair, most vividly. A great cloud of dark curly hair on her head, a small cloud of dark curly hair below."

"Excellent clues. Why, we'll have her rounded up in no time."

"But here's the most serious error, Lara, and only because you weren't aware of it. I didn't sleep through that night, either. At one point I got up and went a mile down the beach. And when I came back I just watched you for a long time. You *were* asleep and I studied your face and your bare shoulders, by the silvery light of the Horizon Motor Hotel parking lot."

"What were you thinking? On the beach."

"Thinking how lovely the beach was in the middle of the night, empty. Thinking about the kids. And I thought about Estragon, and his unfinished joke."

"Estragon in the play."

"My character in it, yes. We were doing it that fall, four shows over a weekend at the Klein. And I had been experimenting with Estragon's voice, his tone and speaking rhythm."

"So what was his unfinished joke?"

"It's the story of the Englishman in the brothel. That's how he leads into it. 'Of course you all know the story of the Englishman at the brothel.'"

"I don't."

"The Englishman drinks too much at a pub, weaves his way over to the brothel next door, bows to the madam ceremonially. The madam inquires, in her extreme Cockney accent, as to whether he would prefer a fair, a dark, or a red-haired wench. And that's it. That's where the joke gets cut off."

"Well then, I see where it qualifies as unfinished."

"Vladimir says, Estop, Enough! Estragon reels back into silence, and the play goes on. It's my third favorite moment in that play."

"Aren't you the coy one! First the unfinished joke, and now the *third* favorite moment. Merely implying the first and the second."

"Favorite moment is when Vladimir, waxing sentimental, reminds Estragon of the old days, in the Macon County, and Estragon leaps up shouting, I never once set foot in the Macon County! I have puked my puke of a life away right here, I tell you, here in the Cackon County!"

"That certainly would not be my favorite moment."

"Second favorite moment is the vaudeville skit at the end, when Estragon's pants fall down. Loose clownish pants that just collapse to his ankles and Vladimir says, Pull up your trousers and Estragon replies, What, you want me to take off my trousers? No no, they *are* off, I want you to put them back on. And so forth."

"Did you have underwear?"

"Loose clownish underwear, yes."

"How merciful. Those were the days when audiences began to be assaulted at every play. By gratuitous nudity."

"I don't know about assaulted. As I recall, people were queuing up around the block to see those shows."

"A transparent excuse for exhibitionists and peeping toms. That's all it was."

"Well, I had big baggy underpants. I was a very respectfully covered theatrical person in that production. Less so in some others."

"Anything for your art."

"In those days, yes. At that age."

"So then you came back to watch my shoulders sleeping. At the motel."

"Yes, but first, as I was walking back, I thought about my dog Lucky."

"Lucky in the play?"

"No, no relation, but good for you, there is a Lucky in that play and that's what got me started on it. That or the beach itself, because Lucky and I spent a lot of hours there. He would fetch a stick from the surf endlessly. If I threw it ten thousand times, he would have fetched it ten thousand. Or died trying."

"A boy and his dog."

"Innocence, is how I would put it. How easy it was for that boy on the beach to be happy, how tricky it was for the man."

"That boy might have grown up in Cambodia. Or Watts."

"Understood. But he didn't. He was a cheerful fortunate son of the middle class. The man was cheerful too, mind you, but he was finally coming to understand that after childhood there would always be elements of unhappiness mixed in with his happiness. Happiness would have to subsume some unhappiness, forever after."

"And such were your profundities as you regarded my sleeping shoulders? That I was the unhappiness inside your happiness?"

"You were also the happiness inside my unhappiness. That was the problem."

"And the solution?"

"There was no solution, as you know. Though I did resolve to get the kids a dog. Whatever else happened, there was no good reason I couldn't get them a dog that summer."

"Bret."

"Yes."

"A name suggested by the boy Bart, perhaps? The one who never existed?"

"Named after Bret Maverick, whose show I used to watch with my dog Lucky."

"But didn't Bret Maverick have a brother named Bart?"

"Plus another brother named Beau. Anyway, that's how I got back to sleep that night. That decision pushed me past the shame of being a bad father. I would present them with a dog. How bad a father could I be?"

"Not bad at all, Calvert. But do you know what I made of it—when Marisa told me that the dog Bret had joined your family? That's that, is what I made of it. The door had slammed shut. The way I saw it, you had just made a fifteen-year commitment, the life span of a mutt. You would never leave Winnie, never leave those kids, and you would *really* never leave a puppy selected in a moment of cavernously deep guilt. In my mind, Bret put an end to any remaining ambiguity after The Twoweeks."

"Ah, but ambiguity never ends."

"Marisa went to see your play. I had carefully avoided knowing about it, avoided reading any reviews, but Marisa saw it and reported back. She ran right through my stop sign, all the way to the dog Bret. Though she did spare me the knowledge that you dropped your pants."

"Did she finish the unfinished joke? Honestly, for years I was asking everyone. I would even rummage through books of jokes in the library, desperate to learn the rest of the Englishman's story."

"You couldn't figure it out? Or just make it up?"

"I knew the Englishman couldn't have made a definitive choice. If he had done that, it wouldn't have been a joke. So he chooses one—say the fair-haired one—and ten minutes later he comes back to the madam with a change of heart. He'd like to try the dark-haired instead. I got that far. I just couldn't see where it ends up."

"That's always the tough part, isn't it?"

Day 8. Halfway through The Twoweeks, seven days behind us and at most seven more ahead. It struck me that for the first seven days, we had been doing addition. Time passing seemed to accumulate in our favor, to bless or validate our plan: we really *did* need this time together.

From now on, though, we would be doing subtraction. Each passing hour would be another crate removed from our dwindling storehouse of time. And this would be more radically true if I opted to cut the deal short, at nine days, or ten.

In the poem "February Snow," I am trying to cast the whole transaction as a fabulous snowman. You create it heedlessly, then watch as your creation comes to nothing. As it literally evaporates. Humans add, God subtracts.

Even though I was the one who pushed for our date with Gerald and Debra, I found myself regretting we had made it. Partly this had to do with C. (if our time together was about to be cut short, did we wish to spend our last two days on couple life?) and partly it had to do with Ian and a flare-up of conscience.

Ian had sent a postcard. It was harmless, just a line about his brother's family and a gentle joke about fishing sixteen hours a day. I know him, and I know he sent it to make me smile, not to make me feel guilty. But I did. Pictured Ian twiddling his thumbs in Idaho while I was out "gallivanting around" (as Mom would have put it) and felt that out of fairness, I ought confine myself to the dull and the normal too.

True, we would be with Gerald and Debra (who are about as dull and normal as anyone that smart can be), but the house presented a problem, or the location did—out on Plum Island, before the greenheads hatched. We had heard them rhapsodize about sunsets on the "portico" (which would turn out to be a porch, as I had suspected all along, albeit a really nice porch) and soft grass running right down to a strip of warm sand the consistency of sugar, blah blah blah.

Anyway, we had the social obligation and we went. Me, C., and my guilty conscience. And though their glowing description would prove accurate, the occasion might yet qualify as dull and normal. Certainly it was tame. Making soup and salad, wading and walking, eating and talking. Or not so much talking as listening to Gerald talk, and then to the two of them arguing.

How they do it is this: he delivers a lecture (he is used to it, breath-conditioned from the classroom, a subscriber to the idea that they paid their tuition *in order* to hear him talk) and Debra listens raptly. She never interrupts until he throws the floor open for questions, whereupon she disputes everything he has just said. Then they argue about it.

At first they argue pleasantly, eventually it gets a tad snippy, finally they have to be separated by the referee. (Not sure how they handle this part if no referee is present.) I must say I witnessed this psychodrama in considerable awe. This is not a good template for marriage, I was forced to conclude. These two people, each of whom I like and enjoy, do not bring out the best in one another.

C. behaved remarkably well. Smiled and sipped his beer, even managed to look attentive for long stretches. Occasionally he tossed off a moderating phrase, like a handful of sand on the bonfire. "You could both be right," he declared judiciously, when Debra equivocated on the nuclear power plant ("It's as good a location as you could hope for") and Gerald ("It's insanity, plain and simple") raged against it.

Because we were expected to stay overnight, I kept waiting for C. to concoct a pretext for our having to change the plan. If a lie was needed, he was the man for the job. He just kept sipping beer and smiling, though, and it fell to me to solve the problem. How (and how soon) could we leave without giving offense?

Why did I care about giving offense? Well, there was the fact we had invited ourselves. This was our idea, or mine. They had responded with generosity and the least we could do was show appreciation. So there is all of that. Anyway, it's not that I *care* about giving offense, it's that I simply don't do it. It's not nice.

"I guess we're not the only ones who have relationship problems," said C. as we headed back to the city. "Whatever happens, we'll be better off than those two."

"I didn't mind them, really. They were just being themselves. I don't even mind Gerald's lectures. And he was funny about his namesake, President Gerald."

"Debra was funny there too. When he said the hardest part of losing Nixon was that no one could hate Gerald Ford and she casually mentioned that he was averaging about twelve death threats a day."

"To his credit, he laughed at that. Our Gerald, I mean."

"Our Gerald isn't like that when he talks one on one. Only when he senses a group has formed, I guess. An audience."

"Debra never disagrees with anything anyone else says, either. How do you suppose they got together? Not to mention got *married?*"

"I bet I know how. They went off together for two weeks and had such a good time they wanted it never to end."

"I'm not sure how to take that."

"What part are you unsure about?"

"Well, does it mean that whatever happens in a Twoweeks is bound to be unreal and unreliable? Or since nothing of the sort ever did happen to them (they met in college, went out for years, married in a church), does it mean that all relationships can be expected to go sour over time?"

"Do you suppose they have any idea how it looks? How it *is*, for that matter—the way they grind against each other. They must have fallen into the pattern inch by inch. You know, if a marriage got just a milligram worse each month, wouldn't it be like a thousand times worse after twenty years?"

"Amortized, you mean."

"Something like that. Compounded?"

"Were you going to answer my question?"

"No. I wasn't going to. But I was going to say thanks for getting us out of there."

"I felt terrible. They had made up the bed. Debra had put flowers on the night tables. I wasn't at all sure I could come up with the words to say no thanks."

"How about, People, we are *outta* here."

"A bit too blunt for me."

"Could have been blunter. As in, Sorry but we won't be free to fuck here, certainly not in the style to which we have become accustomed."

"Well, thanks for not saying *that*. I'm sorry to learn you could think it."

"They say you can't convict a man for his thoughts."

"Maybe they can't, but I sure can."

And I meant to. I was going to punish him by refusing his advances that night. Trouble was, he didn't make any advances. Just went roundly, soundly, to sleep. Then when we both woke in the middle of the night, I was too groggy to remember the lesson plan.

"What woke you"?" he said, distracting me with small talk while he advanced.

"Not sure. The moon?"

"Me too. The moon. In Shakespeare, you know, moonbeams pouring down always translate into love."

"Love, huh," I sniffed dubiously, though we were already making it by then.

"The act of love, if you prefer."

I may have preferred it at that moment, but I was a good deal harder to sway when he woke me an hour later with a bizarre proposition: "Let's get one more in while it's still Day 8."

So he too was counting the days. (And keeping score, since after all he is a male person.) To the extent I was conscious at that hour, I was astonished at how this man manages to appear to be on top of things. Listening to him, you would have to believe he studies the road map, notes the location of gas stations and restaurants—that his journey through life is under control. Both hands on the wheel.

Whereas in truth he is driving with both eyes closed and "Look, Ma, no hands!" scrawled inside the cartoon balloon above his heedless head. He has no control over events, no planned responses, he just trusts that he *will* respond as needed and sometimes I would find myself trusting it too—even as we went careening "ninety miles an hour down a dead-end street."

"It is not still Day 8," I said, fending him off. "It's Day 9."

"Is that a no?" he said, still pressing his request to "get one more in."

How to put this politely. Sex can be so easy. It can be a lot of ways, of course. Fumbling/bumbling with Les, yearning/learning with Vince. Ian, and marriage, with its own stages. Here it was just so easy, almost unavoidable. It's summer, you're naked—all that. Plus you just fit somehow. The logic that makes it happen is the same logic that makes you drink your morning coffee. What else would you do?

"Here's my way of looking at it," he said, after we had so melodramatically finished what we so laconically began. "The day begins when you rise. The sun rises, you rises, and that's the start of a new day."

"Versus the stroke of midnight-plus-one-second, you're saying."

"Right. Midnight-plus-one may be technically correct, it's just not how a day is experienced. A night ends when you wake up. And a day begins. That's what the word 'dawn' means, you know. Beginning."

I got straight out of the bed (no longer, by that point, self-conscious; somewhere halfway between relaxed and sneaky-proud) and went for the dictionary, determined not to be bamboozled. Damned if he wasn't right, though. Dawn was defined as daylight appearing. Also as "the beginning of anything."

"Maybe having a reference book handy would keep Gerald and Debra from arguing so much. They could just stop, look it up, and abide by the verdict."

"Were we arguing?" said C.

"We were disagreeing."

"You were disagreeing. I was merely stating a fact."

"You were doing your thing. Which bears little enough relation to *fact*."

"Of course it's possible they don't want to be kept from arguing. Gerald and Debra."

"Well, I do. Though I wonder, does Day 9 begin when I get out of bed or when you do? When the sun clears the Jacksons' roof or when it comes over Tiny's Variety? The midnight-plus-one approach avoids any such subjectivity."

"So does the dawn approach. Dawn can be as precise as you like. They put it in the newspaper every day: 6:13, 6:16, and so forth."

Whatever it is that Gerald and Debra do, this is what we do. Not so much argue as joust, in jest. We can't stop pushing and pulling the taffy of words and concepts. C. wanted to push the taffy of time, that's all. And if he could find a way to start a day eight hours later, maybe he could find a way to make the days longer, or make The Twoweeks into three weeks.

Because by that morning we were approaching a dangerous place. I was wise to redraw the contract (maybe end at eleven days, though, instead of nine) because by now I had lost track of Miller Road as the place Ian and I lived. It had become the place where C. and I were holed up. In the same way, I was no longer getting the vibe about Winnie, or the children, off C. He too had been lulled.

We could rationalize this (Why miss Ian when I would soon be with him? Why fret over Jake and Hetty when he would soon be frolicking with them?) but we knew something had shifted on us. Whenever it was that Day 8 officially concluded, we both knew the boulder was rolling down the far side of the hill now, and gathering momentum.

⁂

"Just a few quick points. None of them, by the way, contradicting a word of your account."

"What, then? Ignoring it?"

"Amplifying? No, *completing*. By providing answers to a few of the unanswered questions."

"This can't be a filibuster, Calvert. I'm much too tired."

"While we are on the subject of long-windedness, is it my imagination or are these entries of yours getting longer and longer?"

"I don't see why it matters."

"It doesn't."

"I had never kept that sort of journal before. What I had were notebooks, full of scribbled conceits and images, ideas for future poems. Never anything so personal. I had to get used to doing this and I guess I did. So that may be why."

"What made you decide to do it at all? If you never had before."

"Mostly the obvious, trying to make sense of my life. And it did give me some space, that week in Maine. Ian only needed to know I was 'at my desk'—that I was working—and he would give me a wide berth."

"Ian did give you space."

"New poems? he would ask with a sort of rueful smile he had. It's a smile with no teeth and no mirth. An invitation to confess if I wished, no pressure to do so if I didn't. And I would say, Just some notes."

"True enough."

"So went my justification. Plus Ian is a very intelligent man. It wasn't as if he expected The Twoweeks to end like one of his beloved prizefights—the bell rings, the bout-is-over sort of ending. He knew there would be aftermaths. That we would all be concussed. He was absurdly patient with me."

"He was a lot cooler and wiser than the average bear."

"Once, after I had come back from Europe, he asked me if he had made a big mistake. Given me too much freedom and lost me in the process."

"But that was later."

"He asked very little after The Twoweeks. He let me be, hoping I would weather it out."

"Cool."

"He had a ton of pride, which took the form of self-enforced dignity. And I know he was going on the assumption that the sooner he asked the questions, the rougher would be the answers."

"Wise."

"I felt like such a bitch."

"What did you tell him, by the way? Could he have held on to you?"

"If he had said no, there would never have been a Twoweeks. But later, after Europe? Life was going on, spiraling off. I was unstable and unkind."

"So you could tell him he was damned lucky he *didn't* hold on to you."

"That is precisely what I told him, more than once. And each time he would display the rueful smile."

"Wisdom. Coolth. But no teeth and no mirth."

"Sadness, mainly."

"Poor Ian."

"Calvert, don't."

"Sorry. I'll get back to the business at hand."

"Which was what, exactly? I forget."

"We were going over your journal entry. Unless you would rather not?"

"I already agreed, the entries probably did get longer. I might even agree that—unconsciously—I was using the journal as the only available means of being with you still."

"Now there is a rare concession!"

"Oh come on, Calvert, you knew how I felt."

"Never. I never did. Which leads me to the next point, on the subject of sex. Where you write, 'How to put any of this politely?' My question is why bother? Why worry about politeness in a journal? In a private conversation with yourself."

"Because—as it seems to keep saying here—I was, I am, my mother's daughter."

"Sure, but you are not reticent. Your mom wasn't particularly reticent, either. She was just of an earlier generation, verbally speaking."

"One does tend to speak verbally."

"All right, but this was written, not spoken. Why not describe the sex as it was?"

"I didn't have the slightest desire to describe it at all."

"You couldn't avoid describing it a little, here and there."

"There was a tug. I wanted to remember events, including my reaction to those events. But I certainly didn't want to become a pornographer."

"You just didn't want Ian to see it, accidentally. Which was fair enough."

"Forget about sex. If Ian saw one sentence of this, any sentence, he would have been devastated. I knew that and I was writing it down anyway."

"Then why the reticence? You have written poems that I would call erotic."

"Erotic, possibly. Pornographic, never."

"What's the difference again?"

"The difference is words, partly. And directness. You want to be more suggestive than descriptive. I have always hated the words that go with porn."

"He was hard, she was wet."

"And worse, but along those lines. They are so tired and trite they aren't remotely erotic. Furthermore—"

"Did you say *furthermore?*"

"—the more you talk about it, view it, review it, name it, analyze it—anything but actually *do* it—the less erotic it becomes. It's like putting clothes on, instead of taking them off."

"Like your mother and father. Didn't you used to say they did it fully dressed?"

"I could never believe they did it at all. There's proof, of course—me and Liam—but not one pixel of credible imagery. Of the two of them, you know, *touching*. Mom I could see. She danced, she flirted. But my father must have done it without moving a muscle, in suit and tie, dress socks, polished leather shoes."

"Kinky."

"Time to change the subject, Cal, or get back to it. Were there other issues?"

"Amplifications. Clarifications. About this alleged tendency of the male to keep score?"

"The tally, yes."

"I knew the days. Toward the end, I even knew the hours. Only at the very beginning did I have any notion how many times we had fucked—"

"To put it politely."

"How many times conjoined, then, simply because I could remember every one of them. After a few days I hadn't a clue. Could not have cared less."

"What a guy."

"It's just information."

"Fine. So is that it?"

"One last, on the children. Where you say why fret over Jake and Hetty when in a short while etcetera?"

"Right."

"Wrong. The closer we came to Doomsday, to our impending ending, the *worse* I felt about them. My need to be with them was one thing, but the guilt was about failing them, *harming* them. And I knew I'd blown that. I was going to be stuck with the mess I had made, and so therefore were they."

"You didn't show any of that."

"It was being deferred. What wasn't being deferred? But the fact I would be seeing them soon, or frolicking with them as you put it, made me terribly sad. I was on the verge of tears a lot of the time, those final days."

"You never cried. When did you cry?"

"The verge, I said. Though I must have cried at Charlie's Kitchen."

"If you did, it wasn't about Jake and Hetty."

"No. Not that night."

⁓

DAY 10 began with a meeting of the rules committee, or a debate. Resolved: Was it or was it not permissible to repeat an activity? Specifically, having been to Gloucester on Day 1, were we therefore prevented from going to Gloucester on Day 10?

C.'s position was we owed it to ourselves to be creative and original, mine that we ought to be mirroring life, not art.

"If we have run out of fresh ideas in ten days," he said, "what would we come up with over the course of ten years?"

"That's entirely academic," said I. "Two weeks is our portion, not ten years. Besides, people who are together for ten years don't 'come up with things to do,' they have a life. They work and raise children. They do the laundry."

"No wonder they're bored."

"Who said they're bored?"

When I pointed out that our portion was two weeks, I felt a twinge of guilt. I had never mentioned a change in plans, a foreshortening of our contract, and the moment was getting closer. Imminent. That our portion might soon be reduced was what the rules committee should have been discussing that morning, but I hadn't found the right opening.

✍

"Hang on a second, Lara. I hate to interrupt, but can we back up a bit here? There seems to have been a mistake—"

"Cal, I am simply reading this. Word for word."

"Sure. But you are reading about Day 10. You've gone from Day 8 to Day 10. You see the problem."

"Day 9, I suppose you mean."

"Day 9 is missing. Here is the solitary original untrammeled— unfudged?—surviving archive of The Twoweeks and fully seven percent of it has been omitted. Or destroyed?"

"I must have forgotten what we did that day."

"Couldn't remember a thing about it? When you dotted the i's and crossed the t's on every previous day? Look, you've got conversations going on verbatim for ten minutes—sights and sounds, prices, what we *ate*—and now there is this total blank?"

"It would seem so."

"Did Ian get hold of it and burn it maybe?"

"He would never do that. He respects privacy too much, not to mention the good old written word."

"What if that entry contained something about him, though, something that violated *his* privacy. A skeleton in his closet. He cheated on his taxes, or came on to a student . . ."

"Ian Witherspoon never cheated on anything or anybody in his life. He didn't even have a closet, much less a skeleton in it."

"Okay, then maybe there was a poem in that entry, or a fragment. You tore it out later so you could work on it."

"That sounds like a reasonable explanation."

"It does?"

"Sure."

"So where's the poem? Where's the finished product? I know you remember every line of every poem you ever wrote."

"I don't even remember the ones I finished and published, much less every draft and fragment and image and idea."

"Do I believe that?"

"It's true. Sometimes I'll come across an old notebook and be amazed at the stuff I never got back to. Really promising starts, which I simply abandoned and never glimpsed again."

"What about that list of fabulous titles you never used. Do you still have that?"

"I do. And I reserve all rights to use those titles in the future."

"Cool as that was?—it did come as a disappointment to me, Lara. The same way I was disappointed to learn *The New Yorker* has people placing one man's caption under another man's drawing."

"Not with their better cartoons. Never with Charles Addams."

"Do we know that? They have one shoebox full of captions and another full of drawings, and someone whose job is to pin the tail on the donkey."

"I would never use one of those titles unless it was absolutely right for a poem. Which is why they never have been used. I keep that list in knowing sorrow that probably they never will."

"A poem and its title should grow together, like the briar and the rose."

"Agreed. Shall we resume now?"

"Absolutely. As soon as you tell me what really happened to Day 9. I have a right to know about that day, Lara. It's my life too."

"But it's my journal."

"That sounds like a confession."

"To what?"

"To concealing or destroying the entry for Day 9."

"I confess nothing."

"You insist you don't know what happened to it?"

"I insist nothing. Except that my notes for Day 9 are not here. I suggest we go on to Day 10, which *is* here."

"We can go on, but I am not forgetting Day 9. And despite all your disingenuousness on the subject, I don't believe you have forgotten it either."

"Good for you, Cal."

✥

T<small>HAT WAS</small> the hottest day of the year, 100 degrees by mid-morning. Twice we stepped into the shower just to cool off, then sat buck naked in front of the screen door, hoping Mrs. Ridley did not suddenly appear. (A cup of sugar? No problem!)

At some point we recalled that air-conditioning had been invented. This came slowly to our joint consciousness because we both disapprove of it. A whole appliance just to get you through the handful of seriously hot days each year? Air-conditioning is strictly for whiners, it's wasteful, it's terrible for the atmosphere . . . and where can we *find* us some?

The movies, was one obvious answer. Winnie would not be at a matinee, although she could (C. pointed out) be somewhere along our path to the movie theater. She was *somewhere* every second (I pointed out) and therefore might be on the *path* to anywhere. Were we not allowed to walk anywhere?

"Now that you mention it, it would be safer in the car."

"Because she is never in the path of cars?"

"Because she never even notices cars. Whether it was a car or a truck, whether it was red or green or white—much less the make or model. Just doesn't register with her."

This seemed dubious. Not only had Winnie ridden in my car, she had stood at the curb as I pulled up to get her. A faded blue Dart with a bustle of rust around the doors and panels? Distinctive, I would have thought, in its shabby way. Hard not to notice.

Before I gave voice to this, C.'s paranoia had raced ahead to the next potential disaster, that his son Jake had "a dangerous brain." All those specifics that Winnie failed to register, Jake would see clearly and question closely. Places he had been driven past while seemingly *asleep* in the backseat he would later describe with precision. He noted (and retained) the price of everything in every store. Able to read at four, he read (and retained) every road sign and billboard. So there was Jake.

"Has he met you? Has he seen your car?"

"Yes and yes."

"Then you're in the file. Though you may not loom that large."

"What about his famously firm grasp of minor characters? Didn't you tell me his favorite Milne character was Owl?"

"Owl looms large."

Between Jake's dangerous brain and our discovery that the car (smelted all morning in the furnace of the sun) was literally too hot to touch, it seemed a taxi might make sense. Jake wouldn't associate us with it even if he had opened a dossier on the driver, plus it would be air-conditioned.

"It would also cost four bucks each way. Eight bucks."

"Then hop in, cheapskate. I'll drive."

We put sheets on the seats of the Dart and finally got going. The movie houses weren't open yet, though, so we went first to the Gardner Museum. Having skipped breakfast in the heat, we decided to eat something in their (air-conditioned) café. Which was another lovely idea, except that it cost *nine* bucks.

"Worse than a cab," I couldn't help noting.

"But it's not a total loss—which a cab would have been."

"And why is that?"

"Well, because there's no free lunch. Say we made a couple of tuna fish sandwiches at home and split a can of beer. Say we then went down to Tiny's and split a Three Musketeers bar. A minimal meal like that would cost around five bucks. So our real dollar loss on lunch is four."

(Nor would our "real dollar losses" stop there. Tabulating the museum fee, the movie, my popcorn and C.'s Raisinets, keeping cool would prove no cheap endeavor.)

C. had been able to relax on the Cape and on Plum Island. Now he was uptight again. In the café, he positioned himself with his back to the wall, facing the door like Wild Bill Hickok. Afterward, he passed through each gallery portal as Wild Bill surely would have: eyes sweeping the room, guns drawn. No one was going to back-shoot my guy.

He cooled it at the movies—no worries in the dark. It was dark and sparsely populated (a Chabrol, with subtitles, in the early afternoon) and cold! You have to *dress* for air-conditioning, it turns out. It was so cold in there that the butter on my popcorn congealed.

"I guess this comes under the heading, Be careful what you wish for," I said, as we exited into the steam heat. For the last hour, we had been huddled together for warmth.

"Or: We got our money's worth—unfortunately."

"How about, Can't win for losin'," I said.

"Just skate your lane and keep your stick on the ice," said C.

"Can't say I follow that one."

"I thought we were doing clichés. Which always remind me of my high school hockey coach, who spoke exclusively in clichés. 'Keep your stick on the ice and the goals will come' was another favorite. We would sit on the bus coming home from a 7–1 defeat and say, Geez, we must have taken our sticks off the ice. But he had an endless supply."

"And I'm sure you had an endless supply of wiseass responses."

"'Let's play 'em one at a time,' was his standby. So we played 'em one at a time and lost 'em all, anyway."

Back at Miller Road, back into the shower—a shorthand version of our water theme. We did consider the city pool, not far away, a dime a swim. C. had taken his kids there and assured me it was not bad, so long as you didn't mind unguided 50-pound missiles landing on your neck now and again. It was his admission that these missiles (cannonballs and can-openers launched carefreely from the pool's rim) could be hefty 150-pound teenagers that tore it for me.

(Much later, when in a desperate moment we considered taking the last train for Gloucester and sleeping out on the beach, C. said, "That's fine, if you don't mind a 250-pound cop stepping on your neck.")

For dinner that night we had fat pretzels and Colt .45 so cold it was just shy of frozen. Even at nine o'clock that night, you could step out of a cold shower, towel dry, and find sweat beading at your temples. This was one night when no one could possibly want sex to happen—or so I thought.

I was just as certain I would not mention it here either (not after what I wrote yesterday) and yet here goes. The fan was on, Ray Charles was on, and side one was finished before we were. (The record kept going around, making that little drum-brush sound until we finally noticed it and laughed.) "Just for a Thrill"? Ray was right about that, even at one hundred percent humidity.

Sometime in the night the weather broke, with stupendous concussive thunder and tracers of lightning in the yard—the fire-bombing of Boston. Splashed by rain through the screen, chilled in fact, we bundled together and naturally (naturally would be the *mot juste* here) started up. Our attraction seemed to survive both hot and cold.

A factor worth noting is that neither of us ever seems to run low on energy. It's the first thing people say about C., but they have always said it about me too, so combined we must be like pi R squared or something. You have to direct all that energy someplace; and while it is true enough we should have been building hospitals in Latin America, we simply weren't. We were just fucking our selfish brains out.

(Sorry, Mom, promise I'll never say it again.)

✍

"THERE YOU have it, plain as day."

"Have I it?"

"You have, my sweet. A crystal clear reference to Day 9. And not merely that there was such a day—that much we knew, ontologically—but proof that you wrote about it in this very journal. The missing day *referenced*, if you will."

"Can you be more specific?"

"Right here, where it says 'not after what I wrote yesterday.' With the obvious implication that you wrote about sex. Which may explain the book burning?"

"Book burning is a bit strong, though I guess I see your point."

"You would have to be George W. Bush *not* to see it."

"Well, I certainly am not George W. Bush."

"Though you do share a behavior or two with him."

"What a nasty thing to say."

"By purest chance, my sweet. But deceit? Evasion of discussion? Concealment of relevant documentation?"

"You of all people are talking about deceit?"

"I will gladly withdraw the George W. Bush analogue, if you will produce for me the missing—let's say missing, rather than concealed—entry. Will you?"

"Not at this time."

"Because?"

"Because it isn't here."

"You admit it exists, admit you still have it, admit you purposely separated it out, and allege that it is not in this house at this time?"

"I admit nothing."

"Can you summarize for me what it says? What it would add to this story, were we privileged to have it?"

"I can't do that, no."

"Can't or won't?"

"Can't. Won't."

"Can you at least say whether it is a short spicy entry, or a long dreary outpouring?"

"Let's imagine that it's quite short and terribly unspecific. That it doesn't have much to say about what we did that day, which is both why it doesn't add to the story and why I can't summarize it. I mean, I could summarize it easily enough if it said we went to New York, to a Miriam Makeba concert at Carnegie Hall, ate a cup of borscht at the Russian Tea Room afterward—"

"Enough of that. I know we didn't go to New York."

"There you are, then. Maybe *you* can summarize Day 9 for us. You seem to think you recall those days with fair accuracy."

"Was it the night we saw Conway Twitty at Jordan Hall?"

"I believe it was! You could be light years away from the onset of Alzheimer's, Cal. Do you remember that little pink sun-suit he wore? A matching top and bottom, in not even bad but truly *astonishing* taste. Such that I could not believe my eyes."

"Stalwart Conway fan though I am, I too was taken aback."

"Still, they put on a great show."

"The Twitty Birds were in rare form."

"The Twitty Birds! Two guys, right? Bass and guitar?"

"And a drummer floating somewhere in the background. They all wore baby blue sun-suits. The Big Twitty Bird, maybe six foot six, on upright bass, the little one, about four feet high at the shoulder, on guitar. And the opening act that night was—?"

"No idea. Total blankitude."

"Hank, Junior. Who at that point was *only* Hank, Junior— had no hits of his own, sang medleys of his daddy's songs in his daddy's voice. He came out and did a tour de force, though. Playing big riffs on every instrument, including an absolute dead-on Jerry Lee on the piano. He did a very scripted wildman thing—wild yet flawless, canned yet impressive. Hank, Junior."

"We walked home."

"There was a full moon—"

"Now you're making stuff up."

"It could be true. Under a full moon, the city lay quiescent, the river in all its gleaming liquidity slipping beneath the bridge as we stopped at the 49th Smoot—"

"Smoot me no Smoots, Calvert."

"Maybe it was the 50th Smoot. I know we walked over the Mass. Ave. Bridge and I know we waved to a cabin cruiser. Two men smoking cigars and drinking on deck."

"Plumbers!"

"That's right, I surmised they were plumbers."

"Because all plumbers get rich and buy boats."

"Yes, but there was also something about the name of the boat. In Hot Water, or Down the Drain. Something like that."

"It was a beautiful night."

"Very likely you did do something of a poetic nature with it. Then, naturally, you tucked the pertinent material into a separate folder, a poem-in-progress folder. You can admit that, can't you?"

"If I did, would you cease and desist?"

"I would, after the most cursory glance at the material. I'd also like to see the autographed program, which must be in the same lockbox."

"That's right. You actually made him sign the damned thing."

"And I gave it to you. That program is worth big money now, Lara."

"Remind me of Conway's real name."

"Harold Jenkins."

"You tricked him. Told him you had a sick nephew named Jenkins and cajoled him into signing his real name. You lied to Conway Twitty, Calvert. How low can you go?"

"It *was* his real name. I didn't trick him into writing it backwards, or anything, like Mr. Mxpltk."

"He died, you know."

"Mxpltk?"

"Conway Twitty. He's dead."

"A lot of them are. The amazing thing is that the two most likely by *far* to be dead are still going strong. George Jones and Jerry Lee."

"Life is unpredictable. Is that what you're saying?"

"I wasn't, but certainly it is. Take Jake."

"All right, but why Jake?"

"When he was ten, or twelve, I would wonder what he'd become. I had a dozen guesses and none of them came close. A river guide? Come on."

"And a filmmaker, don't forget."

"That's just his way of jacking up the price. They get the trip and they get a film of the trip. It is a nice little gimmick."

"I disagree. Those are terrific films, very much worth having. But what did you guess he would be?"

"Everything except an actor. That was the one thing I knew he wouldn't be. Hetty thought it was glamorous—especially when I was on TV—but to Jake it wasn't a real job. It wasn't work."

"So there you are. He rejects fantasy in favor of bedrock nature. River guide."

"What would you have guessed for Iris?"

"At that point? That she would never exist. We were getting close to the part where we would never see each other again."

"Did I ever tell you that after The Twoweeks—when we were busy never seeing each other again—I would sometimes walk by St. Paul's, just in case you were inside confessing your sins."

"I have to confess: I haven't been to confession since college."

"You might have gone, though. That summer or fall."

"It crossed my mind. It crosses my mind a lot, still."

"But you'd rather go to Hell?"

"Please don't joke about my religion, Cal."

"It's my religion, too."

"Not in any real way."

"Such as going to confession? Living the dogma?"

"I won't try to explain myself to you. Or to any priest, for that matter."

"As I said, you'd rather go to Hell."

"I presume I will go to Hell. That we both will. How could we not be consigned to Hell?"

"If there were no Hell. That would be one way. If God were dead, another. And what if He is alive and happens to be a wise old Jew?"

"Calvert."

"Why is that blasphemous? He was Jesus' daddy, right? Unless He converted, He would by now be a four-thousand-year-old Jew. Who was capable of forgiving sins long before the business wing of the party came up with the Baltimore Catechism."

"Calvert."

"There is one thing He would never forgive, though, and that's concealing the journal entry for Day 9."

"So there you are. I told you I was going to Hell."

✺

Day 11, June 29. Debra called that morning to say, We get it, we like it, you guys seem great together, always did. It turns out everyone at the gallery presumed C. and I had something going on, and would have been amazed to hear otherwise.

I chose not to relay this corroborating evidence of "chemistry" between us to C. For starters, he would have gloated. Then too, the case for my innocence would have become the case for my ignorance, or obliviousness. Who needs that?

"Who else thought that about us?" I asked Debra.

"Who didn't? Henry and June had a pool going on the outcome. Brief affair versus long painful affair versus totally busted marriages versus suicide pact."

"Henry and June should talk."

"They weren't criticizing. It wasn't like that at all."

Debra had called to propose another foursome. Dinner in the city, the 4th of July on Plum Island, the Saturday following, "Whatever works." We had never been the couple they presumed. Before "the Saturday following" rolled around, we would not even be the couple we were two days ago, at their cottage. We would be an ex-couple, or an ex-non-couple. Just a couple of people life chewed up and spat out.

And I would be alone. "Let's give it a few extra days," was Ian's wise prescription upon leaving for Coeur D'Alene. So he would be gone two weeks plus the few extra days—not flying back straight away. Flying back, as it happened, on July 6th, otherwise known as the Saturday following.

Meanwhile, I would be left holding the weirdness bag while C. was reuniting with his family, spending the 4th of July at his in-laws' country seat, as I confess I had begun to call it. Why should he have that to fall back on? Why should the beautiful Winnie also have the most wonderful parents and C's "favorite place in the world" to further skew the competition? What did I have to counter that?

I shook off this onslaught of self-pity and reminded myself I was a happily married woman with no need to "counter" any-one's summer house in the Catskills. All I had to do was get Debra Gordon off the phone. Which would have been simple enough had I wished to explain The Twoweeks to her. It felt too private, though, or maybe just too strange.

She had unfolded so many different scenarios for getting together that there was no easy way around her. I ended up agreeing to another visit without registering that it would be Day 13 (if there even was a Day 13 . . .), and then slipped deeper into obligation by offering to bring salad and dessert.

"How bloody normal can I get?" I complained to C. "Dessert and bloody salad."

"Isn't that what you wanted from them? To feel normal?"

"Plus, that would be Day Thirteen."

As I said this, I became acutely aware that the moment for speaking up had arrived. If I was going to rewrite our timetable, I had to tell C. right then. But I couldn't do it. I froze up and let the conversation roll on, let it flow swiftly past the moment and into a sea of painless repartee. "We can leave early again," he was saying, as I watched the moment bob away and disappear.

"No chance of that. There's some sort of early fireworks display on the beach and it won't start until dark."

"I say the fireworks start right now."

"Hands off until we figure this out."

"There's no more figuring to do. You put us in the quicksand, babe. Stuck is stuck. Best we can do is—?"

"Offer it up," I groaned.

"Right you are. And let's not forget that it was nice of them to invite us. Hey, we might be perfectly happy to go there if we had a few years to fill instead of a few nights."

"And if wishes were horses then beggars could ride."

"If wishes were chickens then beggars could eat eggs for breakfast."

"We'd better tell them the truth this time. Or enough of the truth so they don't blow your cover with Winnie."

"They've never even met Winnie."

"Sure. But suppose you and Winnie run into Gerald and Debra at, say, Buddy's Sirloin Pit. Hellos, introductions, conversations, invitations?"

"They aren't idiots, Lara."

"Suit yourself. Winnie is your cross to bear."

"I don't mind telling them. But what exactly would we tell them? What is the Truth?"

"I just meant the basic situation. That we're a secret and that we're over, or will be. That's all they need to know: not to confuse this with real life."

"Perish the thought."

Meanwhile, we were packing for another day at Revere Beach. Its ineluctable tackiness appealed to a recessive honky-tonk gene we each carried, plus we liked how easy it was. The train goes right there. You step off and stroll down to the sand in one minute flat.

Or down to the gravel that only wishes it were sand. Just so, you wade into the Swimmable water that wishes it were Healthy but at least is not Dangerous, or wasn't, on either occasion. Then it's out past the bobbing plastic bottles to frolic in dramatic one-foot swells.

It's not that bad, really. Looking back in from the water, it's almost picturesque. You see what's left of the old amusement park, and Kelly's, and the Rotunda, all set against the backdrop of a hill rising to the busy streets of the town. It's easy to imagine the place as a going concern a century ago, a lively seaside destination with trains arriving quarter-hourly from Boston, laughing women changing into their itchy woolen bathing suits, braying men with handlebar moustaches flexing their muscles. It makes a lovely black-and-white postcard in my mind's eye.

We lunched at Kelly's. C. went with the clam strips again, I stayed with the scallop roll. *William*, meanwhile, opted for the greasy cheeseburger.

William (chubby, carrot-topped, nine) was C.'s latest surrogate son; he found one everywhere we turned. But unlike Bart's mom, who had seemed attached to her boy, Wm.'s mom was only too happy to loan the lad out. A chain-smoking harridan in gilded slippers, she asked if we would "grab the kid a cheeseburger since you're going up there anyway" and C. grabbed it, though Mom omitted to pay. Can I go with them, ma, can I can I, went Wm. and Mom went, Sure you can. Without bothering to ask *us*.

In her defense, C. did seem prepared to adopt. Long before l'affaire cheeseburger, he had thrown a ratty nerf football to the lad for a solid half hour. "I hope you aren't jotting down his Christmas list," I whispered.

We had mastered the drill, the Revere Beach Shuffle, on both land and sea. Brought air mattresses to cushion the gravel, brought big towels to cushion the air mattresses, and knew to keep our mouths shut in the putatively Swimmable water. One thing you do not get at Revere is that deep sea feeling of being supremely clean, as though scrubbed by Mother Nature. Instead, you make liberal use of the outdoor shower.

You do get shed of Wm. when you swim. Want to come in, said C., and Wm. replied (in full-throated parody of the Boston accent), "Are you guys *nuts*?"

When finally we shed him for good (when Wm. and The Harridan broke camp and started uphill to their "stinking steaming apartment," as she characterized it, after we marveled at the agreeable notion of a seaside residence), C. waved as they receded from view. Wm. did not condescend to wave back.

"Did you even like that kid?" I said.

"He's okay. I mean, given Ma?"

"I found him mildly repulsive."

"Lara, he's a child."

"He is a small male person. Is it your educated guess that he will be a nice male person when he grows larger?"

"I'll be rooting for him," said C. with a grin.

"You know, you may have missed your calling, Cal. Aren't the Cub Scouts always looking for a few good men?"

"That's the Marines."

"Really, though. You are a male person who exhibits patience with kids."

"And has roots in the community! You make it sound like I'm a convicted criminal angling for a lighter sentence."

"Lighter than going to Hell, you mean?"

"Oh, much lighter."

We ate dinner at the Paddock Lounge, nothing but top-drawer venues for us. The place boasts a pervasive racetrack theme (Suffolk Downs one train stop away) with saddles and silks and historic photo finishes on the walls. A very small man sat a few stools from us, alongside a framed picture of the same man in cap and silks, posing in the winner's circle with a horse.

As C. headed off to the washroom (Colts on one door, Fillies on the other) I realized why William had tapped into my uncharitable side. I was jealous. Not of nine-year-old William exactly, and not *jealous* jealous—merely protective of our time, of our fast-fleeting limited exclusivity. Where exactly did that leave me, given my resolve to limit it even more?

Unaware of my unspoken scheme, C. was in a good mood. Clowning around, he improvised a scene for the barmaid, scrolling down the beer card as though it was the wine list in a fine dining establishment and he a connoisseur painstakingly making his selection. Disappointed that the waitress did not applaud (or even notice) his performance, he was further disappointed to find that Rolling Rock was their idea of a snob beer.

"They serve normal beers," I explained to him. "It goes with their normal food."

"Oh well," he said, "we came for the waters, really."

I had a Hey Mabel Black Label with my Portuguese cabbage soup, he had Rolling Rock and the Salisbury steak, we split a wedge of lemon meringue pie. When he hauled me up by both hands and said, "Come on, old girl, time to go home," it was so sweet, so offhandedly affectionate, that it felt right. It felt real.

But I should not have let it pass. "Home" was not where we were going and I should have said as much. And I should have said, right then and there, that we had a lot less time than he thought we did. That not only were our days numbered, they were numbered differently than he thought. Again, though, those words simply were not available to me; the mood was just so powerfully otherwise. Outside on the street, we kissed. Waiting at the T-stop, we kissed again.

The inbound train was virtually empty, with maybe a dozen riders scattered through three cars. Gloomy fluorescent light blanched a bald head; worn signage offered to prosecute your accident claim; dim stations flickered by with their gray littered concrete platforms. At Government Center, where we emerged, a cool breeze swept the vast plaza.

In spite of our heavy imposts, we somehow held hands as we walked. On the Longfellow Bridge, halfway between two sets of pepper-pots, we stopped to watch the river. (This was almost a tradition by now, viewing Boston from the bridges.) Narrowing back toward Harvard's enclaves in the dusky air, bejewelled with golden streaks of light, the river glowed like an Impressionist painting. It was gorgeous. With all our water-going forays, we had never considered the possibilities of the Charles River, so close at hand.

"It's true you can't swim in it. Or fish. I have seen canoes, though."

"Winnie?" said C. "Jake? Hetty?" By which he meant they sometimes strolled the riverbank.

"I forgot to worry."

"That's all right," said C., brushing my cheek.

But it was not all right, it was a bad sign. Just as he had forgotten Miller Road was not our home, I had forgotten Winnie, Jake, and Hetty. Pretty much forgotten their existence. I was bearing down on the schedule, obsessing over the days, without registering the reason why. Without remembering that Cal was not mine.

And of course, I was the one charged with reminding us.

✑

"First of all, I'd like credit for holding my tongue."

"I take it you aren't planning to maintain that discipline."

"Come on, you didn't think I would miss it, did you? The smoking gun? Incontrovertible corroboration of Day 9?"

"You're still on that?"

"'We packed for another day at Revere.' There it is. Clearly there was an earlier day at Revere; just as clearly it has to be the lockbox day."

"You certainly are tenacious of a point."

"And this line about having 'learned the drill' obviously refers back to the day in question. In fact, I recall that you detested Revere the first time. We hadn't been there two minutes when you stated flatly that you wouldn't be coming *there* again. And yet you did."

"I have always been flexible."

"Less so now, though still agile for your years."

"I did not mean in any prurient sense, as you know, Calvert. We ended up liking it, that's all. I took note of the fact."

"We ended up loving it. How could we not? Turds floating past the Swimmable sign? Our threadbare towels laid over sharp rocks? Plus, for a bonus, you got bit on the backside by the Guinness Book of World Records horsefly."

"It left a big red welt on my whitest part. Or so you said."

"Smack dab on the sweetest curve in Christendom, that half-moon slice of lower buttock that mere underwear could never contain."

"It itched like crazy, I will say that."

"And you scratched it like a man: butt itches, you scratch it. But then you were distracted. Right after the horsefly came The Weirdo in the Speedo? Do you remember?"

"Sounds like a distasteful topic."

"We laughed at the time."

"Remind me. Or maybe don't."

"Just a guy who thought he was on the beach at Cannes, or St. Tropez. Prowling back and forth in his itsy-bitsy. And either he believed he looked better than he did or he was wonderfully unselfconscious about his appearance."

"Maybe he was a genuine European."

"One of the thousands of French tourists flocking to Revere Beach? At the time, you called him a weirdo."

"He was behaving oddly, walking on his tiptoes and singing to himself. Didn't I speculate he might be a dancer?"

"One of the many internationally famous dancers flocking to Revere?"

"Either he didn't care how it looked or he didn't know. Like me, that day in Duxbury."

"When you swam in your underwear."

"Only because you assured me it looked like a bathing suit."

"You believed that?"

"The top and bottom matched. It was opaque. It was in no way different from a bathing suit, you assured me. At the time, I didn't know you well enough to ignore you."

"Did I ever tell you how I would check the newspaper—for years, actually—to see if Revere was Healthy, Swimmable, or Dangerous? I would get lonesome for you and recall the greasy clam strips, and the bobbing turds, and *Gamby*. I'd get nostalgic every time I read anything about Gamby in the paper."

"That was our jockey friend?"

"Carl Gambardella, the greatest race-rider in New England history."

"The bartender asked him to sign a shirt for some kid—and then the shirt got wet. Something spilled, remember? Don't let the ink run, Gamby? You sang it on the train, to the tune of 'Wait Till the Sun Shines, Nellie.'"

"I should have had him sign my shirt too. Then you'd have had Harold Jenkins and Carl Gambardella among your collectibles."

"What did you write when people asked for autographs?"

"If there were three or four of them, I made a quick slash, like the mark of Zorro. If there was just one, I would ask her name and put it in."

"Her? Was it always a her?"

"Pretty much. I'm sure it was that way for Conway Twitty, too. With Gamby it might have been different."

"The little guy was a man's man?"

"In a man's world. But isn't memory an amazing feature, how all this stuff comes flooding back? The whole scene there that night: the fish tank; the lady with the ripped cobweb stockings; the bartender with Waylon Jennings hair."

"That's why one keeps a journal."

"Oh, does one?"

"Well, if one did. It's a way to keep from losing bits of your life. Though I wasn't sure about these particular bits. This journal."

"You could have burned it, at any time."

"You don't do that. If you write it down, you hang onto it. You know where you put it, you take it with you when you move."

"And yet here you are, claiming to have never once read it."

"Oh, this one? Not until tonight."

"Honestly, though?"

"Honest injun. I am in the same boat as you are. We are both about to find out what happened on Day 12."

"Lead me back into temptation, old girl."

⁓

DAY 12 was not the day we parted—that whole idea was slipping fast—it was the day we got arrested. And C. acted like a jerk.

The poor cop was just figuring out what the hell to do with us and here's C. holding out his wrists, saying "Cuff 'em officer." Saying, "Cool, we're under *arrest*," because he had lost out at a couple of recent auditions and the standard joke among actors is that they are so overlooked they can't even "get arrested." So to him this was funny. He *was* getting arrested. It would be a story to tell.

A story for Winnie, though? Would she cheerfully post bail for him and serve as a character witness at the trial? Such minor complications rarely cross his mind.

That day started out with bad vibes on Miller Road. Mrs. Ridley no doubt suspected we had murdered Ian and buried him in the cellar. She adores Ian. He's her go-to guy. For power outages, cigarette runs to Tiny's, imaginary robbers, advice on her dialysis . . . she always turns to Ian. "He's my husband, too," she once smiled and said, as he helped her up the rickety stair.

All that morning she had been pacing like an angry red squirrel, wearing a path in the yard. Sounds escaped her from time to time, but she never spoke and she never *pounced*. She started to wrestle with her folding table, even more strenuously than usual, as though to call Ian back from the dead for this, his favorite chore.

When C. innocently offered to give her a hand, she hissed and clawed at him. Maybe I exaggerate, but she definitely rejected his help with a *No Thanks* that sounded like the metal whacking the wood in a rat trap. "She's all yours," he said. "You sort her out."

Fair enough. He and Mrs. Ridley would not be facing off for much longer. Soon enough she would have "our husband" back. The question was, would she tattle on me? Would she take our Ian by the sleeve, as she liked to do, and pour poisonous confidences into his ear? She could never have imagined we were on the up and up, that my betrayal was pre-approved.

C. spent some time with a map, determined to come up with "something good" to do with the day. What he came up with was a lake on the Wellesley College campus, which he said looked promising. To me it looked like a tiny blue smudge on the map.

"I feel there will be images for you."

"Whatever you say, Cal. We'll go out and collect a few images."

"You don't sound enthusiastic."

He had caught me absently wondering if I wouldn't rather go in to work that day. Hypothetically. Maybe I didn't miss Ian, but I did sort of miss my life. And while I wasn't getting tired of C., I was growing weary of our ground rules. So I was not in the best mood, and driving in traffic did not improve me.

Nor, by the way, did being detained by the lake police. But C. was right about one thing. "Comparing Apples and Images" got started that day, or I should say that the seed of it was planted. Nothing (not a word) actually got written during The Twoweeks. Apart from the newspaper, I scarcely *read* a word, which is a far cry from my book-a-day ways.

In fact, getting back to my own habits has been one major benefit of The Aftermath. I may have been free to run around with C., but I never felt free to sit at the kitchen table with a cup of tea and a novel. To do that I needed to be freed from freedom, so to speak, and now, up here, I have been. Plus Ian provides a different sort of freedom, the freedom to be sensible and content. No danger of getting arrested in his company.

C. and I were not arrested either, in the end, though it was touch and go for a while. We broke the law and we got caught. Instead of raising his hands and saying you got me, C. insisted it was a bad law and that bad laws must be broken. "Think Nazis," he instructed the poor red-faced boy policeman. It was not that cute argument that got us off the hook. Nor was it his next sally, that "even if it were a reasonable statute in its way," it was clearly one that called for a wink at the point of enforcement.

The arresting officer did not wink, or Think Nazis. What won the day for us, I am pretty sure, was his embarrassment. He had never liked telling people they couldn't swim here, he confided. As a lad he had jumped into many a pond, not to mention (he confessed) the bottomless Quincy quarry. But to swim naked, in broad daylight, on the campus of a girls' college, simply had to be forbidden.

"Why?" said C., instead of thanking the guy for his consideration and honesty.

"Well, it's obvious why," said the poor blushing soul.

"Not to me," said C., adding "with all due respect, officer."

Meanwhile there I stood, shivering in the heat, towel pressed inadequately to my front. The officer turned toward me, blushing the more, and apologized for the inadvertence of my ongoing nudity. "I'll look away, if you would like to get some clothes on now," he said. I stood behind a tree with the towel clamped in my teeth like a flimsy curtain, and tried to pull my jeans up over my wet legs.

"You're peeking," said C.

"I am not," said the officer, emphatically.

They sounded like a couple of eight-year-olds. But by then Officer Tim Sheehan (stenciled on his shirt) was prepared to cut us a deal. If we would leave immediately and promise never to come back, he would let us off the hook, even though his boss insisted on strict enforcement. It was a warm day. The water was inviting. He understood all this.

Please for once keep your mouth shut, I implored C. with my most potent gaze, and miraculously he did. He gave Officer Sheehan his word of honor and a handshake that may have even been sincere. I know he felt badly once he had stepped out of character. "The kid was pretty nice, really," he said in the car.

"The 'kid' was probably your age exactly."

"Yeah, too bad. A sheriff should be old, bald, fat, and mean. But that's not to say it wasn't a good bust. The kid did his job."

"And you still couldn't get arrested."

"I could have, if it wasn't for you and your wiles."

"Me? I was just cringing the whole time. And concealing myself as well as I could."

"That was the one questionable aspect of the bust, when he ordered us out of the water and you said We have no clothes on and he said Out, Right Now."

"What was he supposed to say? He handed you the towel, to hand to me."

"He should have leaned out the window and said, I'll be back around to this spit in fifteen minutes, folks, and if you aren't gone by then I am going to have to charge you with trespassing, indecent exposure, and murder most foul. And then in his best southern sheriff voice, You hear me now, boy?"

"Maybe he didn't think of all that."

"Maybe he wanted to get an eyeful instead. You made his day."

"I guarantee he was far more embarrassed than aroused."

"We won't know that until he makes confession."

"You're so sure he's Catholic?"

"Officer Tim Sheehan? The only question is how we get the priest to spill. He may invoke the sanctity of the confessional just to stonewall our investigation."

We found a lunchroom at one of those crossroad villages along Route 16, and collapsed into a comfortable red leather booth. Good thing it was comfortable, too, because we might have got the 24-hour Peking duck faster than we got our grilled-cheese-and-tomato sandwiches. It was four o'clock when we ordered, yet we were still waiting as five o'clock approached—and we were the only customers they had. At one point, we got a friendly wave from the cook, through his cutout window; later a visit from the waitress to say our order was "coming right up." Not in this century, that's all.

Most inexplicably, the food was cold when it finally arrived. "We'll think twice," said C., "before we get hungry again."

We had joined the delightful rush-hour traffic jam when I announced it would be safe to get hungry that night, if we ever made it back to Cambridge. "I'll cook dinner. I'll shop and cook. Real food."

"Like a real person?" said C.

That was part of it, admittedly. The rest was that I *like* to shop for dinner and cook it. The same way I like to read. If we weren't going to end after twelve days, we might have to do a bit more normalizing.

"I'll drop you off, to be safe, and then shop at Savenor's."

"Savenor's? To ensure that cooking at home costs as much as eating out?"

"To ensure the food is good. I'll get some chicken, and potatoes, and broccoli, and just do what I normally do at seven o'clock."

"Play the part of yourself."

"If you say so."

"Which you are dying to do after having played some other role for the past twelve days?"

"No, I've been myself. It's just I haven't been doing what I usually do; what I like to do. Why can't I cook dinner? Cooking dinner doesn't fit your definition of the proper exercise of freedom?"

"Whoa. Suddenly this just turned into an attack on me, of all people. I have no objection to the shop/cook/eat option, Lara. None at all. As long as we have enough beer."

"I'll pick some up when I get the groceries."

"Let me get it. Drop me in Central Square and I'll grab a six-pack at Libby's. That way I can be normal too."

That's when I stopped the car. Turned to face him. Was crying, I am sure, by the time I found any words.

"Are we crashing to earth, Cal? Are you tired of this? Of me? You could go home right now, you know. We don't have to stick it out."

"Lara?"

"Think how happy they would be if you walked in with an armload of presents and just said, Honey I'm home, or whatever."

"Are you saying I need presents to get a proper reception?"

It was a laugh line at a non-laugh line moment. It was not an answer, it was not a help. Definitely I was crying by then.

"Lara, I have no idea where this is coming from. Unless it's you who wants to quit?"

"Not exactly. No."

"Well, me neither. *More* than two weeks has certainly crossed my mind. Less has not."

"Just checking," I said, willing to grope my way back toward whatever lightness we could find. Mainly I felt exhausted. Worn down. I knew it was my absolute last chance to change the rules of the game, but I just couldn't summon the strength.

I got some of my energy back at Savenor's. The guys were flirty, the old lady was evil, and the bill was absurdly high. This was all so familiar that it lifted my spirits right up. I was excited to stop Having Fun, stop bearing down on when to *end* the damned fun, and simply cook a nice dinner in my crummy apartment. Putter around my kitchen for one blessed hour.

C. was sitting on the front stoop when I drove up. He stood and bowed and I saw he had flowers in shiny red florist's foil in one hand, a beribboned box of chocolates in the other. Ah yes: the joke about showing up with presents.

"You misunderstood," I said. "As usual."

"No, I didn't. I know you weren't demanding tribute, for goodness' sake, Lara. You reminded me one *could* bring presents, that's all. So then, of course, I wanted to. I wanted to shower you with gifts."

"Well, thank you."

"We've been together almost every second, you know. How could I walk in with flowers, when I was already there?"

"Where?"

"Wherever you were, my wild Irish rose. At all the beginnings, middles, and ends of the earth."

I could not quite resist feeling flattered and pleased by this silly stagecraft he trotted out. C. is an actor, hence in one sense a practiced professional fraud. But I do believe he sometimes uses those patently artificial sallies as a way of saying something genuine. He can't allow himself to go sloppy on me without underscoring it as a joke; yet he is, at bottom, inside the wildly overblown parodies of sincerity, sincere.

In other words, he did reciprocate. My folly was his folly too. There was no chaser and chased, no stronger no weaker. Nor would there be a winner and a loser. We were both going to lose the game.

The radio was always playing those manipulative false-yet-true Kristofferson ballads, the ones that glorify seized opportunities. "For the Good Times" and "Help Me Make It Through the Night" came on constantly. And, no doubt like all other illicit lovers out there in radioland, we couldn't help buying into the illusion that surely this was "our song."

Plus, that was a Sunday, so we could hardly be surprised when Johnny Cash came on to serenade us with "Sunday Morning Coming Down," Kristofferson's most brilliant and depressing song. There's something in a Sunday that makes a body feel alone? That night, as I cheerfully roasted my overpriced chicken, I suspected a couple of bodies were going to feel radically, dangerously alone by the time another Sunday morning rolled around.

$\infty$

"I THINK you were a bit unfair to me about the little cop. Did you really believe I wanted to be dragged into court on swimming charges?"

"What I believed was that you couldn't help bristling. That you were young and male and so was he."

"Is it really that simple? All young men are idiots?"

"Yes. And I know precisely when I learned there were absolutely no exceptions to the rule. It was when Sid Lathrop joined the battle."

"Sid, the funny gay guy at Allison's."

"Funny, but also seriously laid-back. The veneer of uncaring, and then the casual poison dart."

"He did tell me Oscar Wilde was his hero."

"Allison had this big buyer. A player in the city. Owned a big construction company, had a direct pipeline to the mayor, that sort. And he would buy paintings to prove he was civilized."

"An art lover."

"The guy was about to hand Allison three thousand dollars for a Rizzi. Then, Nick—that was his name, Nick—notices an Erlanger and starts giving it the once over."

"Kiki Erlanger."

"Yes, and now Allison dares to hope he will buy *two* paintings. In her mind she's already paying down the mortgage on the Nantucket cottage when Nick says, I like it but it's a little too faggy, don't you think?"

"Yikes."

"And before Allison can agree—which she might have, God forgive her—Sid Lathrop is at her side. Materializes there. I saw the consternation in Allison's eyes, saw her mouthing 'Don't you blow this sale' to Sid. Which Sid does not see at *all*. He is telling Nick, 'Oh no, not a bit faggoty, sir, oodles of blood and thunder here, sir, always with an Erlanger one gets the subtext of blood and thunder and the truly high-test testosterone, why just look at those rich running reds—'

"And Nick looks him over, sizes him up, pegs Sid for a queer making sport of him—and spits on the floor."

"There goes the veneer of civilization."

"Gone. Allison's face is white as King Arthur Flour, Sid's face is the cat bringing you a mouse in his mouth, and I'm wondering, okay what comes *next*. The answer is Sid dropping all irony, all pretense of cool detachment, and saying, 'Is that your notion of masculinity, sir? A gob on someone's carpet?'"

"Allison must have been reaching for her pearl-handled derringer."

"Allison was paralyzed. Nick's witty comeback was a second gob, this one aimed at Sid's shoes. At which point Sid takes one step forward and smacks the brute across the face. Open hand but hard, a real shot across the bow, and within seconds the two of them are wrestling on the carpet, flailing and kicking while Allison yells for help."

"You didn't help?"

"I didn't see any need to. Sid was holding his own. And it all worked out in the end. The next day Nick sent his cleaners over, sent Allison flowers along with a note of apology and a check for the Rizzi. He bought that one after all. Though we never saw him again."

"Well, good for Sid."

"In that case, yes. Nonetheless, I was forced to conclude that if Sid Lathrop would behave that way, any person burdened with a Y chromosome would."

"Did she fire his ass?"

"She might have, absent the check from Nick the Brute, but she didn't. In fact, Sid was still working at the gallery when he got sick."

"He got the invoice."

"Almost everyone did. Jared lucked out, but Sid, Barry, Rennie, Hal, both Georges—pretty much every gay man I knew. Though all that was years later. You do remember we were discussing Day 12."

"I do. The digression was yours, my flower. I was about to address your misrepresentation of that moment in the car. The moment when completely out of the blue you asked if I wanted to throw in the towel ahead of schedule."

"I was just asking. You seemed out of sorts. We seemed out of synch."

"When you came out with that—said we could just let it go, end it early—I was stunned. I was tuned in completely to your happy dinner idea: cooking together, going to bed together, waking up together. And here you were saying you couldn't care less."

"I didn't want to be pressuring you, that's all. I wanted you to be able to be honest with me."

"All the same to you, couple of days more, couple of days less. Whereas in my mind we were in it together and every second was precious. And who knows, maybe the days would keep coming, like the loaves and the fishes, where you have a short supply that expands indefinitely."

"How typically *realistic* of you, Calvert."

"Call it romantic, if you like, I'm okay with that. Call it irrational. But I hated hearing you be so *un*romantic. So horribly realistic."

"Womens learn to protect theyselves."

"Oh, so now we are back around to men are simpletons and brutes."

"Shortsighted might be a nicer way to put it. They see what they want and they do not see the consequences of taking it."

"I saw the fucking consequences, believe me. I didn't like them, so I was hoping time would stop for us. What's wrong with that?"

"Apart from it's being impossible? Nothing at all."

"So there you are."

"Put it this way. You wanted two contradictory outcomes and, because you are a male person, you managed to believe you could somehow have both."

"Which makes me a fool, not a brute."

"We were both fools, Cal. There's no getting around that one."

&#x221D;

ON DAY 13, C. woke from a dark dream, mumbling that it was Friday the 13th, bad luck and trouble. Somehow his subconscious had registered that it was the 13th day? It was a Monday, and we were willfully averting our gaze from the trouble to come. We talked, made love, dressed (always so simple in the summertime), made toast and coffee.

"We could go back to bed if you want," said C., though we had only been in the kitchen five minutes.

"Are you tired?"

"Not a bit," said C., sliding his hands under my shirt as I stood at the sink.

"Tell me how you and Winnie met," I said, and the hands were swiftly retracted.

"Why do you ask?"

"I'm curious."

"Friends of friends," he said warily. "We met at a poker game."

"You won big that night, fella."

"We both felt set up. There were three couples invited that night, plus the two of us. They had all conspired against us, a blind date in disguise."

"I'd say they were pretty fair matchmakers."

"What is this, Lara?"

"I mean it. You and Winnie?"

"All right then, your turn. Tell me how you met Ian."

"We met on a bus. A chartered bus, to a peace rally. Ian hates Nixon just as much as you do, you know. I did hate the War, of course, and I hated the sleazy way Nixon and Kissinger decided to bomb half of southeast Asia more or less for the merry hell of it. So I was on the bus."

"As in you're on the bus or off it."

"Different bus, but yeah. I was willing to march and sing, if it helped."

"So you found yourselves holding hands and swaying to 'Kumbaya'?"

"We found ourselves assigned arbitrarily to get coffee and hot dogs for ten, from a food cart. On the way back, we managed to fumble the food."

"Uh oh."

"We laughed and started rearranging the hot dogs—*composing* them to look right—and never mentioned the mishap. We figured they were already poison, so what the hell."

"Were there casualties?"

"No one even got a tummy ache. Then we swayed to 'Kumbaya,' or more likely 'We Shall Overcome,' and the bombing campaign went on undisturbed. About a year later we were married."

"At Nathan's Famous?"

"At my parents' house. A sit-down dinner, with hot dogs for two hundred."

"Ours was a bit smaller than that—we had four in all. We dragged Fitz and Winnie's friend Gail along to the City Hall as our witnesses, so they also shared in the wedding feast at Cronin's afterward."

"Winnie was okay with it?"

"Absolutely. She planned the whole wedding."

"Did you plan to have a kid, or did that just happen? And then Hetty. Did you have her because you already had Jake? How does that all work?"

"Lara, my bright-eyed darlin', is there some reason you are trying to bring us down ahead of schedule?"

"Honestly, I'm just curious. Though there is the elephant in the room aspect. Pretending the elephant isn't there—"

"That's not what we've been doing. It's more like the elephant *isn't* in the room for two weeks and we're making use of the space he'll take up when he returns."

"Suit yourself. Anyway, I'd better get to the store pretty soon and get stuff for the salad. You do remember, don't you? Mr. and Mrs. Normal are going visiting?"

"That's us. Salad and dessert."

"You know what we haven't done, that would have made us truly normal? Watch some TV together. Hunker down on the couch and catch a few shows."

"You don't have a couch. Or a TV, for that matter."

"We had one when I was a kid. Liam and I used to sit on the couch and watch together, every Saturday night for two hours straight. We had our special shows, that no one was allowed to interrupt."

"Your parents probably thought of it as two hours when you would not be interrupting *them*."

"We could eat whatever we wanted, too. They just closed the door and left us alone."

"Hey, I'll take that deal. Curl up with you every Saturday night for two hours? Close the door? Eat whatever we want?"

"I felt so betrayed," I went on, ignoring his lame joke, "when Liam grew up on me. He turned thirteen and then, as if that wasn't bad enough, fourteen. Really, I never saw him again."

"Wasn't he just here last Christmas?"

"That wasn't him. I never saw him again *as he was*. Because he was never that way again."

"Nor were you, presumably."

"He went first, and by a substantial margin. When he was thirteen, I was ten. So I watched alone on Saturday night, with my icebox cookies and milk. My mother felt so sorry for me she would sometimes come in and watch with me, even though she never liked westerns."

"Did she like icebox cookies?"

We weren't due at Gerald and Debra's until four, so we were not really in a rush. I voted we curl up and read, but C. was restless and hustled us out to the car, where for some reason he insisted I drive.

"Why?" I asked, only because this was an unexplained change.

"It's your car."

"It was my car yesterday, too, and the days before. All of which you drove."

"So obviously it's your turn."

"All right, fine. Tell me where we're going."

"Nope. You drive *and* you choose."

I might have protested such outright tyranny (not to say weirdness) on his part and I did, in a way, by choosing a destination he had previously rejected, Walden Pond. I didn't believe it was risky on a weekday, plus I knew that Monday was Winnie's dreaded long day, concluding with the dreaded endless staff meeting.

I expected the paranoia anyway, but C. kept me off balance by letting it go. As we were riding out to the pond, I came up with several theories to account for this relaxation of the red alert. Theory #1 was that he had painted himself into a corner with his cavalier behavior. He told me to choose, I chose, and he was stuck with it.

According to Theory #2, we had both been growing reckless. Secrecy is wearing and you do come to hate it. How much freedom have you grasped, after all, if you have to skulk and hide? Plus, after two weeks in which we had spent virtually every second together, we felt less the subjects in a crazy experiment than like lovers working through the kinks and knots of a compelling relationship. We were minding our own business, why should anyone mind us?

Theory #3 was the most radical, or psychologically complex. According to this one, C. actually wanted to be found out. I was mindful that as yet he had not lost me *or* Winnie, so he was doing pretty well here, but just maybe he craved to put an end to the lying. Underneath the swagger and bluster, C. is a very decent human being (it turns out) and so (according to Theory #3) he wanted to come clean. Deeply reluctant to cause pain and havoc, he could not bring himself to act on this impulse, yet he could wish (subconsciously) for it to happen.

It was even possible that, subconsciously, he wanted to keep me. Jettison the Twoweeks agreement, ditch both our spouses, and be "together forever" on grounds that we were so right for each other it was worth any devastation we would leave in our wake. I did not want to even consider this possibility. The Twoweeks contract was what gave me a way to handle my emotions and I knew enough to stand behind it.

Nevertheless, as we circumambulated the pond (quickly past the strewn sunbathers, making for the more isolated shore below the railroad tracks) I was stunned to think we had exactly one day remaining. The Twoweeks was about to conclude the way a movie does: the familiar words appear—THE END—the reel runs out, and everyone goes home.

And this would happen simply because neither of us ever expressed the notion we ought not *allow* it to happen. Shouldn't we at least discuss the matter? What did C. feel, at this point? What did I feel? Something had pulled us past all intention, and convention, past all *sense*, into this foolhardy experiment. And then the experiment proved the pull was awfully strong, that together we might have a rare connection, something transformative. Hard to describe this, much less justify it, but I was pretty sure we both felt it.

I resolved to leave these difficult considerations behind and try to enjoy the moment at hand, enjoy Walden, which is still a lovely place to be on a July morning. Maybe they did sell Thoreau pencils there a hundred years ago, and maybe you see a few too many cars in the parking lot now, but the place retains a trace of magic. Thoreau's verities (and America's refusal to learn from them) suffuse the atmosphere. It's a small pond in New England; no one would ever mistake it for Disneyland or the Santa Monica Pier.

Mainly it's mothers and small children devoid of agendas other than sun and water. None of the mothers seemed concerned about how they looked in their bathing suits and few of the children were old enough to know wherein self-consciousness lay. We had left them all behind in any event, back at the public beach. Rounding the toe of the pond, where it pools into a narrow lagoon, we floated our blanket over a pallet of pine needles, on a sunny knoll above the water's edge.

"Thoreau was onto something here," said C., "though I have to admit I don't know his deal that well. Simplify simplify? And that the cabin cost about thirty bucks to build."

"I'd say you have grasped the essentials. All you are missing is his reverence for natural beauty, common sense, peace, and poetry."

"Hey, I've got at least an hour in which to expand my education."

We played childish games in the water. Splashing games, ducking games. He disappeared underwater and butted me gently with his head. He yanked on my bathing suit bottom, pulling it down, and I scolded him though none of it mattered. We were acres away from anyone else who even might care.

C. does like to push the envelope and my reflex is to resist his nonsense. Then there is the side of me that hates being predictable and so was tempted to call all his bluffs. That was the side that let him pull the suit off. *Now* what, was more or less my game. Me testing him back.

The letting-go aspect does interest me. What happens in a tug of war when one team completely releases its grip? What happens to the balance the struggle created? In this case, what would this wise guy do with half a bathing suit in his hand and a bottomless girl in the water?

I had called his bluff and what he did in response was to call mine. He walked out of the water with the suit, looped it neatly onto the branch of a sapling, and lay down on the blanket. Soon pretended to fall asleep, snoring extravagantly. Making it my move.

So I called his bluff again. Faking a devil-may-care blitheness, I emerged from the water bare-assed and sassy, as though nothing could be more natural. (Which is true, after all, or was true, in the Garden of Eden.) I stretched out beside him on the blanket. Making it his move.

I guessed he would sprint off with the suit, waving it and teasing me. After all, weren't we being perfectly childish? Instead he went into what I suppose was one of his Beckett routines, feigned innocence and indirection. He did not react to (pretended not to notice) my state of undress. Took out an orange and peeled it. Casually offered me sections.

Then we spotted a yellow Labrador retriever sniffing and snuffling on the opposite shore of the lagoon, and heard voices trailing close behind. We were about to have company and now C. tossed me the suit. He was ready to conclude our tricky little skit. But was I? Why should he get to make the rules? Why should it be up to him who gets to be naughty, and for how long?

Moral edges, psychological angles. These were the silly symphonies we had always played—as acquaintances, as friends, as lovers. Wrestling for meaningless advantage in the name of fun. But where, I had to ask myself, was the fun in mooning a couple of complete strangers? If only for their sake, I decided it was time to step back inside my thin veneer of decency.

Catching the suit as he tossed it, I was struck by how minimal it was. It was like catching a butterfly. A tiny weightless thing, it disappeared inside my hand. If I'd had a pocket, it would have fit inside. This garment was nothing, or next to nothing, and yet it seemed that without it I was by definition a wanton woman (indeed, a criminal), while with it I became a harmless cipher, a dull normal.

Though when I gave voice to all this, C. flattered me in his fashion: "Never dull, hardly normal."

As planned, we picked up salad makings at the farm stand in Lincoln. Not a lot of their own stuff yet: it was pretty much iceberg lettuce, iceberg tomatoes, iceberg onions. Clearly it would have to be an iceberg salad. Debra would give us a pass, Gerald would lament that we hadn't gone to the Haymarket, as he always did, for his ingredients.

Considering how snippy snobby we had been about going, we ended up having a perfectly nice time with them. Gerald made a wonderful stifado (a far cry from the gourmet hot dogs C. had prognosticated) and a gooseberry fool. The fool gave rise to a symposium on desserts, and what exactly was a gooseberry, other than a "berry word" that provides lovely assonance with the word fool? And then, what was a fool? As for pastry, what differentiates a crumble, a crisp, a crunch, a brown betty, a pandowdy, and so on ad infinitum. We looked them all up in a dictionary, struggled to refine the hazy dictionary distinctions.

"Only in Cambridge," Debra remarked, to which Gerald replied that while we might be *of* Cambridge, we were not technically *in* Cambridge.

"Cambridge, for sure," Debra persisted. "I mean, can you imagine anyone wasting time on this sort of thing in say Lincoln, Nebraska?"

"Regional snob," I said, with our own snobbery still on my mind.

"People in Nebraska tend to be sane, that's all I meant. Whereas we are clearly insane."

"Speak for yourself," said Gerald, never neglecting an opportunity to contradict his wife. "We are this nation's lonely truth-seekers."

"A great man once said that anyone seeking Truth is by definition insane."

I provided this pearl, though I knew of no such great man, or quotation. I made it up! Fortunately for me, Gerald demanded no attribution. Then C. had the last word before the fireworks began:

"Whatever else is true, that was one hell of a fool."

On top of one blanket and snuggled beneath another, we were pretty darned normal that night on the beach, and pretty darned happy. It was both impossible to remember and impossible to forget that THE END was near. Impossible to believe it. My consciousness would disappear into the showers of orange sparks and the smoke floating over the dark surf. Then I would look at Gerald and Debra, amazed that they could be together forever while we were counting down our final hours.

The fireworks display was modest and brief, as befits a July 1st celebration. We stayed long enough to help clean up the kitchen, thanked our hosts with all the sincerity of our contrite souls, and hugged them goodbye in a larger sense than they could know. In the car, C. joked that we would be home in time to watch our favorite TV shows. We could pick up some icebox cookies at the all-night Star Market, and he could play the part of my brother Liam. "The radio can play the part of the TV and you can just play yourself."

Which self, though, pray tell? The one who after a bit more of pretend would be sensibly married to Ian Witherspoon and resume her sensible life free of turmoil, angst, and longing? Or the one who keeps trying to shake Cal Byerly from her mind like a puppy shaking a baby's blanket? Who can't let go when the thrashing is such fun.

At dinner, Debra had asked if we might make it to their Labor Day party. Nothing fancy, she assured me. Gerald would grill kielbasa and chicken, they would build a small bonfire on the beach, where a dozen compatible souls would gather . . .

And again, for an instant, I forgot who we were. "Sounds good to me," I said, glancing at C. the way I would have glanced at Ian, to confirm spousal alignment, unanimity.

C. may have blushed. I had never seen him blush (had been led by Winnie to believe he was incapable of blushing—"unembarrassable" was her word) so maybe not, too dusky to be sure, though he definitely did something one could only call hemming and hawing. It's a phrase one rarely sees now. Hawing? I must look that one up.

He hemmed, he hawed, and he emitted a little click of demurral, like a coded indication of some unfortunate scheduling conflict. Perhaps we were committed in Seattle that week, alas, touring behind the Godot.

We were "otherwise engaged," C. regretted aloud, and I picked it up from there.

"Too bad, too. I'd much rather be here for the kraut and kielbasa. Just don't tell me you'll be toasting marshmallows. I couldn't bear to miss that."

"For your sake, I'll pretend it's never been part of the tradition," Gerald chuckled, smugly. "But I do expect we'll have a nice plum duff that night."

"Thank God it's not a plum crumble," I said, as the pastry joke rolled on.

"You can always come at the last second," said Debra, "if you change your minds. It's just two more indentations in the sand."

"It's not our minds we would need to change," I remarked, flippantly.

But in fact it was. Granted, to change our minds was to change our entire lives into the bargain. That was not an easy question to confront, so we had not confronted it. We hadn't even gotten around to leveling with Gerald and Debra about The Twoweeks, what it was and what it wasn't.

In bed that night, I found myself compiling a list of all the people we would seriously harm by such a change. Winnie, Hetty, Jake, and Ian were obvious, and of primary importance. But what about Ian's parents? (And Winnie's.) What about my brother and Jessica, Ian's brother and Anne and their kids? Our nephew Bradley adored Ian, ran to him like an excited puppy whenever we visited. For that matter, Bradley's *puppy* loved us. Not to mention friends, dozens of friends. The list kept expanding outward.

A *lot* of people would be hurt, a lot of stuff would be screwed up. Would they survive? Sure they would. They would survive if we died, for goodness' sake. But the alternate reality screamed out for attention: who would be hurt if we did *not* change our lives? And the answer was no one.

Or no one beyond the two of us. Would *we* survive? Sure we would. I could not easily imagine Cal with Winnie, nor quite imagine myself reunited completely with Ian. But that would change in time, wouldn't it?

At that point it was necessarily a question without an answer. It still is, except now I am wondering more specifically how *much* time. When does one form a conclusion? Because of course time goes on forever.

❧

"That was right on, about being unable to imagine going back. I was in the exact same place."

"You more than imagined it, Calvert."

"Unless you can live with someone and still be unable to 'imagine' being there."

"That's pure gobbledygook."

"It really isn't. I started living that very distinction, the day after you wrote those words."

"I wrote them several weeks later."

"You know what I mean. 'When we two parted, in silence and tears.' When I went back to Winnie."

"When you were there but couldn't imagine being there."

"I was physically present. My mind, my spirit—whatever you want to call it—was elsewhere."

"Did Winnie notice?"

"Sure. I mean, we had been apart for two weeks. She was trying her best not to stand in judgment, but obviously she was wondering who the hell I was. What I was feeling."

"Still with no idea where you had been."

"If she had known that, she might have had a better shot at what I was feeling. At understanding my distance, and my odd—"

"What?"

"I don't know. Listlessness? I was like a dead man walking."

"Not with the children, surely."

"I hope I managed to put a better face on that, but it wasn't good. There were too many times I felt trapped. At the same time I was grateful, because they kept me from just blowing away, like a kite that gets lost in the sky."

"You wax poetic!"

"Not at all; that was literally how it felt. I was a kite, sailing above my own life looking down, hoping someone had a hand on the string—"

"I'm sure Winnie did."

"I could see the kids screaming and chasing after me, as I went sailing off into space."

"This is sounding more like a dream than a poem now."

"One night we went out to dinner with Fitz and Carrie. Best friends, a nice night out—and I was miserable. Totally distracted. I sat there remembering the good times *we* had with Gerald and Debra, who were no one's best friends."

"They were our only friends."

"I began suggesting we go home early, the kids wouldn't like us being out so soon after—"

"After what? What did you call it?"

"Cal's sabbatical. Carrie named it."

"Did she know?"

"She did not. That became the big joke, my sabbatical. Maybe Cal should take an annual sabbatical, maybe everyone should . . ."

"Because you came back so invigorated. How did it go in bed, by the way?"

"I can't believe you are asking me that."

"Yet I am."

"I can't believe you would think about it, or want to hear about it."

"I certainly refused to think about it at the time. But I would like to know now."

"It changed, of course. It was never right. Even when it went well, it felt wrong. Sometimes I had to get prepared for it the way I would for a scene. Get ready to play the love scene."

"Good old technique and training."

"What can I say? People must do that anyway—act, I mean. Sex can't be totally spontaneous for someone married forty years, can it?"

"Don't ask me, ask someone who has been married forty years."

"All right, ten years then. How long were you and Ian married?"

"Five years."

"And? You don't have to answer."

"I don't know the answer, or rather the question doesn't resonate with me. Personally I never acted, with anyone. I never prepared myself for a 'scene.' To be honest, I've always found myself surprised by sex."

"How so?"

"That it could be not-happening and then suddenly be happening so emphatically. I have always found sex to be a very strange transaction."

"What's the novel where someone catches a glimpse in the mirror, as he and his lady are going at it? And he starts laughing at how ridiculous they look."

"What novel is this?"

"I was asking. It doesn't matter, it's just the idea. It's along the lines of what you were saying, no?"

"Not really, no. I can't say I ever pictured it. Plus, people do it in the movies all the time and it's usually not that funny-looking."

"The book was written in the '50s, before anyone was allowed to do it in the movies. Back when Rock Hudson and Doris Day stayed on their assigned sides of the bed, in their incredibly thick pajamas."

"Only later did we find out why."

"Rock being gay, you mean? Or Doris being stuffed?"

"Calvert, I'm afraid we have wandered far afield by now. Why don't we turn the page and finish up?"

"I'm not so sure I want to relive that last day."

"It's okay, sweetheart, really, it's okay now. But I appreciate the compliment. My journal must be mighty vivid to have such a powerful effect on you."

"It's not your journal, Lara, it's you. I don't want to lose you, even thirty-two years ago."

∽

On Day 14, the theme was emptiness. Even the fridge was empty. We had let it go down to zero, or past zero, to green cheese.

A more serious emptiness was looming, although the fridge led us briefly into distraction, via the long, unlikely, mildly diverting tale of Fitz's brother. As C. told it, this person Philip Fitzgerald once evaded arrest by hiding inside a refrigerator.

"He wouldn't fit, Cal. Not to mention that he would be awfully cold."

"He had emptied it out and unplugged it. Really empty, I mean, took out the bins and shelves. He had done this before, you see."

"What had he done? I mean, what crime did he commit?"

"He robbed a chain of liquor stores. Well, no. The liquor stores were unaffiliated. It was more a chain of stickups."

"That's an important distinction."

Phil Fitzgerald's life of crime was the topic: drugs, robberies, refrigerators, prison. It was a topic that did not touch on our situation, was in no way related to our final day together, and could therefore forestall the reality we both were dreading. It would have cut closer to home, I said a bit dramatically, if Philip Fitzgerald had been on death row, about to order his last meal.

We alternated that morning: whenever he drooped, I tried cheering us up, whenever I drooped, he took a crack at it. We agreed there was no point in wasting "fully seven percent" of The Twoweeks—and then continued wasting it. Continued morbid.

"Do you think anyone can enjoy a last supper," I said, "knowing the executioner waits at dawn?"

"I was hoping to enjoy my breakfast first, until we went and opened the damned fridge."

"We did close it pretty fast," I offered.

Hypothetically, we had two ways of evading the executioner. I could weaken (and sign on for an affair) or Cal could strengthen and break with Winnie. Not a word was spoken of either possibility. The deathwatch continued to inform all our maunderings.

For instance, should we make love under the circumstance, or would that prove "too sad?" We actually *discussed* this. We could easily have found out, and eventually we did. The answer varied. No tears in the afternoon, copious tears at midnight, then back to no tears in the morning when with a grim sobriety we set about memorizing eyes, memorizing skin.

There was a baseline absurdity to reckon with, in that we were doing this to ourselves. It was "unbearable" to part and yet we were about to do it. At times, I was overwhelmed by the stupidity of it. Why undertake to do this (The Twoweeks) if it was only going to depress us? The most obvious response to this question, of course, was that we should *not* have undertaken it. We were idiots who made a major miscalculation.

All we had by way of rebuttal was poetry—variations on Gather ye rosebuds while ye may, the *carpe diem* defense. Gamely, we summoned every romantic cliché known to man that day. Pretty much every sentiment we uttered was a cliché—*we* were a cliché, though it was hardly a help to know that. The jukebox at Charlie's Kitchen that night was a veritable archive of cliché, the ultimate repository.

We had gone there for our final meal. It would be Charlie's double cheeseburg special, $1.99 including the salad and the frosted mug of no-name beer. We sat in a booth and played the cantilever game with their saltshaker, sliding it back and forth whenever we weren't clasping hands or feeding quarters into the jukebox.

Our delightful battle-axe of a waitress, who knew her job well, told us not to worry, she could always tell when it was true love. Told us that whatever our current problem was (she could see there was one, wouldn't "nose around after the details") we would get through it just fine. Time cures everything. Love conquers all. Clichés on the half-shell, cheap beer by the pitcher.

"Nice of her not to insist on the details," said C. "Since she isn't really our mother."

"She is perceptive," I said. "You have to give her that."

"Perceptive? You mean she picked up on our jukebox selection?"

"It may have given her a clue."

We had taken to playing one song over and over, a great song, magnificently rendered by Linda Ronstadt, bodying forth an editorial stance we had thoroughly internalized:

> I've done everything I know
> to try and make you mine . . .
> And I think I'm gonna miss you
> for a long long time.

So gorgeous, so sad, and *such* a cliché. If country and western music didn't already exist, we would have had to invent it that night.

At some point we realized we were trying to get drunk, needing to, and so switched from no-name beer to rotgut bourbon. We joked about finding a veterinarian who would agree to put us down.

"On to a better world," said C., lifting his glass at the prospect.

"Heaven, this would be?"

"Sure. Don't you insist you still believe?"

"Heaven is a tough one. And the idea of you and me getting in? We have already discussed those odds."

"No shot, you think?"

"Unless we reform. Radically."

"Radical reform is coming, babe. Tomorrow at sunup."

"Hush," was all I could say as the song concluded yet again:

> And I think I'm gonna love you
> for a long long time.

Somehow (maybe it was the bourbon) we managed to sleep that night and wake to a world that did not outwardly resemble death row. It had rained around midnight and now a mist was burning off. The backyard was a pool of bright fog. This sequence, late rain and early sun, had sweetened the scent of Mrs. Ridley's roses and honeysuckle. The chickadees, nearly as populous as leaves in the Japanese maple, sang their two-note song. The gallows was nowhere in sight.

We woke to this handsome, fragrant world. We were young and strong and fortunate in every way. There were people waiting who loved us, there were things we loved to do. There was no justification for the terrible sinking emptiness we felt.

We hugged, or clutched, for five minutes at the gate before I pushed him away. Launched him. He brushed my cheek with his hand and drifted toward Western Ave. I did not stay to monitor his progress.

Back inside the apartment, I started cleaning for no reason. Took a shower for no reason. Fidgeted and paced, fighting off every thought that attempted to enter my head. Suddenly life, which had been so full, was empty. No other word captures it. And this emptiness was visceral; I felt eviscerated, hollowed out.

I wanted to believe the condition was temporary. That final night at Charlie's Kitchen, Gladys had assured us that time cures everything and why would Gladys lie? I continue to believe her now, a month after she brought us our check, with a frowny-face scribbled at the top and a smiley-face, the antidote, at the bottom.

Maybe I will go consult her, when we get back to town. It's always darkest before the dawn, Gladys will reassure me. It's better to have loved and lost, she will remind me, than never to have loved at all.

❧

"Kɪɴᴅ ᴏꜰ a weak curtain, don't you think?"

"It's not a play, Calvert. It was never meant to be seen, much less *evaluated.*"

"It could easily be a play, though. The Twoweeks? All it needs is a stronger curtain."

"Do you have specific suggestions?"

"Not me. I play 'em, I don't make 'em up. But I should think a high holy hush ought to fall on the two figures as they part. Snow maybe? Falling fast, blanketing the ground?"

"In July?"

"Well, it doesn't have to be July. It could be set in December."

"You would lose the water leitmotif."

"Freeze it. They ski. They skate down frozen rivers and canals."

"You'd lose the sex scene, on the island."

"They ice-fish. There's a bob-house, with a woodstove. Snug little ice-fishing hut. They huddle inside for warmth."

"It seems you do make 'em up after all, old chap."

"Or you could set it in autumn. The hush could be October leaves rustling in the wind, as the camera pans to a streaky salmon sky. A large bird flies over, an eagle—no, I've got it, an *albatross*!"

"Camera, did you say? Am I to understand that our play, which was a journal, has now become a movie?"

"Why not? And here's an even better idea, a stronger close. Want to hear it?"

"No, thanks."

"Let's say you do. It involves the Missing Day. Remember the Missing Day? We put it at the end and let it stand, saying whatever it is you didn't want Ian to read."

"I didn't want him to read a single word of this."

"Okay, then, whatever it is you don't want *me* to read. Or yourself, perhaps, to ever read again. Whatever it is, that would be the finale."

"What's so bad about the real finale? The clock ticking down to zero, Linda Ronstadt singing through the credits, the two of us going back to our respective lives . . ."

"You went to Maine."

"A bit later, yes. Where did you go?"

"Home. Visited for a few days in Bearsville, then started looking for a job the next Monday. I had the Beckett to prepare for, but I had no real paying work."

"That's when you started at the bookstore?"

"Eighty dollars a week, for thirty hours. I kept telling Pete Wellington it was an invitation to embezzlement. If he paid that poorly, everyone would rip him off and feel completely justified."

"I'm surprised he didn't fire you on the spot."

"He thanked me. Assured me that everyone would rip him off anyway, and at least now he knew I wouldn't."

"Brilliant. So you were free to rob him blind."

"No, Pete won that one. He was pretty damned good at psychological chess. And it was an okay job. The people were fun. It was a lot like working at the gallery, except minus you."

"There must have been someone."

"Someone like *you*?"

"Someone to distract you from me."

"There was one reasonably attractive girl. I forget her name. Nice blue eyes, wrote short stories. Apart from me, everyone there was trying to be a writer. A bookstore, you know. But I wasn't looking for a girl. My goal was to survive my obsession with you and not take it out on Winnie. Going off the rails altogether was not my goal, and it isn't fair of you to suggest it would be. Did I accuse you of looking to replace me with meaningless, transient love affairs?"

"You didn't accuse me, but I did try that. I tried to replace both you and Ian with them, though that's another story."

"Tell it to me."

"Forget I said that. There's no story to tell."

"The same way there is no entry for the Missing Day?"

"Will you please stop with that, Cal? Just let it be?"

"I'll make you a deal. I'll let go of the Missing Day if you let me read about how you tried to replace *both* me and Ian. Is that it there? The blue folder?"

"That's private. You cannot read it—or you may not, I should say."

"I love the title."

"Hands off. And it's not a title, it's just some words I scribbled on the folder."

"I remember the phrase, though. You said it on the last day of The Twoweeks, when I was telling about Phil Fitzgerald hiding in the fridge."

"Remind me."

"You didn't want to hear the story. Said you didn't know the guy from Adam, and that anything Fitz's idiot brother did was as relevant to you as the news that a man in Sicily had just changed his shirt."

"That wasn't me, it was E. B. White."

"I'm sure you supplied the proper attribution. And I pointed out that if you went to the movies, and the opening scene happened to be a man changing his shirt in Sicily, you would be intrigued and want to know more."

"Maybe so. But a work of art has intrinsic interest, whereas the shenanigans of someone's nutty brother may not. In any case, I did listen to the story. I was intrigued, and I did want to know more."

"Meanwhile, you haven't chosen. What'll it be, The Missing Day or your Shirts in Sicily folder? We'll 'pick up on one and let the other one ride.'"

"I have so chosen—to go up to bed."

"Fine. As soon as you drift off to sleep, I'll creep down and have a peek."

"Open that folder at your peril, Calvert. No means no."

"You have a point. It is late, and I too am a-weary a-weary and fain would lie doon. We'll have plenty of time to discuss the Shirts tomorrow morning."

# ✑ 5 ✑

# *Shirts in Sicily*

## (1974–5)

$W$hen The Twoweeks ended, I had no idea what would happen next. Ian had spent time with his brother and with old friends who no doubt ridiculed his tolerance. By now, they might have all convinced him to throw me out like yesterday's fish.

And Cal Byerly was gone. As the man on Charlie's jukebox put it, "Gone gone gone and cryin' won't bring him back." He might even love me, whatever that meant, and still he'd be no less gone. So instead of having two wonderful men to choose between, I might have neither—have no one.

Which might not have been so terrible. Maybe I was too immature to understand that I must not love either of them, Ian *or* Cal, and that until I met *Heinz*, or Heathcliff, I would not know the true meaning of love.

It seemed more likely that I loved both of them, Ian *and* Cal, and needed to move on all the more. Because whatever I felt for Cal, whatever he felt for me, he was not available. I did not have the option of choosing him. (Gone.) And while instinct told me I might still be permitted to choose Ian, I also might have destroyed the best of what we had.

I did figure inertia would be on our side—not that inertia is the greatest motivation for lifelong commitment. Still, we were married. Even without children, without real estate or money in the bank, to become unmarried was a process, arduous and ugly.

Who would allege what, as grounds for divorce? Who would get custody of the friends and relations? Would I get Ian's mom on alternate Sundays?

Whereas if we simply lapsed back into our old life (cooking side by side, strolling up to the Orson Welles and the Plough on Wednesdays, visiting his parents to whom we would present ourselves as happily married) divorce could shape up as arbitrary and unwelcome. I might be able to have him.

Technically, as I say, I did have him: he was my husband. If he came back east and did *not* throw me out like yesterday's fish, I could surmise he still loved me. Whether he could ever trust me again was another matter entirely. Even if we got past Cal Byerly, every man I met might loom (to Ian) as a potential relapse. If you let a woman get away with murder, what's to keep her from killing again?

Another fair question was whether I loved him in the way he deserved to be loved, as the kind and brilliant man who had never done me the slightest harm. I began by arguing the affirmative. After all (I argued) I would have loved him Forever (wouldn't I?) had Cal Byerly never opened his big mouth. If I had lost touch with that older abiding love, why couldn't I find my way back to it?

The first obstacle on the road back was the extent to which I *was* in touch with my chaotic feelings about Cal. I was too involved there; embroiled would be a better word. One minute I would picture him content to be back with Winnie and be rattled by it, angry at the very idea. The next minute I'd picture him miserable with Winnie and want to rush over and save him. I knew I could make him laugh, even if she couldn't.

My emotions lay close to the surface, my tears barely below it. Nearly anything could start me crying. I cried at sunup and sundown, cried when I dressed and undressed, cried when I fried an egg. At my most pragmatic, I cried in the shower.

As events began to unfold, Ian and I shared a real determination to make it work. We did cook nice dinners and eat them on the landing, welcoming the sunset with cheap red wine. We did march up to the Welles two consecutive Wednesdays, and mosey over to the Plough after the movie. Mrs. Ridley watched us come and go, like a wily detective waiting for the perpetrator to make a mistake. Though her skeptical gaze demanded it, I refused to overdo the wifey part for her.

When we went out to see his parents in San Carlotta, I was more willing to lay it on. I owed it to Sebastian and Sally more than I did to Mrs. Ridley, and it was hardly a stretch with them anyway. It felt genuine to be part of Ian's family and then to be the two of us *coping* with Ian's family in all the old ways, for here came his dreadful sister Lydia and the nephews from Hell. Here, in their wake, came the bedraggled misused abused Peter.

In keeping with tradition, we would flee to the mall, of all places, for peace and solace. Cultural snobs to the core, mall haters from the first jump, we took refuge in the Mexican café we had always rationalized did not belong in a strip mall because it was "authentic." The lovely couple who ran it worked so hard and charged so little that we tipped like crazy to help balance their books.

"Maybe we should move out here," I said one night, after two tequilas at the café.

"Move here?" said Ian.

"Well, move. From Cambridge."

"Where I work?" he pointed out.

Rick Ruane had his imaginary handbook, his comic map of all the places "people like us" could feel at home. Sixties people, we were being called. Meaning what? That we liked music and art and literature and personal freedom? That we believed in Civil Rights and emphatically did not believe in a grotesque misbegotten war? Which among those values could any decent, intelligent American citizen reject?

Still it was valid, the Ruane Map. We all knew it was, even as we laughed. Cambridge and Berkeley, Madison, Santa Fe, Austin, Ashland, Homer. Greenwich Village carried an asterisk, as I recall, and Des Moines a footnote of some sort. Parts of certain cities had qualified, neighborhoods, like Dinkytown in

Minneapolis. We could find a good fit somewhere. Maybe Ian could get a teaching job in Dinkytown.

If we had normal jobs we could be forced to move willy-nilly to places well off the Ruane grid. Liam and Jess had lived that way for ten years. They had been "relocated" by Liam's company to Fort Wayne and then again to Charlotte. Children go where I send thee, sayeth the man who writeth the checks. If they could survive it, why couldn't we?

After we returned from San Carlotta, where in five days I shed not a single tear, the weepies returned. Out west, my mind could go to other places, larger spaces. In Cambridge, I might run into Cal anywhere, or hear news of him from mutual friends. If willpower was all that kept us apart, propinquity generated danger.

I never did see him (nor, mercifully, did I see Winnie) but I was constantly keyed up for the accidental meeting. Mainly I did not want to be taken off balance, so each block I turned down became a nerve-wracking affair. Even at home, I found myself staying alert. The telephone unnerved me whenever it rang. The doorbell posed such a threat that I took steps to disable it.

Cal wouldn't just appear at the door, would he? To take a careless shot at finding me alone or (conversely, perversely) to make a clean breast of it with Ian. If he did find me home alone, would he be there to apologize or to commiserate? Or to propose! He could propose anything from a walk in the park to marriage.

I did assume Cal was mired in the same emotional swamp as I, yet what if he wasn't? What if appearing at my door was the farthest thing from his mind? I couldn't even know whether to love him or hate him. Not that I had any proper business (nor anything to gain) doing either. So it was a mess, and I was a mess.

It's a mystery to me where Ian finds his equanimity. He won't even take credit for it, insists it's nothing but common sense. But his Someone Else Entirely idea (which started during our week in Maine) made no sense to me. We were almost okay for a while, almost ourselves, except perhaps in bed. Really, the worst part of it, and the most surprising, was how bad we felt when it was good in bed. It worked! we all but shouted, as if neither of us believed it could.

Soon it came clear that it had only worked technically. It had not drawn us closer, as it should have, as it always had in the past. Instead it shouted right back at us, You have got a problem here, kids.

Ian, with his bottomless equanimity, was determined to confront said problem head-on. He brought Cal right into the bed with us, albeit in a lighthearted way. What do you think of *that*, Calvert, he said, after we finished one night. Another time it was Uh oh, better cool it, girl, or you'll make Calvert jealous.

At the restaurant in Damariscotta I happened to notice this guy in the kitchen. The dishwasher? The cook? I saw him through the portal, a good-looking guy with thick brown hair and a blow-'em-down smile. Ian noticed me noticing and said it again: "Careful now, or Cal will be jealous." Going with the joke, I assured him the experience was purely visual, like looking at a movie star.

He was being too easy on me. His reward? I was getting annoyed with him, bitchy and critical. What did I want him to do, for goodness' sake, slap me around and stuff me into a trash barrel? What could he do to please me if being wry and sweet and supportive failed to do the trick?

It didn't, though. Ian could do nothing right in Maine, and by the end of our stay there he had grown weary with trying. So over a dessert, which Handsome Harry, as we had taken to calling him, delivered to our table (and incidentally my movie star was not so good in close-up—his skin was pitted and he had taken a fatal overdose of peach-scented cologne), Ian introduced the Someone Else Entirely theme.

To him, The Twoweeks was known as The Hiatus. How went The Hiatus, he asked on the day he returned, hale fellow well met, as though we were not a marriage in crisis but voyagers returned from separate pleasure cruises. Now he was suggesting a longer version, Hiatus Squared.

"You might need a complete change of air, as Henry James might have phrased it."

"The air here is just fine, thank you."

He persisted. I might not need him *or* Cal Byerly: "You might need Someone Else Entirely. Which sounds too formal. Why don't we just call him 'Someone' for short?"

"Ian, please be serious. And please don't bring the busboy into it again."

"Oh, he is much more than that. I've seen him dress salads and answer the phone. He could be anything from the great factotum to the restaurateur."

"Please?"

"Fine. He shall be designated Noone. As opposed to Someone."

This was Ian being snippy. He was smiling and making witty, but I knew him: these were shots fired. He wanted me to experience them as such, without pegging him as the shooter. In his subtle, indirect way, he was finally lashing out, and I could hardly blame him.

Nor did I. The trouble was I didn't care enough. It didn't *matter* enough that he was angry (truly, it made perfect sense) and though his being hurt certainly mattered, even that didn't have the desired effect on me. It simply doesn't work that way, the heart. To my shame, "heartless" is probably the word that best describes my failing.

Heartless and imbalanced. One evening we noticed a beautiful wooden sailboat anchored off the point. Boats had come and gone all week, dinghies had come ashore. With the binoculars we would read their names, scope out what sort of people were aboard. This time, absurdly, I imagined Cal Byerly might be on the new boat and that after Winnie was safely asleep he would bring the dinghy in.

Even more absurdly—insanely?—I kept a close eye on this "situation" past midnight. I took a walk down to the jetty, to check on it. I recited (to myself) Browning's lovely brace of poems, "Meeting at Night" and "Parting at Morning," as I pictured Cal rowing in by moonlight, then rowing back "as the sun peeked over the mountain's rim." My mind was shot, and we would be stuck in Damariscotta for two more days.

Those were rough days. Days that would make us look back nostalgically on our first weekend there, when the weather was splendid and when we believed we had come there to heal. We were confident we could work through this crisis and preserve (or revive) a marriage we had never before had cause to question. Instead, we were doing the worst thing a couple can do, waging guerrilla warfare behind phony smiles. Ian's subversive sarcasm crashed against the walls of my bizarre indifference. It was so awkward and out of synch; the opposite of dancing.

There was a last supper which felt exactly *like* a last supper (Judas, the betrayer, within me) and a last night on which we were as likely to reach for one another as corpses were. Not to mention a last breakfast at which Ian could not eat a bite, while I shamelessly gobbled up his bacon. "We'll get you something on the road," I said, as though he wanted not my love but a better cheese danish.

About a week after Damariscotta, more or less out of the blue (we were on the landing at Miller Road, watching the sun start down) Ian said, "You should call him."

From Mrs. Ridley's door, one storey up, you can see across the river to the Boston side. From our level, you just get sky pressing on the treetops, but the colors can be spectacular, shot through with beautiful pollutants, multilayered, varicolored. This was something we had always done, watching the sky change at that hour. It was a designated affirmation of life.

I guess I sighed. Exhaled, anyway. A moment earlier I had entertained the idea we should simply drink more, drink as much as it took, and end up in bed. A wall had bloomed between us there. Night after night, we either fell asleep quickly or pretended we had. It had reached a point where we needed to utilize the bed for its other special function before that function became vestigial.

*"Can* you call him?" Ian went on.

"Who?"

"Oh come on, Lara."

"Winnie is the one I should be calling, you know. She must be wondering why I haven't."

"She hasn't called you, either, in case you haven't noticed. Which might provide a clue as to her likely attitude if you do call her."

"Yikes."

"Yikes indeed. I'm saying something different: that you need to talk to Cal."

"I don't. There is no provision for checking in. It's done with."

"That assumption isn't working for you, Lara. Maybe it isn't working for him."

"He'll have to make it work, and I'm sure he will. I'm pretty sure he has."

"Because he hasn't called?" Checkmate, said his pained, twisted smile.

"No, because he doesn't want to call. Doesn't want me calling him, either. Knows what it was and knows it's over."

"I see," said Ian, cranking the hideous rictus a notch or two tighter.

He was not having a lot of fun. He was very apt to say the hell with it; to hell with waiting while I completed my "evaluation" of our chances. Ian is an eminently sane man. He is even capable of choosing sanity, or *order*, over love. Whatever love is.

"All right, so how are we going to do this, Lara?" he said now.

A chill went down my spine. (Cliché, yes, and yet there it was, a chill.) Sudden tears blurred my vision. I didn't bother to feign ignorance. I knew what he was saying, though I could not say anything.

"Do you want to hear my idea?" he said.

"Oh, Ian."

"Obviously I could get a place, or you could get a place. One of us could stay with friends for a while. Alternatively, you could go to Mexico, file for divorce there, and be free in a week."

"Ian, please."

"My idea, however, is that you take a trip on your own. Go back to France, if you still want to. But dislodge yourself from Cambridge, one way or another. Travel, brood, write some poems—and find Someone Else Entirely. To get clear of the immediate situation."

"You make it sound so simple."

"Well, it's simple enough to do it. To book a flight and get on it. Easy for you to meet people. If you wanted to go to London, you would already know people. Ben and Lila. Katia. And of course, they know tons of people."

"Quit my job?"

"Sure."

"Money?"

"We can cover it."

"You would foot the bill for me to run off and look for 'Someone Else' in Europe?"

"Someone Else Entirely. Yes, I would pay my share."

"Am I that horrible?"

"Not horrible, just unhappy. And not sufficiently yourself for me to even recognize you, if I needed to place blame. It's not Lara Cleary making my life miserable, it's this lookalike replacement they sent from the temp agency."

"Ian, I'm really sorry. So sorry, for doing this to you."

"I think we would both benefit if you took the trip."

My reflex was to contradict him, to walk him past a low moment. Cheer him up, win him back. In any case, not *lose* him. I hated the idea that Ian could stop loving me, even if I had stopped loving him. Did that mean I had not stopped?—or did it just mean I was a narcissistic bitch?

I did try to console him. I did not find any useful words (or none that would have rung true) but I hugged his head, stroked his hair, wrapped him in my arms. I took him to bed and there

I took down the wall, which it turns out I had put up by myself. Yet as we lay there hip to hip, each a tick or two more optimistic, I was already musing on the shape such a trip might take. On the relief it might provide.

Not at all on the opportunity for cheating on my husband. Ian had convinced himself that a brief affair could break through the binary equation in which we were currently imprisoned. He was always bound by logic, and now his logic told him we had already lost what such an affair might be expected to cost us: the closeness, exclusivity, and trust.

At the very least, he logicked, what we stood to gain was clarity. And he was willing to gamble that, in the throes of total freedom, I might find I wanted nothing more than to have my old life back. His logic told him our marriage might start looking pretty good after a while. Ian never kidded himself—that was never an option, not a part of his temperament—but on one level he simply could not believe anything looked better than what we had.

Cal and I had spoken once of our early loves, youthful adventures in romance—or his. From early on, earlier than he felt ready or even willing, he had been sifting through offers. He wasn't ready and he was picky. Apparently, there were only five (count 'em, five) girls he found attractive in his high school and not many more when he got to college. But reciprocity was never the problem. The ones he wanted seemed to want him too.

Whereas there were plenty of boys good enough for me—or so I assumed. Since I was not deemed good enough for any of them, it was hard to know for sure. I did not have a hint of a boyfriend until just before senior prom when suddenly (and to this day no one has ever told me how or why) I was everyone's first choice.

Something had happened. Somehow I had won the lottery and suitors began pursuing me. You would have thought I just moved to Braxton, that they were all getting their first look at me. Certainly they were looking through a new lens.

I hardly knew where to begin, so I began by snubbing them, cutting off my nose to spite my reappraised, upgraded face. I did this more in confusion than in vengeful retrospective anger at anyone. The effect was to make them even more eager to win my previously worthless heart and hand.

The transformation was real, apparently. I was an altered, improved commodity. Even my mother commented on it, and my favorite Uncle Satch (Louie, to his friends) was bombarded with good-natured wolf whistles and dirty old man jokes when he danced with me at my cousin's wedding that summer. A famously graceful hoofer, he had danced me all my life, at first in the air, then on his feet, playfully. Later, when I was the ugly duckling, Uncle Satch would take care to shield me from wallflower status, though in truth I felt perfectly at home with it.

Now he was dancing with an eighteen-year-old in a scary backless dress and he could not stop telling me how wonderful I looked. He meant it, too. They all meant it. I would enter college with a clean slate. No one there would know I was an ugly duckling. To them I would be this other creature—no beauty, God knows, just a girl who had something that worked. Something that gave her power over boys, whether or not she could bring herself to believe it.

At first I did not believe it, or trust it to continue. I had never even fantasized such a state, never dreamed a boy might want my company. Convinced I would remain flat-chested all my life, I was surprised and grateful when small (almost normal!) breasts snuck up on me senior year. I didn't have them at fifteen, when everyone else did, so I had given up waiting, stopped noticing, didn't much care. I never wanted to be Gina Lollobrigida, I just wanted to be sufficiently normal that no one *would* notice me.

I was shy, a "reject," and the only sort of boy I could imagine being interested was a corresponding reject, someone like Timmy Gabrielson from French Club. Tim looked a lot better too, by the by, when he got rid of his braces and came back from the Peace Corps tanned and confident. Teenagers just have a hard time believing in the future. The present can be so overwhelming that it feels solid and permanent.

In my teen incarnation, I ruminated less about boyfriends than about a peaceful spinsterhood or (more vividly than that for a time) *sisterhood*—an actual nunnery. It seemed a solution of sorts. A nun is not a reject, after all, she is the one who rejects, or renounces, the world. She takes herself out of the running in a way that serves only to enhance her stature.

It was easy for me to envision a sedate life of reading and prayer and poetry, walking in the hills, tending to animals. It would be pleasantly lonely, like my real life, which I knew how to enjoy. Meanwhile I would be serving the poor, serving Jesus and the Church. A nunnery was not a bad fit for the old version of me, the girl who could hardly be surprised when no invitation came for the Homecoming Dance.

I tried researching the sisters of mercy who had written poetry, and when I found none (or none that were known to the world) I turned to monastics and ex-monastics, reverends and near-reverends. Anyone who had set his holy struggles to meter, against a backdrop of natural beauty. Gerard Manley Hopkins became not merely my favorite poet but my absolute polestar. God's Grandeur was never so grand as it was in his hands.

But then came the sea change, and the flood of eager young men. It was almost like one of those Hollywood comedies, where a noisy flock of foolish suitors come elbowing past one another, hoping to catch the ingenue's eye. As soon as I got to college, the past receded and a new world order beckoned. Pretty quickly I started having fun with it, especially once I saw that nothing more was required of the new Lara than that which the old Lara always had to offer, a quirky intelligence and a cheerful disposition.

I soon suffered an embarrassment of riches. So many of those college boys wanted me; the question became which ones did I want? This was a problem radically unfamiliar to me. Seth wrote poems and had pretty dark brown eyes. Ben wanted to make a film about Sylvia Plath and had pretty pale blue eyes. Enzio's accent was irresistible, especially when I laughed at it and he protested that no no no, his English was "long ago perfected."

There were others as well and my policy, freshly shaped, was to sample them like candies, commit to nothing, refuse to worry. When pressed with buzzwords (steady, exclusive, future, *love*) I simply backed away. Even Ryan Weissman (to whom I am still attracted, in absentia, a decade later) had to be dismissed. And the amazing aspect is that my arrogance in dismissing them only added to my "mystique."

Boys, or men, were supposedly allergic to commitment. Instead, I was hearing (at age nineteen) from each of two accomplished seniors (ripely aged to twenty-two) that I was the chosen one to bear his child. To me this was laughable, for I knew what neither Seth nor Austin knew in proposing marriage and parenthood, namely that a very short time ago I had *been* a child.

By junior year the novelty wore thin, the dance of dating lost its savor, and I met Ian, to whom I was neither the princess nor the duckling. I was a friend to have coffee with after our "Revolution and the Age of Reason" seminar, and then, gradually, something more than that (dinners, long walks) as the friendship moved in what I took to be a natural progression toward true love. What else would it be? When we put an end to my unexpected career as a femme fatale, I had no regrets, only a sense of relief.

Now that he was proposing to throw me back in the ocean, my instinct was to resist. His strategy was not only counterintuitive, it was insulting. To me, and also to Cal. It trivialized *our* connection. Whatever Ian needed to believe, affairs in the abstract held no appeal for me.

Traveling did appeal, and getting away did make some sense. Nor did going alone scare me a bit; on the contrary, it excited me. I had always enjoyed my own company and the concomitant freedom to troll for poems. And if there were occasions when that apparent freedom generated unwelcome encounters, I now had a rock-solid fallback position: "Sorry, I am a happily married woman."

Moreover, as I began to entertain the possibility of a trip and to imagine the shape it might take, I noticed I had ceased to troll for Cal Byerly. Ceased to anticipate him at every intersection. By pushing me in a new direction, Ian had successfully redirected my gaze, which was fine by me. I had been unable to manage it on my own.

Even so, as Ian's suggestion began to morph into a plan of action, I could not quite suppress the urge to communicate the plan to Cal. Whether this was because I wanted him to suffer or wanted to relieve him of suffering, I honestly hadn't a clue. There was just this nagging sense he should be informed.

Somewhat ruefully, I recalled a chance encounter with Cal shortly before Ian and I left for Paris that summer. Cal was virtually a stranger to me at the time, yet I couldn't contain myself and crowed about the fortunate days awaiting me. How joyous I was on the eve of that journey, how joyless on the eve of this one. Maybe I wanted to inform Cal because he was to blame for the change. Because of him, I was being banished. Because of him, Ian was footing the bill—financially *and* emotionally.

And what was Cal doing all this while? Reading Estragon's lines to Winnie in bed at night? Flipping a Frisbee to his son? I could hardly avoid blaming him a little.

Though maybe I would end up thanking him. To me, after all, Ian's scheme was another grant, a chance to get some work done. I would go back to Scotland first, hole up in some Highlands coaching hotel where (seated by a peat fire, cold rain battering the glass) I would carve out a dozen new poems. Maybe two dozen. I would work.

My days would have a shape. Up early and into the hills (or possibly onto the strand at Anstruther, into the stiff spray of the Firth of Forth) and then back to the peat fire and the poems, shepherd's pie and Scotch ale. Variants on this outline would unfold in London or Paris, places where I would feel almost at home. It was not such a bad assignment.

Mighty strange, however, in the carrying-out. For we did carry it out, going so far as to plan many of the details together.

Ian kept dragging out maps and train schedules, reckoning distances. Overhearing us, you would have guessed we were preparing for a vacation together and I would have been glad if we were. To the end, I remained ambivalent about the wisdom of this enterprise.

It was comforting that the trip would begin in Scotland, for I had long romanticized that country and in particular the Scottish autumn. My family had lived there during the sunniest three months in their history, a freak happenstance for which my father, teaching that semester at St. Andrews, was given full credit by his colleagues. He was the only variable, they insisted, therefore the only plausible explanation. We arrived and the sun arrived with us; we left and there ensued one hundred consecutive days of rain.

("Come back, come back," one postcard read, with a picture of four sodden golfers huddled under a tree with a flask, waiting out a downpour.)

But those later rains were unreal to me, the brisk bright days were the ones I had experienced. I was nine at the time, Liam twelve. Each afternoon we would rush home from school and with our little posse ride bicycles over roads with no traffic, through villages with no visible population, to beaches and deserted moors we virtually owned.

We experimented with lawlessness. Like St. Augustine, we stole pears from a tree near the St. Andrews campus. We removed a man's hat as he slept on a bench and hid it behind a fountain. Liam and our friend Nigel hatched a plan to commandeer a yawl from the Pittenweem pier and sail it across the Firth to Edinburgh.

We spent hours plotting covert actions inside Edinburgh Castle. Liam and I had not yet been inside, but Nigel had, and he spoke knowingly of a secret passageway leading to a suite of long-abandoned rooms, with Gothic-arched stained-glass windows overlooking the cobblestone alleys of the Old Town. All this he illustrated lavishly for us. He drew up a floor plan of the concealed apartment, pinpointing locations for the trapdoor and the wall safe.

It hardly mattered that this was a fantasy or a hoax, not when Nigel wore such nice sweaters and spoke in a dazzling accent that brought me this close to understanding a foreign language, albeit that language was English. Liam wanted to *be* Nigel and I wanted to marry him, for this was before puberty and long before I considered pledging myself to sisterhood.

It was the loveliest time, then and ever after, for Scotland had burrowed deep and stayed with me. Scotland always loomed. The notions and images I accumulated there would crop up again and again. The chance to revisit them, to augment and perhaps revise them, comprised the positive side of my ambivalence.

The wild oats part of the package had shrunk from my view entirely. I tended to forget it was the centerpiece of Ian's scenario, whereas he would keep coming back to it. He is an academic and academics get very attached to their little hypotheses. If I questioned the logic, he would insist that logic did not pertain. Or that the logic was "firmly based in illogic." How do you argue against *that*?

When I said it wouldn't work, he assured me I would see how it worked as events unfolded. Medicine was one of his cute little analogies: you might hate the taste, yet you needed to take it if you wanted to get better.

In the end I felt like the skinny girl my parents had packed off to summer camp against her will, in the face of her dread. Not quite kicking and screaming (I was a tad more dignified) and certainly not clinging and crying, I would yet require a final shove onto the plane at Logan.

I am a crier, though, and did a fair bit of drizzling out over the Atlantic, to the point where a gentleman alongside me surrendered his entire packet of "sneezies" to the cause. He was otherwise reserved and respectful, and for the next four hours maintained a polite silence. Then as we were circling Heathrow, he just as respectfully wondered if I had a place to stay in London.

I looked at him for the first time. Really, he had been a head perched atop a suit, with British rather than American inflections, nothing more specific. Now I saw the suit was bespoke wool, the briefcase was leather with debossed initials, the ring finger was bare. Was I expected to swing into action this quickly? Had Ian *planted* this guy?

"I'm connecting to Edinburgh," I said, by way of politely declining. "Off again in an hour. You live in London?"

"More or less. Wimbledon."

"The tennis place."

"Yes," he laughed, as though absolutely everyone said this and he didn't mind in the slightest. "That's just two weeks out of the year, you know. The tournament."

"Two weeks can be a long time," I said, mostly to myself.

"Yes, I suppose it can. Well, then. Glad you've dried up, in any event. They'll have a fresh box of sneezies inside the gate."

"I'll get one, as a precaution. I'm fine, really. No one died on me or anything, I'm just a congenital weeper. Tears close to the surface."

I noticed myself lapsing into his British cadence, teetering there, you know. Tears close to the surface, you know. Didn't take me long, now did it?

"It's best that way," he said. "Not keep it bottled up inside."

"No chance of that."

Standing at the baggage carousel, I reconsidered him as a prospect. Which, to begin with, he was not. But was this how it would go? Men would materialize, my mysterious superpowers would assert, invitations to come away and sport would result (polite ones, as with Sneezie Man, less polite in other instances) and I would fail to see the earthly purpose? Not be attracted in the slightest?

It was too soon, of course, and Sneezie Man was a dark horse at best, hardly a fair test case. Alternatively, Sneezie Man might prove to be my only offer the entire time. There was no telling how that would go, and I was taking my assignment too literally in any case. It was just that being thrust so suddenly out into the field, so to speak, I was pressed into questioning the premise anew. Here I was emotionally involved with two men; how in the world was I supposed to make room for a third?

The city of Edinburgh had changed less than I expected. It was recognizable, even familiar. Now, as then, I marveled at the dramatic ravine demarcating the old city from the very old. The contour of that landscape, the deep defile, prepared your eye for rushing water down there, a river making for the sea. Instead, you still looked down on a cavalcade of glowing, glass-gabled train sheds.

Now, as then, loomed the castle, which presumably would Never Change, not when they could boast of its history on profitable guided tours. Taking one of those tours, early on, I found I still craved to go bounding up the roped-off stairways, stood eager as ever to ferret out Nigel's secret passageway. I pictured myself dropping back from the small pack of tourists and stowing away past closing time so as to effect my reconnaissance under cover of night.

While I never believed that Nigel Patrick had glimpsed anything which remained a secret to the wider world, neither could I quite shake the sense there must be *something* to it. Even as a child I had never understood pure fantasy. Never could make anything up out of whole cloth. Every line I write is drawn from concrete observation.

When we were a bit older, and Nigel's transatlantic letters were tapering off, my dear brother began pointing out some of our friend's more outrageous howlers. Even then, where Liam scoffed at the idea of Nigel horseback-riding with the royals at Balmoral Castle, I quietly calculated the distance between St. Andrews and Balmoral and found it plausible for a weekend visit. Liam wrote me off as a dead loss.

Meanwhile, our tour guide Robbie was not about to let anyone out of his sight, least of all me. Maybe he read my mind, maybe he just knew a potential stowaway when he saw one, but every fascinating tidbit our Robbie recited, he recited to me personally. Making firm eye contact, awaiting my nod of assent. At every turn he took my elbow, as though I had lost all capacity to steer myself. On one steep step he all but lifted me up, while older, feebler tourists hauled away on the iron banister. Were the superpowers at work, or was he merely suspicious?

In my memory of 1957, our guided tour had taken hours, traversing *acres* of cold stone-bound space. No doubt the world seems larger to a child (and time limitless), but Robbie's tour was compressed down to half an hour, much of it spent on a narrow parapet, where we snapped photos of one another. In '57, we had strolled freely through the Cemetery of Soldiers' Dogs. This time, we had to read the headstones (Major, Scamp, Yum Yum, and the rest) from an overlook. No one tried the velvet ropes; no one ducked from Robbie's sight lines.

There did come an invitation to lunch, which I politely declined in part because he looked so unhealthy. (Lara: "I am a happily married woman." Robbie: "But you are traveling alone." Not a bad summation.) Never have I seen a paler face or such pale yellow eyes. Even his lips were pale. As pleasant a fellow as he was, Robbie definitely needed to get out of the castle more.

Or out of town. That week, at least, Edinburgh was not the place to mount an attack on the problem of pallor. There may have been a sun somewhere above the earth, but apart from the presence of wan daylight (implying the orb), no trace of it was discernable at ground level. I could only conjure it up in daydreams, most of which derived from The Twoweeks. Fenway Park, Revere Beach, the Concord River.

At first I did not, as the Scots say, "muckle mind" the weather. Generally the rain was soft and sparse, so I could wander my way between cafés and bookshops. During one stronger downpour, I holed up all afternoon at James Thin, Bookseller, seated beneath a clock as big as the Ritz, and was enormously pleased to find myself working through a new poem. Suggestible as ever, I wrote about clocks, or how clock time ceases to dominate the human equation once a person steps outside her normal haunts and patterns.

James Thin, Bookseller, became my normal haunt. By the time I saw Busse (Swedish, despite the dark hair) there for the third time, we felt old-friendly enough to chat. He brought over scones and coffee, behaved graciously, and included with his dinner invitation a pledge to ask "no personal questions." This was an odd promise (almost odd enough to intrigue me) until he added that what he would in fact ask were "questions about your political figures, Nixon and Eldridge Cleaver."

Busse was tall, dark, handsome, and nice. The trouble was I believed him. He really wanted to know about my nation, not me, and he had genuinely concluded that "Nixon and Eldridge Cleaver" would be the place to begin. Sorry, Ian: not this one either.


Then came Julian.

Neither a Scot nor a Swede, he hailed from Frieth, west of London, and he was staying at hostels while writing a sociology thesis on The New Youth. We gravitated together as a category (postgraduate) in an establishment where the clientele ran about eighteen years of age and management twenty. Management (two pallid bony lads and pallid stocky Stella) judged me doubly insane: first as an American (therefore sex-crazed and bloodthirsty) and then as an old lady putting up at a youth hostel. Not that there were *rules* against it. It was just, well, you know, *weird*.

Not to Julian. He considered it the luckiest thing that had ever happened to him—or so he testified. It could be pure unadulterated poppycock, a line he used once a week and twice on Saturdays. "I could have gone the year without meeting a woman," he said, as we sat in the dank, dark breakfast nook, sipping tea. "And I could have gone a lifetime without meeting a woman like you."

"Meaning what? What am I 'like'?"

"Gorgeous. Brilliant. Game."

"Game as in willing to have sex with a stranger?"

Here Julian blushed becomingly, for that was precisely his meaning. And "game" put it quite well, for he could hardly say exciting or sensuous after what had basically been my disinterested observation of his transports. He kept praising me (I was wonderful in bed, so lovely in bed) where in truth I was not much better than an inflatable doll might have been.

That was in no way Julian's fault, no more than the bad weather was. Had the sun appeared on the day we met, I would never have consented in the first place. All we had to spur us on were the cold dark skies over Scotland and Ian's voice in my ear saying this might be your best chance. Surely Julian qualified as "Someone."

Someone I liked, that is. I liked the way he was both foreign and familiar to me, culturally I suppose I mean. I enjoyed his bemusement at the academic pecking order, and at the silliness of his thesis topic. "The New Youth seems quite like the Old Youth," he said with a puckered grin, "albeit with a bit of fresh slang, some insufferable new tunes, and superior contraception."

I liked him well enough to walk with him in the Pentland Hills (bringing a bag of crisps that we ate in a chill wet wind at Arthur's Seat) and well enough to sleep with him a second time, mostly out of charity, just before I left. I didn't want him feeling he had let me down, or failed any tests. He was so sad to hear we would not "continue to be together in every way" (amazed less that I was leaving than that I would consent to sex while planning to leave) that I wished I could concoct some sweet lie to ease his distress.

In lieu of that lie (which I could neither invent nor deliver) I gave it a better try between the sheets. I was "good in bed" to a slightly greater extent, both for Julian's sake and to give this amoral arbitrary wanton sex a fair chance. It's bizarre, really, how one can be so uninvolved, for lack of a better word, in an act so intimate. Was there something wrong with me, a unique flaw, or did I just need to see the sun?

I sailed (they call it that) across the Firth that afternoon, confident the sun would greet me on the other side, in the East

Neuk of Fife, where it never failed my father and his golfing buddies. And a few minutes out over the water, it did seem brighter. Away from the gray stone and the gray streets, the gray sheets of glass in shop windows and the gray faces reflected in them. Here at least, in the unenclosed unpunctuated sky, was a more luminous sort of gray.

Faces looked brighter too, almost ruddy in the spray. One of those faces belonged to Harriet, an older Scotswoman who caught me looking at her and looked me right back. Normally, a woman would have looked away. Harriet not only met my gaze, she introduced herself and offered me a pull from her flask. Though I declined the libation, we were already friends by then. "I know you," she said, nodding.

After another pull, she turned palm reader and pronounced, "You are searching for something here. Your head is full of questions."

Boy, was it! I had to laugh (at her preternatural insight, or at her presumption) before asking her a couple of easy ones. Nothing about the meaning of life, more in the line of local color. "I'm a word person," I told her. "Maybe you can help me out on some of these."

Oddly, she could not. When I wondered about the difference between a firth and a bay, she shrugged and waved the issue away, saying only "It's more like a fjord." And when I pursued the definitions, or differences between a gate, a lane, a wynd, and a close, she winked and said, "Well now, that all depends, doesn't it." Harriet was not a word person.

Then she was gone, the instant we docked at Anstruther, and as soon as she was gone the gray fog closed in again. Everyone else on the ferry had a clear destination. Two by two they left the ark and marched resolutely toward buses and cars, while I stood on the sea-wall watching them go. I was in no hurry. I had no destination and I was transfixed by the rolling and bobbing of the boats at anchor below.

It was nearly twenty years earlier that we bicycled to this village—Liam and I, Nigel and his sister Katy—and surveyed this precise scene: two dozen fishing boats, most of them faded and worse for the wear, riding the waves below our feet. They lay so close and accessible, we were tempted to jump aboard. As tall green waves swelled against the breakwater, I was tempted to dive in.

Then we were off, pedaling around for hours. At five o'clock Nigel's dad would fetch us in his big station wagon. Meanwhile we had all day to explore the small village, eat fish-and-chips from a greasy paper bag shaped like a cone, eat ice cream, play hide-and-seek in a steep wood.

When finally we coasted back down to the harbor, the boats were gone. Which was not so surprising, except that the water was gone too. An alarming expanse of rippled mud had replaced the Firth of Forth. And to me this was a powerful Biblical scene, like the Red Sea parting. If the sea had run dry, then surely the world must be ending. Apart from the darker teachings of my church, this was a common fear in the 1950s.

In reality, of course, low tide had arrived. Very low tide. The surf stopped so far out you could walk halfway to Edinburgh without getting your knees wet. And the fishing boats were right where they had been, sort of. The sea level had dropped fifteen feet and so had they. You saw them down there, scattered on sandy mud, when you stepped closer to the railing.

Liam wrote me off that time too. It was Nigel, though, who broke my heart when with the best intentions he patted my head in sympathy. Or pity. His kind gesture marked me as a foolish child, being consoled by an older wiser man. The wedding was off. Apart from thanking Mr. Patrick for riding us home, I don't believe I spoke to anyone for three days.

The Anstruther Arms, pretentious nomenclature notwith-standing, was a small informal hotel two blocks up from the waterfront. Someone had taken the trouble to paint it a dark brown from top to bottom, in keeping with the principle of dull depressing monochromy established by the weather.

Each day there loomed a single iron-gray cloud the size of the sky (of the universe, the galaxy) and from this cloud would issue forth a froth of cold drizzle, unless (the lone variation) that drizzle thickened into a soaking rain. It reached a point where the lighter sort of rain qualified as fine weather. "I believe it may be clearing" was a straw much clutched at around dusk, when it was harder to tell.

One gloomy afternoon, I broke our rule and telephoned Ian. That was not an afternoon where anyone believed it might be clearing, more one where you were apt to believe it *never* would. I was lonely (and wondered how Ian was faring), but it was also about using this particular phone. Planted by a sign marking the road to Crail, it was your classic boothy, red as legend and dense with architectural detail.

We were only to communicate in the case of emergencies— Ian's ironclad rule. After a dismal week in Edinburgh and six dismal days on the East Neuk of Fife, I felt justified in defining it as an emergency.

"I think I'm ready to come home."

"Because it's *raining*, for God's sake?" said Ian.

"Raining and cold."

"Get thee to a pub, for goodness' sake. Sit thee down by a fire."

"Tried that. And trust me, I'll try it again. But even the fires are cold here."

"Order up a hot toddy, and some nice hot food."

"Mostly it's been the cold smoked salmon."

"So there you are."

"I know. That's the problem. Here I am."

"Get thee to the Costa Brava, if all you want is weather."

Was weather all I wanted? I had come to think it might be. Being cold is like being hungry, the way it can block out your sense of everything else until you solve it. I was hardly the only victim. Even Angus (my landlord at the Arms, who testified he loved "the wet" and boasted of fishing in the rain at Loch Tay "where the salmon seem to rise to it") had become fed up. He talked about heading south, if he could only convince his cousin to take over the hotel for a week. South, to him, meant London, where he reckoned you could count on one dry day in four.

I asked Angus if he recalled a year when the sun didn't shine for three months. "I recall quite a number like that," he said, with a smile that bespoke fortitude, not humor.

He was kidding, I guess, about going away, because I offered to run the place for a week if his cousin couldn't make it, and he backed off. Couldn't afford a holiday, could he then? Had I not noticed there was only myself and two other guests at the inn, only a fistful at the bar, an armful in the restaurant? It was so bad he might have to shutter the place up and join the fishing fleet.

Or so he said. When I trotted out this gossipy detail at the Waterloo, I was quickly set straight by the old girl behind the bar. "Angus says that a lot. He has been about to shutter it for twenty years now, and I'm told his old man was about to do the same for thirty years before that. Angus will join the fishing fleet around the time I get me to a nunnery."

Her too? But no, she winked as she said it, and appended a broader wink for a couple of genuine fishermen holding down the curved end of the bar. They had the shiny mahogany slab pinned beneath their pint glasses and their heavy elbows.

It was clear which of the two was keeping her from the nunnery these days (the older one, "my good man Flatley"), and even clearer when his buddy slid down to chat me up. He too was a winker—a winker, a drinker, and (understandably, given his profession) a bit of a stinker. When he finally got around to inviting me onto his boat for "the grand tour" I was tempted, not so much by Hergy as by his boat. I could board it, case it, and later boast about having done so to Liam.

"Maybe tomorrow," I said, dodging. "I'd rather see it in the daylight."

"Such as it is," Hergy grinned. He was just going through the motions. He would have been stunned blind and dumb if I'd said yes to him.

In bed alone, under a thick pile of thin blankets, I broke a cardinal rule of my own making: I allowed myself to think about Cal. I wasn't fooling myself when I called Ian earlier that day. I knew it was Cal I wanted to call. Cal whose company I wanted at the pub rail, and Cal whose arms I wanted around me now at the Anstruther Arms. Denying this had not worked; admitting it didn't do me much good either.

I did what I could to shape a small independent life. Each morning I would go down to a tea shop where they had terrific currant scones, strong coffee, and the *International Herald Tribune* with its three-day-old news. It was all news to me, as I had lost track of public events completely.

After a ritual hour there, I would brave the rain and ride out on a bicycle for miles. I rolled down every gate and close and lane and wynd (however these might be defined) in a joyless solo reprise of our carefree childhood Saturdays. Back at the Anstruther Arms, I would "lie down for a minute" that invariably lasted two hours. Then it was down the stairs to Angus' sparsely populated dining room, where with reheated coffee from his morning urn, I set myself up at the window table to write. Trying to justify my existence—but to whom?

After a walk to the docks, I'd come back and curl up with a book, working my way toward suppertime. To Angus' chagrin, I took to eating my smoked salmon sandwich at the Waterloo, where life was a bit livelier. Hergy turned out to be a decent guy, happy just to gab. He and Flatley and Georgiana, the bartender, were always ready with a wink. And there were others, a crew of locals.

I expect they were debating whether to categorize me as a harmless lonely woman or a dangerous escaped lunatic. What on earth was I doing here? Too polite to ask, they waited for information to emerge. The problem was I had no information to offer. What *was* I doing here?

I have never been a complainer. To the contrary, I drive people nuts with my ceaseless good cheer, and I gather I'm most annoying on the subject of weather. Isn't this a beautiful day, I can't help exclaiming, on a day that Ian or Marisa might classify as bearable. Every day was beautiful to me. It just was.

So what was wrong with these days? What was wrong with me? Reluctant to let it be Cal Byerly, I attributed it to the unrelenting rain. By any objective standard, these were not beautiful days—they were extreme, they were awful. To meet my few fellow travelers (teams of Germans going about, a few Londoners, one Nigerian Brit with a quiet American wife) was to listen to a litany of woe-is-me's. Their day was ruined, their trip was ruined, their lives were ruined . . . So it wasn't just me.

It came as a revelation that the Germans' English was easier to understand than the Scots'. While I could puzzle through Angus' harangues and nod approvingly at Hergy's cheerful utterances, the literal wording tended to escape me. "Would you mind writing that down?" I took to requesting, for on paper their Scottish inflections would evaporate and I would find myself looking at perfectly familiar nouns and verbs.

Whereas the Germans spoke it clearly. Franz (and yes, while no Heinz materialized, a Franz actually did, one evening at the Waterloo) not only spoke it well, he wrote—in English—for a living. "This is my market," he shrugged, indicating the four walls of the pub. He was writing a book about darts for his London publisher.

"A whole book about darts?" I said.

"Yes certainly darts," he said in his clear, brusque and always *unpunctuated* English. I had not seen his written material, but conversationally he had yet to acquire the comma or the dash. "My third whole book and many many articles and so yes I would say so."

A darts writer, then. He did have a faint guttural burr to his speech, like the actor Maximilian Schell, but his boldest national marker was baggage, the sheer volume of it. Like all his countrymen traveling around, Franz carried three rooms of furniture on his back. To watch a German board a bus was like watching a complex circus act—part juggler, part strongman, and part contortionist.

Franz was tall, with lank brown hair and soft round eyes so dark they looked more black than brown. I don't know exactly what is meant by the phrase "a skier's body," but Franz reminded me of a skier, or an Alpine guide, the way he held his head and neck, alert and swiveling as though racing downhill, swerving past flags. He was traveling alone, he confided, because this was his work and because "to travel is not an activity people can do together."

This postulate (originally stated as ironclad fact, 2 + 2 = 4) turned out to have a corollary, less stringent in nature. People *could* travel together "for a few nice days quite successfully," and Franz suspected he and I might accomplish as much, starting out in the morning. He would be driving to Birnam and Dunkeld, then on to Aberfeldy, where he swore you smelled salmon on the air "the way you smell horses in a barn." It would be his privilege to show me these sights and smells.

Could anything be crazier than signing on for such a journey? To be out of touch, in a foreign land, and consent to drive off with a man about whom I knew practically nothing? I didn't even know for sure he wrote about darts. (Even if he did, what kind of weird obsession was that?) He could be a sociopath, or a collector of Nazi memorabilia. He could be a *cannibal,* for all I knew.

He struck me as a gentle soul, though, and honest. "I have of course a wife," he said, by way of refining his terms. There were to be no deceptions, no illusions.

"I'm glad to hear it."

"You are glad?" he said, inclining his head as if to better hear me, though possibly he was just swerving past a flag.

I confirmed that I was glad, without mentioning why, namely that it tended to confirm he was honest, and just possibly normal—except I suppose for the honesty.

"Don't you want to know if I have a husband?"

"What difference does this make? When I propose marriage then yes it makes the difference and then yes I need this fact. Why not let us first go see the Birks of Aberfeldy."

This was Franz' ticket to ride. He was "a writer who need not make anything rhyme. Dart fart tart no need." But I was a poet and Robert Burns was a poet and roaming the birch forests of Aberfeldy, Burns had set down some of his best rhymes. With pleasure Franz would show me the Birks of Aberfeldy. It would be his privilege.

He had rented a car in Glasgow and, in fact, would be driving back there by way of the Highlands, if I wished to come along. This would be within the limits to which people could travel together, I gathered, and Glasgow too, he speculated, surely had its lyrical side.

"Why not let me first come as far as Aberfeldy," I mimicked him, "and maybe just as a friend. We might be taking two rooms."

"A fair arrangement. I am content to clear the premier hurdle. Possibility is possible yes? Nothing more asked."

Except that we became lovers an hour later, still in Anstruther. The not-asking worked. It got to a point where I was comfortable with Franz and his quiet uncomplicated delight in everything, and at the same time a point where I had much drink taken. On my way upstairs I teetered between concluding the entire enterprise was an ugly immoral business, on the one hand, and just rolling with it on the other. In a seriously twisted way, I was offering myself up.

In his rented room (at a house nearby) I expected Franz to shift gears, to accelerate and mount a Luftwaffe-style attack, but apparently something traumatic had happened to the Germanic male, or so I extrapolated from the handful I met. They were so terrified of repeating the past, or owning it on a personal level, that an undiscussed gentle hesitancy, most commonly expressed as excessive politeness, had taken root in their souls. While they did charge around the continent in a commandeering fashion (ve vill do zis, you vill do zat) they left the moral choices to others.

I chose against intercourse. "It's a middle way, for us Americans," I explained, and he nodded and smiled, saying (without punctuation, as always) "Sure I get it sex but no fucking" and that is what we engaged in that night.

I also chose to return to my own bed later on, as I was already sobering up and revisiting my decision to leave with Dartman in the morning. Gloomy as it was, I had grown attached to the Anstruther Arms. I had grown fond of grumpy avuncular Angus, plus I had achieved a hard-won order to my days there, a nice balance of melancholy work and melancholy play.

At bottom I am a nest-maker, and here I had woven my nest. It was lonely and tinged with mildew; still it was a nest. To hit the road with Dartman, who was only *presumptively* not a cannibal, represented a radical flight from that nest.

"Save my room," I told Angus in the morning. "I may be back tomorrow, or even tonight. Don't bother washing the sheets right away."

"I'll have no trouble saving it, my dear, the competition being slim as it is. But I shall place a plaque on the door and reserve it in perpetuity. No man, woman, or child shall ever lay a hair on your pillow, forever and aye."

"What if you shutter the place and join the fleet?"

"Then I shall put in the terms of sale that Room 6 is sacred space. But for a day or two? Truly, dear, don't you worry."


So away we went to Birnam Wood. Right off the bat, in Birnam and Dunkeld, we established a pattern whereby each morning we would poke about together, each afternoon we would be writers (he researching, I rhyming dart with fart), and by night we were dinner companions and unconventional bedmates. Our dinners were invariably taken at the same pubs or coaching hotels where Franz had done his daily research, since every small village in Scotland has precisely one such hostelry. If you wished for your smoked salmon, your Tennent's 70 Shilling Ale, and your dish of whinberry crumble, you knew right where to find them.

Franz never did vary from his gentle manner, never pressed for more than I offered. Until the heavy wheeze of sleep set in, he even remained a respecter of boundaries. Only then did he become territorial (the Hun will out?) and occupy by increments an impressive percentage of the bed. The Sudetenland fell, Czechoslovakia fell, the Russian border loomed . . . In Birnam I elbowed him with mixed results; in Aberfeldy I ended up sleeping in a mouldy armchair.

He was right about the salmon. Every stream, all the water-falls and woven rapids, carried that salmon perfume. Every tree and rock exuded it. Small processing plants and backyard smoke-houses were everywhere. This part of Scotland was as saturated with salmon as it was saturated with rainwater.

The ceiling of cloud might lose coherence long enough to allow a teasing slice of open sky to appear. Once, as we wandered among those birches of Aberfeldy, past the ropes of falling water, along a winding stream-crossed trail, the *sun* appeared for twenty minutes and we gazed up with mouths agape, like children staring as Superman flew over. Otherwise, the rain continued.

In a tea shop in Dunkeld, I managed another poem, and though dart and fart were nowhere in evidence, I did near-rhyme, to some effect, tubers and hubris. We had come over the ancient toll bridge behind an astonishing potato truck, or a truck loaded to an astonishing extent with potatoes. It had no cover, not even a loose canvas, and though the spuds were piled so high and wide they *cantilevered* over the rickety wooden sides, not a single one fell off. A million potatoes, yet stable as the ancient unmortared stone walls. This visual image took root, grew into a metaphor, ended up a poem.

In that same tea shop, I had the next in a series of odd encounters with small assertive Scotswomen. There would be three in all, beginning with Harriet, the woman on the ferry who looked me in the eye and told me my head was filled with questions. Now came Mrs. Cameron, however, and soon enough I would be meeting Tiny Nurse. So three of them. Given the numerology and the harsh admonitions each of them bodied forth, they seemed in the aggregate portentous, like Shakespeare's trio of witches. It was not lost on me that we had come to Birnam Wood.

I incurred my fate, if that's what she was, while sitting down at one end of a long table anchored at the opposite end by Mrs. Cameron. This was the custom when the smaller tables were taken; yet the instant I sat she rose, as though we were on a teeter-totter. Blushing, I stood right back up, to apologize: "I didn't mean to scare you off, madame."

"No one scares me off, dear girl," she said with considerable flintiness and the thinnest arc of a smile. She continued on to the counter for more coffee ("petrol" was what she called it, and black was how she drank it) with an impressive spring in her white-sneakered step. From ten paces away, she seemed a small agile athlete. Close up, despite the almost frighteningly blue eyes and a row of small perfectly white teeth, she aged thirty years. Threadlike blue veins lay close to the surface of her paper-thin skin, like a map of rural waterways.

"Don't you ever, *ever*, let anyone scare you off, either," she said, shutting one eye for emphasis. We were both on the same end of the teeter-totter now, our faces two feet apart.

Harriet had provided only a first name, Mrs. Cameron gave only a last. In Mrs. Cameron's company I felt obliged to be Mrs. Somebody too, an obligation I resisted. I remained Lara, didn't let her scare me off—though it was a close call.

"I come here each day for my dose," she explained, "while Mr. Cameron goes and stands like a happy fool on the rocks of the River Tay, and once every blue moon arrives back home with a catch I can cook him."

As we talked, I felt a new amorphous guilt creep into my soul. Because I spoke of places and schools and jobs, and because these implied freedom and money and middle-class opportunity, I presumed the guilt must be cultural. Not that any residue of hardship lingered about Mrs. Cameron, who spoke of a house and a garden and two boys "in the city, very successful." It was just that she had been born a mile from where we sat, had married in a church we could see from where we sat, and had never lived or even traveled anywhere else. The lone variable in her life was whether or not Mr. Cameron brought home a fish for her to cook.

"You might call me provincial, dear," she said (like Harriet, reading my mind with ease) "and you'd be right enough. I believe in depth, not breadth, you see. I never meant to alter course, and so I never have."

"Good for you, Mrs. Cameron."

"You don't mean it, but that's all right."

"I do mean it. You've made your choices. Controlled your own destiny."

"That's utter nonsense. But I've not altered course."

"No," I said, much chastened and increasingly wary of the blue gleaming eyes, one of them so fixed and fierce it might prove to be a glassy.

"We set our course, Mr. Cameron and myself, a long time ago. Fifty years next month, not all cakes and ale, plenty of the other. But we've not altered course."

"No."

"And so we shall reach our destination. Stay on course, dear girl. Don't scatter your brains to the wind, like some do. I can see you have more sense than that."

"One hopes," I said—modestly, she may have thought. But *sense*? If anyone was keeping score, only the schizophrenics could be racking up lower totals.

In all likelihood Mrs. Cameron had seen a few mini-skirted London birds cavorting on the telly, or perhaps she knew of a local beauty rendered pregnant by the itinerant drummer. That was the sort of cautionary tale to fit inside her rubric "like some do."

As we were swapping histories, I found (perhaps because I was so eager to reassure her) that mine was to a remarkable extent about Ian. The ways in which I had recently altered course were somehow expunged from the historical narrative. She had not seen me with Franz, knew nothing of Cal. What I did a week ago with Julian Kelman would have caused her to pitch her petrol in my face.

Not-alter-course remained the bedrock refrain, the homily. Mr. Cameron, the happy fool on the riverbank, was a given. She could hardly criticize her own choice, could she now, having made it freely in God's sight. So she would live with it fifty years and beyond. My choice was Ian. Only a careless spoiled American child would question it; only an ingrate or a dope, who would come to no good. Mrs. Cameron's implied judgment, her power to withhold grace, felt almost like a memo from God.

The memo cost me another night's sleep. Franz didn't help. We had done our non-conjugal dance and, in what is usually accounted to be typical male fashion, Franz was sound asleep mere seconds after his bliss subsided. I had no such luck and would squirm in discomfort throughout that long salmon-smelling night, through the hours of his radical sprawling and snoring.

But I have not been fair to Franz here. As I look back on those confusing cloud-choked days, I cannot recall a single way in which he deceived or disappointed me, or a single thing he did to earn my snotty sarcasm. Franz was a generous and good-natured companion, who seemed to lack entirely the reflex of complaint.

He never objected to my Papish evasions in bed, never remarked my moods or contradicted my odd choices: everything was good by him. Silly faces I made (expressions I would have categorized as standard American banalities, such as thumbing my nose or rolling my eyes) he found absolutely hilarious. Something gained in the translation, perhaps, the way any European accent can charm us by its linguistic imprecision.

He was just so relaxed. And why not, I suppose, if he could make a living playing darts in pubs and writing about it—not to mention stay married while taking lovers. (*Widening* course!) Still, nothing ruffled Franz' feathers.

An example. Leaving a pub one night, we discovered we had brought no cash with which to settle up. In that brief flash of reckoning at the bar rail, I knew exactly how Ian would react: poorly concealed panic and then some elaborate strategy to circumvent his embarrassment. Cal Byerly? I guessed he would have a laugh about it and then escape through the bathroom window.

Franz simply chuckled as he turned his pockets inside out to pantomime our situation for the landlady. Trained to think like Ian, I was about to propose I stay behind as collateral while Franz went to fetch some money. Such a solution, with its implied mistrust, never occurred to Franz or to our creditress. No flint-eyed close-with-a-dollar Scot was she. She shrugged, he shrugged, and everyone in earshot nodded, as though we had all been friends for decades.

"It's four and six, as things stand," she said. "It'll stay at four and six for a while before the interest begins to accrue. This one" (she was pouring us two fresh pints) "will be on the house."

All I mean to say is that Franz was faultless, that the fault lay all with me, for my sketchy participation and now this retrospective sarcasm. Much as I liked Franz, the truth is he remained a sort of shadow figure to me. One morning as we rambled the hills near Fort William, I had a flash of concern I might have strayed too far (from signposts, from fellow humans) and might find myself in danger. Somehow I had managed to forget that Franz was hiking right alongside me.

Worse than failing to register his presence, I could be embarrassed about it when I did. On one level (that of the high school cheerleader I could never have been?) I regretted that a world of strangers might presume Franz to be my consort. In a bizarre twist of vanity, I felt an urge to explain myself: It's not what you think, this man is just a casual friend.

And there it was again, not just the vanity but also the nagging truth that Cal Byerly was still on my mind. I would not have wanted to explain Cal away. If I had to be viewed as someone's appendage, defined by the company I keep, Cal was the companion by which I wished to be judged.

And this despite the fact no one was judging, or even noticing me.

I took to writing Cal postcards. There were things I simply had to tell him. In Arrochar they laid a trout out on my plate, the entire fish, with a maraschino cherry inset like marquetry in the exposed eye socket. How could I not relay this incident to him? How not share with him the stark realization that one is not "eating fish," one is eating *a* fish.

Composing these postcards was therapeutic. After writing the day's card, setting down such details as the cherry-eyed fish or the overloaded potato truck, I could let go of Cal for a while. Breathing comfortably again, I could remind myself that Ian was my choice; that I had not altered course.

I had no intention of mailing the cards. The only question was whether I would save them, and it was not much of a question. They were newsworthy, I rationalized each time I added one to the packet, sliding the thick rubber band back into place. They comprised a quirky secondary record of my travels. For one thing, they were never selected for standard fare wish-you-were-here scenery, but rather in diligent pursuit of offbeat local color, as with the photo of four lanky pocky lads from Crianlarich, The Hilltoppers, duded up in rhinestone suits, playing country-and-western music.

Who knew, by the way, that in the Scottish hill-country one could wake to the strains of Conway Twitty himself singing "Hello Darlin'" on a radio down in the hotel kitchen? This particular song I understood to be nothing less than a postcard *back* from Cal. I had sent none of mine (and he had no idea where I was) yet surely that explained this unlikely emanation, this poignant comic reminder of our night with the man née Jenkins. As I strained to listen, I had a clear vision of the Twitty Birds: the little Twitty with his eyes shut tight as a televangelist in his transports, the big Twitty rocking so far forward he threatened to topple like a tree onto the front row patrons.

We had walked home after the concert that night, walked across half of Boston, across the Charles River, then across half of Cambridge, singing as we went. Back at Miller Road we devoured a bag of fat pretzels and drank Colt .45 malt liquor—our fallback meal—and jumped into bed. Recalling this, I found it jarring to think that right now Ian Witherspoon was sleeping in that bed.

His bed though! His home. (Or our bed; *our* home. We had lived there for years.)

I telephoned Ian a second time—from Crianlarich, that morning—to tell him our marriage was over. Fortunately, there was no answer. The marriage might well prove to be over, but Conway Twitty should not be allowed a voice in the matter. And even if I proved capable of reaching such a decision on my own, I ought not pass it along via an awkward, time-staggered, transatlantic phone connection.

Once again I tried to peer calmly, realistically, into the future that would accompany such a decision. Chaos, loneliness, misery—and then *dating*. The loss of family, loss of friends. Ian's mom would not remain my friend. Ian would not remain my friend, either. Who would? I made a list of those who would tilt toward Ian and who toward me. And when my calm began to crumble in the face of such depressing assessments, I simply pulled back from the notion that a confused, dejected, rejected girl spinning her wheels in a foreign land was fit to make important decisions.

Was there really a decision to make, though? However bleak the prospect of leaving Ian, was staying in the marriage a realistic choice at this point? It was in the context of this inquiry that my encounter with Tiny Nurse (my third, and final, and *scariest* witch) was particularly disturbing.

I was reading a book with my dinner and so was she, two women dining solo in a drab coaching hotel. There was only one other party in the room and the instant they decamped she came over to join me, as if our encounter was scripted. (Enter stage left, witch number three.)

No introductions at all this time. She never gave her name (not in the script, I guess) and so I never gave mine. She only became Tiny Nurse to me when her profession and her weight ("seven stone soaking wet") emerged. She was an alarmingly thin woman, with skeletal hands and a razor's edge to her facial bones. Before she uttered a syllable, the restlessly flexing muscles in her jaw and a cold spark in her coal-dark eye marked her as an angry woman.

At a glance, at a given moment, one could miss it. Lavishly decorated with turquoise earrings, a delicate gold neck-chain, and silver rings on every finger, she was quite pretty when she smiled. The smiles came unexpectedly, quick flickers that fixed you, threw you off the scent. Nonetheless, Tiny Nurse was clearly choked with anger.

Not at me, mercifully. I was merely her confidant for the evening, the chosen recipient of her widely ranging complaints. In this regard, she was the polar opposite of Franz. He had no complaints, she had an infinite list. It began with her back, the sacs and discs and spurs all so painful and so hopeless in ways clinically detailed, one failed procedure after another.

Then there was the oppressive, underpaid, thankless job she had just quit. "Be assured, thirteen years with the acute insane was enough for me," she said, as though I had disapproved of her decision to leave. One wondered whether so many years of proximity to the insane was enough to have rubbed off on her to some extent.

There was her father's final illness, forcing her return to the north, to John O' Groats, to care for him, though he was an awful man and the people of that town were "awful *nosy* people, through and through." She turned her head in disgust at the very thought of them, and for an instant I feared she might spit over her shoulder.

Dear God how she needed to drag herself upstairs, to soak her back in a tub, to sleep ten hours if she could. I encouraged her embrace of this program: the hot bath, the warm bed, they could only help. But she would not go. Instead she rambled on about her love of solitude, her preference for dining and drinking alone. "The doctors all decry drink," she said, narrowing her eyes in almost comic exaggeration, an expression culled from silent films. "Then what do they do? *You* know what they do."

They drank, the doctors did. I figured that out. But I could not figure out this difficult woman. I would pick up the scent, then lose it again. She would grant me the pretty smile, then tense up and glare. What did Tiny Nurse want from me? She kept reprising the hot soak upstairs and perhaps a massage, which raised the possibility of a come-on, her love of solitude notwithstanding. But this was neither linear nor consistent, and none of it was ever clear. I could not decide whether Tiny Nurse was nice or nasty, sane or insane, heterosexual or lesbian, a rustic or a cosmopolitan.

Not that it mattered what she was, other than a severe caution to any woman in grave danger of cutting herself loose from the safety net. A woman such as myself. In the garbled outline of her life, one did see what the world could do to a woman alone. How inexorably it could reduce her to a set of small sharp bones and a litany of complaint verging on the "acute insane."

Tiny Nurse was safely away for John O' Groats before I came downstairs the next morning, yet she would accompany me across the North Sea. The lurching bumpy flight from Glasgow to London could not shake her loose, the freezing green swells could not drown her. Even in Montmartre, where ten days later I took the tiniest room (with the tiniest window ever fabricated, a window the size of a magazine cover), there would be space for Tiny Nurse to lodge with me. She fit just fine.

I had selected the room more for its price than its charm. (Apart from a pleasant café two doors down, it had no charm.) But you never know. I did get a poem out of it—out of that minimal window, as a matter of fact, for while very little light came in, one could gaze out upon a visual cornucopia. Through that single page of daylight, I could see the fenestrated bell tower of a church, a dozen tiled roofs (shaken into Cubist planes I tried in vain to understand geometrically), and a world of sagging wires that cross-hatched my patch of sky. There were doves coming and going from their nest in a cornice, and the regimented tops of Lombardy poplars at a nearby park.

The one thing I could not see was my future; that was a window too small. I understood I was not thinking of Ian the right way. I didn't miss him in the right way. Never wondered or, by implication, cared enough what he was doing there without me. It was George Eliot who declared that "we fall on the leaning side." Had I been capable of leaning toward Ian, my life would have been a great deal easier. What could be better than the uncomplicated affection I had counted on from him for so long, and the security? That in the grip of my loneliness and gloom I could be leaning the other way, toward difficulty and insecurity, made my indecision seem primarily a crisis of courage.

Then one morning I bumped into Guillaume at the book-stalls, and what a pleasure it was to see him. A familiar face, a friend, a diversion from my binary bind. I might have looked him up if I'd known how. But I had no address for him (he never stayed anywhere for more than a few months, in any case) and he had never had a phone.

He still didn't. His principles remained firmly in place. No car, no phone, two meals a day. Half of any money he earned still went to charity. The trust fund, yes, he supposed it still existed. It was somewhere, in someone's capable hands. Someday he would accept his share of the family wealth, just so as to give it away responsibly.

Guillaume had not spoken to his parents since turning twenty. He was in touch only with Marianne, his younger sister, whom I had met briefly and liked enormously. A beautiful sprite, with a mischievous smile and merry green eyes, Marianne had grown up and was now at the Sorbonne.

"In the system but okay," he told me. "She is what you would call pre-med."

"So what would I call you?"

"Still nothing," he shrugged. "As you can plainly see."

I could see he was a good deal more than that. Apart from being extremely handsome and (for a Frenchman *and* an ideologue) surprisingly amusing, he was an utterly dedicated human being. His "job," which he performed without a scrap of sanctimony or self-congratulation, was to help his fellow man. As we sat at a sidewalk café, under a translucent awning that ushered the rain past our table like a shower curtain, he reaffirmed all of this in his matter-of-fact fashion.

True, one could never cure the world of irreducible, Biblical truths. One disease gave way to another, one war ended and another began. Indeed, there were 20 wars going on as we sat drinking our coffee, he assured me, and most citizens were unaware of 19 of them. The newspapers could only handle one at a time. Alone among men I have known, Guillaume could be forceful, even unequivocal, without being aggressive. It was almost a parlor trick.

On the other hand, he went on, it was so easy to help people every hour of every day. To bring food to a hungry family; to help a man find work; to translate documents or fill out forms for refugees; to tutor children; to volunteer time at the health clinics. Sadly it was all one could do, fortunately it was also the best thing to do. There was, he stated, no morally sound argument against it.

I stayed with him that night. Not that I was in thrall to his ego-free virtue, much as I did admire it. I knew it was for real. It may have been good old Catholic guilt (combined with a lifelong distress at his father's guilt-free greed) that had spurred him in the direction of saintliness, but a saint is a saint is a saint. If all Guillaume had to eat was a Hershey bar, he would either split it with the next hungry person he saw or give the whole thing away and go hungry himself.

No, I stayed with him because it might please him and because it cost me no additional sin to do so. Guillaume was my other transgression; Ian knew about him. He had been surprised that July afternoon, and no doubt dismayed. (Betrayed so *casually*.) I so wished I could have lied to him. Denied the obvious, to protect him. Why did I feel a need to wound him with my honesty?

"So that's how you spend your time while I'm holed up in the carrels," Ian more or less snapped, as he more or less glared at me.

To Guillaume, though, he was polite. He extended a hand (thankfully, did not offer a mocking version of the bilateral air kiss) and said with just the slightest twist of the blade, "Is it okay if I call you Bill?"

Guillaume, confused, blushing (he blushed easily, didn't believe affection between human beings could be wrong, hoped there were no hurt feelings), said, in English, "Sure, why not?"

I blush easily too, and was above all embarrassed to have slept with him. I hated that Ian could see me as such a clichéd *type*, the unsophisticated American girl who goes abroad and takes to bed the first handsome European who comes along. Spare me the thirty worst movies that hinge on this scenario.

My embarrassment should have been the least of it. I was guilty of a cruel and careless act, likely the result of too much free time on too nice a day in Paris. Neither of us had been unfaithful and the understanding was that neither of us ever would be. To be honest, I felt Ian would have been within his rights to strike me. I almost expected it. Would I not have struck him, had our roles been reversed?

Not surprisingly, he was far more restrained, limiting himself to a few cutting remarks, the worst of which ("I suppose Little Miss Poet was out gathering experiences?") he seemed to find amusing. He let go of it; he let it go. So for a while at least, embarrassment could trump guilt in my hierarchy of self-flagellation. I could face my husband more readily than I could face myself.

This time around, when neither guilt nor embarrassment figured in, depression would trump distraction. Guillaume was just one man too many, on one too many wet afternoons, and I proved unequal to the occasion. Unwilling. I had set myself a goal of cheering him up and fell well short.

"Why are you crying?" he asked me softly, in English.

All I could say was, "I'm not. I'm not crying."

"You don't like your Billy any more?" he said.

"I do," I said. "Very much."

And then I cried some more, doubling his confusion. How could he possibly know how irrelevant he was, when we were such friends, were—his favorite word—*compatriots*. He saw us in common cause. Artists, he contended, give humanity a gift every bit as valuable as food and shelter.

Guillaume's assurances notwithstanding, I don't know what I was giving humanity besides a big pain in the backside. He cried too when I said we should leave it at that, one evening for auld lang syne. (The Scots were still with me.) I had persisted in believing I was nothing special to him—just an American girl who said yes—until he confessed he had tried all that year to paint my picture. He was not a painter, he simply wished to have an image, life-sized at that.

He went so far as to enlist Marianne's boyfriend, who *was* a painter and who produced a large portrait on the basis of such police-sketch-style details as they could reconstruct. Guillaume had almost no furniture in his current room—a bed, a chair, a table, none of which he owned—but the big painting was there.

"This is you, no?" he said.

I could only hope not, as I gazed upon the sister I never had, on the worst hair day of her life. Still, it would have been even creepier if the thing did look like me.

Shortly after parting ways with Guillaume, I ground to a halt. My energetic rambles became perfunctory walks, my meals (consisting of the smallest pellet that could sustain me) were better suited to an astronaut than a gastronome, and the poems were getting lousy. Because it depressed me to write badly, I stopped writing.

I also stopped sleeping at night, for fear of more house calls from Tiny Nurse. More than once she had left the bedside of her ailing father in John O' Groats and come to mine in John O' Dreams. These dreams were so powerful and realistic that I would wake in a sweat. Shaking uncontrollably the last time, I sat up and ran tests (recite the Ten Commandments) to reassure myself I had not slipped onto the roster of the acute insane.

This was no joking matter. Absent sunshine, absent companionship, absent the ability to bail myself out by writing a decent line of verse, how long before I too was materializing at dim-lit tables in windswept coaching hotels like Tiny Nurse? I thought of Boris Karloff's grave-robber Gray (in the original 1945 *Body Snatcher*) dropping by to say an insidious oppressive hello to his "old friend Toddy McFarlane" in a tavern which scant moments earlier had been the vision of coziness. I was constantly alert to the boundary line where comfort meets terror at the door, where sanity stares across a table at madness.

Naps felt safer. Tiny Nurse would not expect to find me asleep before nightfall. Sliding under the blankets at four o'clock, I would read myself to sleep and those moments, with a page of my novel giving way to oblivion, were invariably the sweetest of my day. Hours later, I would take myself (and my book) to the Café Soleil for a glass of wine and a bowl of onion soup.

As soon as they unfurled the awning the next morning, I would be back at the Soleil for a bowl of coffee and a boule. As I say, astronaut chic, French style.

At times I blamed Ian for those aimless days and endless nights; blamed him for sending me away and siccing those scary little women on me. At the ragged mental edges of my chronic fatigue, it seemed that Tiny Nurse and Mrs. Cameron might well be in Ian's pay. Always seeking to be fair, I blamed Cal too, for taking me off the rails and leaving me in a ditch. He should have kept his big mouth shut and left well enough alone.

In more lucid moments, I understood I had only myself to blame. Though my world was far wider than Mrs. Cameron's, I had been sheltered from the vicious winds that battered and shattered Tiny Nurse. I was comfortable with Ian, and better than that I was *happy*. All I needed to do was not alter course. Such a simple prescription and yet I was unsure how to fill it.

I could hope that only my marriage was wrecked, not my life. Relationships end all the time, people survive. Back home (and how wistfully I intoned the word "home") on familiar turf, I might regain my footing. Walking the orderly, epicene alleys of the Bois, I idealized the early October day when I flew east, away from the sprawling sunlit forests just beginning to hint at orange and scarlet.

The picture in my mind's eye was dated. The grass is always greener on the other side of the ocean, but by now it was late November in New England and likely as gray there as here. Moreover, I would have to face Ian, have to field both his affection and his hostility. Half heartbroken and half disgusted, he would surely require coherent responses to the serious questions he had waited to ask.

I considered fleeing to the west, beyond "home" to a new home in Southern California, where no one is expected to have coherent responses. I craved sunshine, after all, and Lynn Carruthers had been renting a cute cottage in Laguna Beach. Her life there was a constant postcard of sun and surf, or so it seemed from a distance. Lynn would take me in for a while. Laguna could become my home too. It wasn't as though I hadn't been there; I knew its charms.

But I had been there as a visitor. Now that it was to be my home, I found myself worrying that poetry might prove impossible there. Seriously, I could not dredge up the name of a single significant Southern California poet. Maybe this was simply ignorance on my part, but it occurred to me there might not *be* any.

One had to go pretty far back (Joaquin Miller, Robinson Jeffers) or further north (Ferlinghetti, Snyder) to even start a California list. And there might be reasons for that. Through my mind like the unshakeable refrain of a catchy tune ran the lines of a Louis Simpson poem, one which stood as a weighty caution to any would-be Southern California poets:

> Here I am, troubling the dream coast
> with my New York face,
> bearing among the realtors
> and tennis-players my dark preoccupation.

There was Florida. Florida was the Sunshine State, an entire state predicated on palm trees and warmth, but there it was again: who were the great Miami Beach poets? Who, for that matter, were the mediocre ones?

Problematic as it might be, home to me was New England. My mother was born in Connecticut, educated in Massachusetts, died in Vermont. The line for me reads born Vermont, school Rhode Island, living Massachusetts. It did not matter if we *liked* New England; no such inquiry was ever undertaken. To "love the seasons" was our assignment, our lot in life.

And maybe a poet requires winter. Robert Frost may have been born in (northern) California, but he was no kind of poet until he had absorbed New England and New England absorbed him. Might not the complete absence of winter explain the absence of poetry in Laguna or Miami?—if there was such an absence.

East, west, south . . . north! Whirling in my mind, I pictured going to Maine with Cal, hunkering down at Hartley's Cottages for a week of bad weather. Was Winnie willing to spare him for one more short stint? If so, I would see if Cal took over that cottage in winter the same way he had taken over my apartment in summer. See whether or not the two of us felt "right" there too, in a place where Ian and I had felt so wrong. Such an experiment could tell me a lot.

Meanwhile, something told me I might be losing my mind for real, although, ironically, I took some comfort from the possibility. After all, everyone knows that crazy people feel perfectly sane—and I did not. Right there, in the paradox, was an argument of sorts for my sanity. I was capable of grasping at such straws.

My father called me crazy when I passed up Princeton for RISD. Lynn called me crazy when I turned down the Hardwick Grant and went with Ian to Cleveland that summer. And Ian himself calls me crazy all the time, though with him it's only a figure of speech. It means we disagree.

None of those cautions had troubled me. I had my reasons for reaching those decisions. Now though, unable to decide anything, for any reason, I paid closer attention to the charge, even if (apart from the disdainful night waiter at Café Soleil) I was the only one making it. There was no shortage of substantiating evidence: I had stopped eating, stopped sleeping, stopped walking, stopped working. I looked like a zombie. At this point, Ian's Someone-Else-Entirely would have fled down the street screaming at the sight of me.

I analyzed my reflection each morning, fearing I would see the final transformation, the sharp scary facial bones of Tiny Nurse blooming in my mirror.

Something told me to go home right away and for once I listened. I managed to get on a plane eight days early, and although I hate flying, that flight was heavenly. I relaxed. I let go of everything. I positively devoured my dinner of phony mashed potatoes and tough-as-turtle Chicken Kiev. With my second complimentary glass of red wine in hand, I read and then I slept (dreamlessly) inside that brief safe corridor of air somewhere west of the Azores and east of East Boston.

Back home it wasn't raining, it was snowing.

Or it had snowed. In the ensuing week of sunlight, the landscape was such a brilliant white that for days my face got locked in a squint. I was constantly off balance. The seasons were out of kilter too, as above the glistening meringue of snow still flew the yellow flags of late-hanging leaves, on birches and Bradford pears.

From the minute I landed at Logan, things with Ian were tricky. Running through my mind as the plane taxied toward the terminal was the latest draft of my speech about our impending separation. Then I spotted Ian at the gate and my heart brimmed with unforeseen tenderness. I was uplifted by his familiar smile, nourished by his familiar embrace. I could hug him easily because I had always hugged him. I could make love that first night because we had always made love.

Stunned by this turn of my emotions, I rendered no state-of-the-relationship addresses that night, or in the nights to follow. Nor, fortunately, did Ian debrief me on my travels. I was not ready to offer him a useful narrative, other than to say with a smile that his Someone Else initiative had been a fiasco. Where we stood in the wake of it went undiscussed.

Discussion did not seem necessary until I had settled in and the days began collecting on us, like dust. Because as we went along without definition (one week, two weeks, three) it emerged that we had not made love a second time. At first no significance attached. The initial reunion carried us for a while, and after that we could fall back on jet lag and fatigue. Soon enough we could add the wearing effects of my job search—all that legwork, phoning, interviewing.

"What did you have in mind?" I was asked by a Miss Grundy lookalike at a private school that had advertised for a remedial reading assistant. Hmm. Clearly, the correct answer was not Remedial Reading Assistant. Was I expected to submit my salary demands? My ground rules for classroom protocol?

I never found out what *they* had in mind, as Miss Grundy was kind enough to provide an opening—the job would start immediately—and whatever anyone had in mind, whatever the job was, I used that opening to back out the door graciously and race over to the Patisserie where (in keeping with recent routine) I sat with my coffee, boule, and book until it was nap-time.

What did I have in mind? I really was jet-lagged, and fatigued, and at the very least *confused* by the job search. Then I was sick for a week. The weary phrase "under the weather" gained fresh resonance. I might have been exaggerating this illness (who even knew?) but I was definitely under the weather. I had been under it for months.

Christmas came bearing down on us, all sorts of plans and parties and visits demanded my attention, and when the smoke cleared after New Year's it emerged that we still had not made love a second time. Not only that, a Thursday loomed. Ian had only one lecture to give on Thursdays. He would be on campus until noon. Even if he met a friend for lunch, he would be home by two o'clock.

So it had become unavoidable: my cough was gone, the holidays were over, we would have to make love that afternoon. (The alternative was to define it as a problem and *discuss* it.) Why was this so difficult, though? I had cross-examined myself any number of times, on those nights when we slid past it in silence and stillness, pretending not to notice the disappearing moment. If I could make love with Julian or Franz, why on earth could I not do so with my husband?

I could, of course, and I did, that Thursday afternoon. But the outcome of my self-interrogation came clear as we held each other sadly, immobilized, though the apartment was getting very cold. With those others, sex was unimportant. Though this had never been true for me at any time in my life before (and I was sure it would never be true at any time thereafter), it was true in Scotland. Sex was no different to me than having a beer with those guys, or not as significantly different as it should have been. Composed in equal parts of propinquity and momentum, it presented itself as a sociable moment of a sort one typically resists. If one does not resist, it might end up happening. That dynamic can be remarkably uncomplicated.

Whereas sex with Ian was more than important, it was life and death. The life or death of our marriage, of my soul, and of his happiness, I feared. I hated lying to Ian. Rather than do so, I had put him through the terrible suffering of The Twoweeks and its aftermath. Now, in his hour of need, I could not allow myself to say I loved him—in case I didn't. Even a potential lie I would not utter. Consequently, fewer and fewer words were uttered.

We could discuss the chicken or the wine at dinner, and the news of the day, Haldeman, Ehrlichman, Muhammad Ali. We could take up my work search, his actual work, his mother's impending 65th birthday. At breakfast we could share the *Globe*, as always, reading one another the outrages and follies of the day as we came across them. Concerning ourselves, and our peculiar impasse, we had nothing to say.

By the following Thursday we had reached a point where Ian would never have taken the initiative in bed, not if he sensed my reluctance. He would just up and go, walk out the door, before he would pressure me. For me to make it happen was a sort of lie, I suppose, but I was humbled by his suffering and by his sense of honor. Plus, as I say, it was another Thursday. The devil really is in the details.

I lied far more egregiously that night when I whispered "Goodnight, love" as we rolled apart. Though I tried to rationalize it (I had not said I loved him, exactly), the truth is my simpleminded moral discipline had broken under the weight of his pain. I so badly wanted to comfort him, to make him *feel* loved, that the word seeped out under the iron gate of my will.

To my mother, pride was the worst of the deadly sins. "Self-centered" was the dirtiest word in her vocabulary. When at age eighteen I was transformed into this woman who magically attracted men, she was quick to inform me how lucky I was to have this power arrive late in life.

"Late in life? Mom, I'm eighteen."

It was late enough, she explained, in terms of character formation. "You'll never be too proud. Not when you've seen how superficial it all is, how arbitrary and fickle. You were a sensitive child, and you will be a sensible woman."

Now here I was manipulating my husband's heart like a puppeteer. Mixing the sauce of our lives like a chef—a shot of Tabasco, a splash of lime. Steering our ship toward the shoals, clinging to the tiller though I lacked all skill and had no plan.

Every second-rate metaphor applied to my ceaseless, useless self-excoriation. Whoever I loved, I knew who I hated: myself.

To make matters worse, I had not written four good lines of poetry since leaving Europe. I understand that nothing could matter less to the average person. It's also true one could publish a hundred poems and count oneself fortunate if a dozen people bothered to read them. They might not even be worth reading. But to a poet none of that matters.

And by poet I mean nothing highfaluting, nothing more than a human being who chooses to write poetry. I render no judgments. My mother's pal Jackie Loughery wrote a poem every Saturday morning for decades. She had them tucked carefully inside the pages of each year's calendar, and those poems were what any critic would call doggerel, or worse, drivel. Lilacs in May, cute kittens, the soul on fire.

But Mrs. Loughery was deeply pleased by each one she fashioned. She was completed by them, in a way neither her Sunday morning churchgoing nor her Sunday afternoon golf games could approximate. Church was her duty; golf was her fun; poetry was her fulfillment.


The one thing I did get right was steering clear of Cal Byerly. I knew his routes and haunts, so the temptation was there to run into him "accidentally." Then there was the lesser temptation to check back on reviews for the Godot play, see how his Estragon had been received, possibly learn what was next for him. I did not do those things and I didn't ask any third parties about him. My hands were clean.

I did run into Gerald Gordon one afternoon at the Grolier, where he greeted me like a long lost friend. Where had we *been*? I knew Gerald's "we" encompassed Cal, not Ian. We never did get around to explaining our strange arrangement to them, The Twoweeks, so they had drawn their own perfectly reasonable conclusions.

"How is Calvert?" he therefore asked. When I put my index finger to my lips to shush him, then shook my head no, the only reasonable conclusion Gerald could draw was that I had lost a few marbles since he last saw me.

Into the maw of this fine mess came Cal's note. The envelope arrived sometime after we had both left for work and before Ian would be getting home. Had Cal spied on us? Had he gauged our comings and goings to make sure I saw the note first, or had he thrown caution to the wind, carelessly relying on dumb luck? Even a passerby would have seen it from the street: a bright white rectangle pinned to the blue door, like a public notice of the hanging.

I wondered about this even as I was snatching the envelope and jumbling it in with the day's mail. Wondered too if Mrs. Ridley had observed my sleight of hand from her front window. Had she watched Cal come and go? She had an uncanny knack for being at that window any time you hoped no one was looking. Ian was careful never to pick his nose, for fear Mrs. Ridley would catch him in the act and tell him how disappointed she was. Disappoint her, I shrugged, but he would never.

I used to think I was a reasonably mature woman. College, travel, jobs, marriage. Oh, and I own a car. Technically, what else is involved? Children? I felt ready for that too. One shameful day in Paris I had fantasized Winnie's untimely death, and a call for me to step in. Jake and Hetty would need me there, Cal would want me there. I felt capable of taking over, accepting the challenge. I didn't wish for it, it wasn't that sort of fantasy; more like a what-if, or an anything-can-happen.

Mature, though? This note whittled me down to a jittery teenaged girl, and just the sort of teenaged girl I had never even been: volatile, and vulnerable, and fearful without knowing why. Too fearful to tear open that envelope. Instead, I set about the breakfast dishes, gave the junk mail an unusually close reading, put on a pot of coffee I had no intention of drinking. Swept the kitchen floor, only to find myself sweeping it again.

It's the pattern I fall into when I have a response from a magazine. The poem might be a hopeless stab (sent in cold to *The New Yorker*, where they remove unsolicited poetry from one envelope and put it into another in a single graceful unbroken motion) or a fifty/fifty shot at *Treetops* or *The Low Plains Review*, each of whom had taken poems in the past. No matter. Whenever I find myself standing at the gates of Acceptance and Rejection, my approach is to stall.

But what would constitute rejection here? For that matter, what would constitute acceptance? I could not come up with anything on either side of the equation, and yet I was sure such a judgment must be contained within the envelope.

I sat, I stood, I paced. I locked the back door against the possibility of Mrs. Ridley bursting in, wagging her big loose index finger in my face and seizing the document before I could read it. I poured some of the coffee I didn't want, doctored it with cream and sugar it wouldn't need, checked the pilot light because the kitchen smelled of either mildew or gas.

Finally I sliced the envelope open and peered inside cautiously, as though peering around a dark corner in a bad neighborhood. It contained a single page, crowded with word clumps organized by topic.

> Sorry. I didn't mean to write, then didn't intend to deliver what I'd written. I wrote it, I delivered it, I'm sorry. I was seeking catharsis.

> Music. Day 14 was the day the music died. Never again for me the work of Harold Jenkins and I may require surgery to get Linda Ronstadt out of my head. It's been a Long Long Time *already*.

> Water. I am grateful for winter, for frozen ponds and rivers. In a movie it was summer and the troupe of laughing skinny-dipping actors made me sad. I just wanted to get arrested, with you, at that lake in Wellesley.

> Poetry. The book you gave me. I wanted so much to love it, and I couldn't. In my head I keep apologizing for this failure and trying it again. No dice.

The T. Never took it before you, haven't taken it since. There is a curse on every T-stop. I get depressed just walking past the entrances. Before The Twoweeks I would not even have noticed them.

Miller Road. Your neighborhood is cursed too. I turned down a dinner invitation on Brainerd Street that might have led to a part at the Wilbur. It was too close. What if I had veered off, detoured down Miller Road like a homing pigeon, climbed into your bed?

Gerald and Debra. I sort of miss them. I think of the "good times" and I think of Gerald and Debra? Uh oh. But of course who I really miss is you. Every hour, pretty much.

This note. "Hope this finds you well." I have tried to keep it short & snappy, not too awful an imposition. In fact I cut it by 92% because a famous editor (are there famous editors?) supposedly said that was the whole trick. Honestly, Lara, you should have seen the first draft.

Though it bore no salutation and no signature, it was obviously From Cal, With Love. It was a love letter, whether he knew it or not.

But it was not a help. Not to me anyway, and not likely to Cal either. The letter indicated that he missed me, wished life could be different, and was struggling emotionally. Confessing as much would not change anything, or for that matter provide catharsis, it would only slow our recovery. It was a sweet confession and a stupid thing to do.

The note upset me terribly. And it frustrated me, because I had such a powerful impulse to write back. I was burning to respond, to drop a note in the *pneumatique* instantly, by return mail. I wanted to deliver the entire packet of postcards I had written him.

It was my duty to resist this urge, for his sake and mine. Our movie was over, whether or not we liked the ending. Catharsis lay nowhere on our map, however frustrating we found that to be. There was only quicksand on our map, in every direction, and we would be fools to wade in any deeper.

I did resist writing back. I *resisted* even thinking about it. But I felt invaded by that damned note. From that moment on, Cal was hovering just outside my door. How could I ignore the fact that this time he had actually been there? He had been on my street, on lots of streets, and he was on them all still. Once again he was like an invasive species, like kudzu, spreading through the city.

The note saddled me with brand new guilt, as well. Maybe it was not my fault it came, but until I brought myself to tell Ian it had come, anything else I said to him would constitute a lie. To ask if he had slept well, how his lecture went, whether he liked the idea of pine nuts in the salad—these were all terrible, trivial lies.

"I have had a note from Cal," was the single tellable truth. Any other words from my mouth simply compounded the original lie with blather.

# ⤳ 6 ⤳

## *Tea and Coffee*

### (December 26, 2008)

It wasn't why she woke before dawn, but it was her first thought upon waking: would Cal find the page she had removed from her Twoweeks journal? Somehow she had forgotten how persistent he could be.

She had made no serious effort to conceal it, merely placing it out of the way, slipping it into the "current" file because that one was handy. As she did so, Lara had asked herself why it mattered, why she cared so much to keep Cal from seeing now what she had been feeling way back then. For that matter, why did it matter then?

Well, there was all that fencing with him, jockeying for position: it was always a chore holding your ground against Cal Byerly. Lara, who had never cared to be (or even appear to be) vulnerable to anyone, had perfected a surface insouciance as protective coloration. There was a ditty she sang to him more than once in those difficult days—"Got along without you before I met you / Gonna get along without you now"—and she used it, or the stance the jaunty lyric represented, to maintain a balance, both within herself and between the two of them. Sometimes, she believed it was a true sample, the way she was, but at all times it was how she presented herself. So there was that.

Downstairs, Lara lit the burner under the kettle, hushed its whistle the instant it rose, handled the glass and spoon like brittle eggs, kept the quiet. She was tired and could have slept hours more, had further sleep been obtainable. She took her tea to the study and sat stilly at the desk for a moment, hands enclosing the steaming glass, absorbing its heat, eyes shut. Then she sipped twice, opened her eyes, and saw it was darker inside the house than out. The moon, still high, spread its light evenly over a surrounding sea of snow.

She switched on the lamp and settled into the corner chair, holding her tea in one hand and the foolish page in the other. Lara had glanced at it the other day. Had leafed through the manuscript and taken out the page describing (or not describing) what they had done on the ninth day. She did not read it. As she told Cal, she had not looked at any of those notes in thirty-plus years.

> I can't recall if it's Leverkühn or another character, but someone in Mann's *Dr. Faustus* defines love as "the astonishing change in the relation of one's self to the external world." There must be a million clever definitions out there, but that is the best one I have ever seen, especially as it pertains to Day Bloody 9.

> The crux of the matter was Revere Beach. Had I gone there another time, presumably with Ian, I would have hated it. Ugly and filthy, with threats to one's health on all sides, it could hardly be called a pleasant place to spend the day. *What were we thinking*, Ian and I would have said, to come here? This isn't a beach, Ian and I would have agreed, it's a rubble-ridden sandlot, which just happens to have the Atlantic Ocean for its eastern boundary.

> On Day 9, however (and this is all I will have to say on the subject of Day 9), I loved Revere Beach. It seems there had been an "astonishing change" in my relation to the external world. I could try to ignore this conclusion. I could (and will) set depth charges

of rationalization and denial designed to undermine it. But it was pretty damned clear that afternoon. Revere Beach was all the proof I needed to conclude I was doomed.

Not that life will cease, or even cease to be rich. And though the "astonishing change" may be lost to me now, who can say that won't be for the best? There is a strong case to be made that losing love is more apt to save a woman than doom her. Besides which, Adrian Leverkühn (as Cal would be quick to remind me) is a fictional character. No way to ask him whether the phenomenon he so perfectly defined leads to salvation or to doom. Thomas Mann was real enough, though, and didn't he choose to pass love by—difficult, immoral love—rather than see himself devoured by it?

As she set the page aside, Lara felt faintly embarrassed about it. She had been terribly melodramatic—Adrian Leverkühn, for goodness' sake, and *doom*—and on top of that she detected a rare note of self-pity. Maybe this alone was sufficient reason for suppressing the entry: not so much to hide her vulnerability as to hide the lapse of common sense. Honestly, had she given a single minute of her life since then to pondering salvation, doom, or the best definition of love? It was jarring, really, to discover how young she was when all this was happening.

The strange part was that she felt more committed, not less, to keeping the page private. She might very well have reasons, but she felt no need for those. Lara had always loved the Richard Wilbur line about "the winter way of doing things for reasons." A wonderful line and a wonderful excuse, always, whenever one preferred to be steadfastly irrational.

If she needed reasons, she had another one in Cal's insistence. He could almost bully you with charm; certainly he could wear you down with logic. Say no to him nine times, say yes the tenth. Unless, like Lara, you refused on principle. What exactly that principle might be she did not care to specify, even to herself, at what was now nearly six A.M., with the dogs moving around outside her door, the day apparently begun. She was content to let go of the inquiry, let it end and the day begin.

"Self," she said, nonetheless, as she carried her empty glass back to the kitchen, where she was greeted politely—they were gentle, well-trained retrievers—by both dogs, and was surprised to see Cal dressed and standing in the side yard, or what was left of it, given the snow. He had already walked and fed them, already made himself coffee. He could be quiet, too.

But that was the principle, she told him, albeit he could neither see nor hear her as she shaped her statement. It might have any number of arms and legs, subsets and corollaries and whatnot, yet it was as basic as could be. *Self*, and the right to preserve it, always.

# A Dazed Child

## (1974–5)

Jake kept bouncing the basketball off his foot and then, even more uncharacteristically, thrashing around in frustration. For months he had it on a string, like a small white Earl the Pearl; he even had the spin move and the crossover; *never* lost the handle.

So what was this? Did ball-handling come and go in stages? Could growth spurts cause backsliding? I always thought it was a nice straight line in sports. You mastered something, then you had it. Went on from there to master the next thing.

Free-throw shooting, maybe. You might hit a spell where your shot went off, it got into your head, and for a week or so the stroke just wasn't there. Not that Jake could shoot free throws. Shooting wasn't his thing yet, ball-handling was. Forget the Pearl, he was a small white Marques Haynes.

It crossed my mind he might be shamming, goofing up on purpose. Hey, the little guy might be *acting,* a chip off the old block. But why? If he was doing it on purpose, what was his purpose in doing it? To punish me, somehow?

Kids can be just as tricky to deal with as grown-ups. Winnifred is a smart, savvy woman who seemed to have no clue my soul was AWOL. She's busy, she's trusting, and yes, physically I am there. "Present," when the roll is called. The four of us sit down together at the dinner table, the bedtime stories get read. I eat, I read, I am there.

The four of us went sledding at Fresh Pond: I slid, I laughed, I was there. Winnie had no idea she was watching a wounded beast lurch across the landscape.

But Jake saw it. I'm not so sure about his sister. There was the unforgettable incident at Morning Glory—and I will get back to that—but Hetty is younger and it's pretty much still the case you can overcome her moods by tossing her in the air. Rough-housing can distract her, hugs and kisses always comfort her. She feels the love, takes it at face value, and goes back to her crayons. Jake is watching me. Blocking out the love.

That day at Fresh Pond, I happened to notice a couple jogging on the path below. The woman was about the right height. Her hair, streaming out from under a blue wool hat, was about the right color. I was assessing her stride when I heard . . . "Dad?" . . . and realized I had heard it a couple of times before realizing it was being directed at me. By my son.

There was Jake with arms spread in an interrogator's stance. What's up, man? Where's your head at? Not that he said those things, he just held the pose. What he said was, "Do you know those people?"

Fair enough. Yet I felt more than curiosity behind the question; I felt accusation. We were supposed to be sledding, not people-watching. How could I let my attention wander when we were enjoying this time together as a family?

"I thought I might," I shrugged, and we remounted for our next downhill run. Father-and-son redux.

The distaff jogger was not Lara Cleary, not even close. I had to laugh when the couple came back around the path and I got a better look at them. The woman was at least forty, with what I call a Barbara Stanwyck face. As appealing as Stanwyck was, you knew that if her lip curled a tiny fraction more, if her nose was a tad bonier or the eyes a pinch smaller, she would have been almost ugly. This one didn't cross the Stanwyck Line, but she was a far cry from Lara Cleary.

My relief was disproportionate, over the top. In fact, I couldn't stop laughing and no one had a clue why I'd started. "I'm just happy," I told them, "I'm in a good mood. The sun is shining, the snow is sweet"—I gobbled some snow for the kids—"and Hetty hasn't crashed into a single solitary tree all day."

Hetty giggled, Winnie beamed, Jake stared.

What would I have done if it had been Lara? What would *Winnie* have done? She had not seen Lara since last April, their friendship had lapsed completely. Was that sufficiently strange for me to conclude Winnie knew more than she let on? Almost. Yet if she knew, if she even suspected, how could she be so easy-going and affectionate?

One day Carrie Fitzgerald asked her about Lara. Was Lara still abroad? My ears perked up at the odd usage (going "abroad" was what my parents would have said) and the even odder possibility that Lara was gone. I had always pictured her on the back stair landing at Miller Road, with her book, or with Ian, chatting up the nosy old lady from upstairs. I hadn't even adjusted for the cold weather. To me, Lara was right where I had left her— perhaps because I was right where she left me.

Winnie told Carrie she had no idea, had been out of touch with Lara, should give her a call. (Which she did not, ever again.) Maybe it was pure paranoia on my part, but I thought I saw Jake's ears perk up at the mention of Lara's name. A dog can't articulate what he's sniffing after, but he always knows when he is getting close to it.

I wanted to lift him by the lapels, by the two wings of his winter coat the way I used to, and tell him, Hey, man, lay off will ya? I'm here, aren't I? We are here. Can't I be allowed to suffer in silence? Do I have to answer for trying to be good, trying to do right? And silently Jake said, You sure do, Dad. You have to answer for deserting me and for not loving my mom.

I was trying to do that too. Why couldn't he grade me A for effort? In my mind I would list all her assets and virtues. I noted the fact that there was absolutely nothing on the negative side of the ledger. Winnie was not merely blameless, she was lovable. As a person, as a mother, as a lover—she was the winner in anyone's lovability sweepstakes. There was only the one problem, that I could not seem to love her.

When we saw the *Globe*'s review of Godot, Winnie marched right back to the Rexford Spa and bought every copy they had, twenty newspapers. "Why?" I smiled, as she started clipping and mailing them out, to family, to friends. Everyone needed to see the original, not a xerox, so they could see my colorful rags, my red wig. She handed me her shortlist and asked, "Who am I forgetting?"

Was she daring me to say Lara's name? I bore down on the list and was relieved to discern a pattern. "I guess you are only sending it to out-of-town friends?"

"Of course. Everyone here will see the *Globe*. And they damn well better go see the play."

"What about the McCarthys?"

"Yes, definitely. Anyone else?"

"Shooey Delaney?"

"God, how could I have forgotten Shooey? This is good, Cal, keep thinking. I can get more papers at Nini's if I need them."

Would Lara have seen the notice? Would she come see the play? For that matter, had she been out there in the dark on opening night, in Seat 12, Row H? For yes, I had scanned the audience hoping to spot her, hoping not to spot her. Why did it matter more to me that Lara hear how well it went than that Winnie was through the roof with pride?

But this insidious habit of mind was not exactly unfamiliar. Why did the Turtle Café remind me more of Lara than of Winnie? Why did I think of Lara when Winnie read me the headline about a Red Sox trade? The question was more and more a rhetorical one, as I tried to love Winnie and couldn't seem to. Tried *not* to love Lara and couldn't manage that either, by a wide sad margin.

It was a real shot in the gut when Carrie Fitzgerald dropped the word "abroad" on me that night. Lara and I were done. It should not matter where she was, yet it did help to know her whereabouts, to know we were at least in the same town. There was consolation in our propinquity. To lose that, and have no idea where she was, took loss to another level.

What if she was "abroad" permanently? I might have no news for a year, for several years, and then learn she had been in Copenhagen the entire time, raising children there, walking dogs. My Estragon, or the upcoming Pinter—my career, which might have served as a point of connection, of indirect communication— would be, in her memorable words, of no more relevance than the news that a man in Sicily had changed his shirt.

I might find myself reading *her* reviews. A first volume of poems would appear, then a second, with a spate of readings announced back here in the states. I would ponder the risks of going to hear her. Going to see her—after five years, ten years— and see if I even recognized her. If the germ could still be running rampant in my bloodstream.

It had not been years, though, it had been months, and the likelihood was that she and Ian were still living on Miller Road. That they had taken a trip, and returned from it. Maybe he had given a paper, or whatever it is academics do. They went, they came back, and the rest was fantasy and fearanoia.

Five months? Probably she was back to writing poems and sending them to magazines nobody would ever read. "I never read them either," she had told me. "You find out they exist and you try them, that's all. If you're lucky they send you ten dollars and two copies of the issue." At Out of Town News one afternoon, I leafed through a dozen such magazines, checking for Lara's name. This was contra-indicated, as the generals say, yet harmless enough.

Less harmless, for sure, than my scouting outing to her neighborhood. That wasn't planned, or intended, I just found myself gravitating there. And although I did understand that I was flirting with dangerous boundaries of discretion and sense, I could not seem to restrain myself. It took good old Mrs. What's-her-name, the nosy neighbor, to restrain me.

That woman was always either in her apartment or in the backyard. She never set foot off the property, so it was amazing to see her at the corner of Brainerd and Miller—stationed there like a sentry. Or a guard dog: Cerberus at the gate to Hades. She gave me a silent two-stage scowl. One, Don't I know you, and two, Sure I know you, you're the bad seed that tried to replace my Ian.

I gave her an innocent, friendly wave, to forestall her from coming after me with a scythe or a broom. Then I continued past Miller to Finnerty, as though that had been my trajectory all along. When I sauntered back past the corner fifteen minutes later, she was still at her post, on full alert. She looked like someone who had shooed away a cat and was making sure the mangy animal did not come sneaking back.

The animal came back much later, under cover of darkness. I needed to confirm that Lara's ancient Dart was parked in front of her house, as only she could park it, two feet from the curb, at a preposterous angle. As soon as I saw the car, I relaxed. A great weight came off me. She was there. Not in Copenhagen, not gone forever.

Why, my son Jake demanded to know, should that matter? Wouldn't it be easier, my son pointed out, if she *was* gone forever? This would happen sooner or later, after all. They would move on. Ian had no shot at tenure here, but he would get it elsewhere, in Iowa or Indiana, at some college where they were not quite so stingy with tenure, and that's where they would go. Tenure was the goal. After that, Ian was fond of saying, Higher Truth could come back into focus.

My son was right, and I rooted hard for his preferred outcome. For a month after I had chalked Lara's tire, so to speak, I steered wide of the entire Grayling neighborhood. For two months, possibly. Now and then I contemplated a stroll over that way, to see how we were doing. See if the Dart was gone, if Lara and Ian (freshly tenured) were happily relocated to Indiana.

"I'm coming with," Jake would say, whenever I broached it. "I want to walk too."

He came with me everywhere. If I started toward the closet, he was up and zipping his coat. If I insisted he wear boots, he would not protest (as in the past) "But *you're* not wearing boots," he would simply jam them on. He accompanied me to places he had traditionally disdained, the post office and the grocery store. Come on, bud, I used to say, we'll hit the Stop & Shop (Winnie going, "Do *not* let him choose the cereal") and he would head for the bathroom with a sudden bellyache.

Not these days. These days he was waiting for me by the door: booted, coated, muffled, mittened. Always happy to mail a letter, or help me capture the bread and milk.

Hetty, meanwhile, had laid her qualms to rest. She had relented. Initially, immediately after The Twoweeks, she was the scary one. The worst of it, the low point of my entire domestic history, came on my first visit to her new daycare center. She had started going to this place during my time with Lara, so I had not yet seen it. More to the point, it had not yet seen me.

Morning Glory, it was called. Jacqui and Lesli, they were called. They greeted me warmly, smiled at me approvingly, for here was Dad getting involved in his little girl's education. To Jacqui and Lesli this was not "daycare," it was school. They were not glorified babysitters, they were teachers. Fair enough. As a parent, I honored their profession above all others.

Then Hetty did her thing. I was the guy who had made the oatmeal to her specifications at seven A.M. I had squashed her banana precisely as she required it be squashed, and I had tied her shoes, in clear violation of Winnie's Rules and Regs about Making Her Do It For Herself. Then Winnie had whisked her away, six hours had passed, and here I was picking her up. Me, Cal, Daddy. The same guy who had squashed the banana and tied the shoes. I looked the same, hadn't aged a day.

Yet my daughter said to Jacqui—with absolute conviction— "That's not my daddy."

Jacqui flinched as though lightning had struck her crotch. Inside her skull, keening sirens tore through the quiet afternoon. Lesli was back in a flash, kneeling, taking both my daughter's hands in hers and asking, "Are you sure, Hetty? You're kidding us—right, sweetheart?"

"I don't know him," said Hetty. "He's not my daddy."

A dazed child woken from her nap at a new daycare might well be disoriented. She might not know who *anyone* was, herself included. But my darling daughter appeared clear of eye that afternoon. She stood calm and firm in her testimony. The best lawyer in the world could not have shaken her on cross.

Lesli looked as though she might know a little jujitsu, Jacqui looked like she was ready to call the cops. If I wasn't the daddy, then *geesh*, who the hell was I? This could be a serious, dangerous moment.

"Call my wife," I pleaded, and for brownie points recited without hesitation the inside line at Winnie's office. "Please call her."

Hetty was transported like delicate crockery to a cot where she lay facing the wall, while a young teaching aide named Brandi stroked her back and cooed. I was advised not to approach. "Why don't you wait over here," said Jacqui, taking me by the arm (bravely, I suppose, if she truly believed I was some sort of molester psycho creep) and guiding me to the holding cell, a kitchenette, where I set about washing a sinkful of pots while awaiting the verdict.

Finally Jacqui appeared and summoned me to the office. They had Winnie on the line and wanted to listen in on our conversation. Winnie must have been busy and hassled by the interruption, because she sounded uncharacteristically impatient. "Can't you just bribe her with an ice cream?" she said.

"Well no, dear, the problem falls well shy of ice cream. They won't give her to me; won't let me take her home. They think I'm a child stealer."

"I vouched for you," she said, softening. "I told them you were probably wearing a brown tweed overcoat. Were you?"

"I were," said I. My best molester outfit.

And at that point I felt a tug at the hem of my frayed tweed overcoat and saw Hetty reaching up her arms, waiting to be lifted. Joke over.

Well, it was a big relief being sorted out and released from custody, and it was useful to learn I was far from the best actor in the family. We were all accomplished thespians, it seemed, all except for Winnie, who was there to keep us grounded. To *vouch* for us.

Away we went, Hetty and (yes, confirmed) her dad. I figured we would need to do some further sorting out at the playground, begin dealing with this troubling incident. (What was *that* about, you little twerp?) I was prepared to meet it head-on (discuss it, resolve it) because it was not a joke at all; it was serious and it had to be about my absence, about my being a stranger to this school she had attended for all of four days. Apparently, this was grounds for punishment.

I was okay with punishment. My concern was making sure Hetty understood how much I loved her, because the stunt she pulled struck me as an expression of doubt, or anxiety. That can't be my daddy because my daddy loved me. My daddy would never miss fourteen whole days of my life.

But Hetty had no interest in addressing it head-on, or even acknowledging it had occurred. (Maybe she really had been a dazed child, or a sly joker.) If there was no way to address the stunt directly, there was still a need to address its wellsprings, to banish any underlying anxiety by loving my daughter extravagantly. And this I could do because, thank God, I did love her extravagantly.

So Hetty got unlimited songs and stories until the repair seemed complete. Unlimited everything. If she wanted a hoist-up to touch the ceiling, then up she went. If she wanted ten more hoist-ups, ten it was. Was I a terrible parent for behaving this way, for spoiling her? Maybe so, but doubt was put to rout.

She did not reprise her "That is not my dog" routine, knowing that Jacqui (not to mention Lesli and Brandi) could vouch for me now. I had what the courts call standing in the community. There would be no further disturbances at Morning Glory, but none at home either. Hetty was mine again, my special baby who would fly up to my neck in greeting, whose hand would find its way to my hand as we walked. Her eagerness to show me the world (look at this, look at that) was fully restored.

We did hit one small bump during preparations for the Pinter. That got pretty intense, the schedule tightened like a noose, and as opening night approached and rehearsals ran later (specifically, when I was missing in action at bedtime), my standing became shakier. One night Hetty tackled me outright, entangling my legs like heavy rope as I tried to leave.

"I want you to tuck me in," she said. "You papa, you you." We were two hours shy of tuck-in time at that point, and I was already late for the first dress rehearsal.

That time it was Jake who rode to my rescue. He played the man for his little sister. "I'll tuck you in, dust-mouse," he said, and then whispered, "And I'll trick Mom into giving us extra cookies."

Well done, lad. Winnie had baked a tray of peanut butter cookies, the cookies Hetty would kill for. The standard dose was two cookies and then (after the spate of fraudulent firmness) one more. Jake would push the total to four, maybe even five cookies. He would make it a numbers game. A few kisses later I was out the door and clumping through the slush to the Klein Theatre. I could address the resurfacing of Hetty's separation anxiety in due course: message received. For the moment, I was being allowed to work.

The price for this liberty was mild enough. At breakfast the next morning, Jake grilled me over our raisin toast. Not quite seven years old and he wants to know if the lady in the play is "as pretty as mama." Wonders if he should perhaps *attend* tonight's rehearsal, just to see how things are going. Is greatly relieved to learn that although there is not one lady but four in the play, none of them are exactly pretty (sorry Cora, sorry Jennifer, especially), much less as pretty as his mother.

"Are they nice?"

"Now that is the right question to ask."

"What's the answer?"

"Well, there are four of them, so some are nicer than others. But none of them," I smiled as I poked him in the ribs, "is half as nice as your mama."

The Pinter wasn't half bad. We sold the seats, we were liked, Barry and Joan seemed pleased. It ran just a week, though, eight performances in all, and I had nothing else lined up until the spring.

I read for a part in New York (waste of train fare), worked some stuff up on my own, and helped reconstitute our Thursday night ensemble. We had no stage, just the big back table at Cronin's, where either we were all the business they had or we scared their other customers away with our stentorian tones.

I had left the bookstore by then and taken another part-timer, manning the front desk at the Howard Johnson Motor Hotel on the river, three 8-hour days a week. This was a choice role in itself, as there (in jacket and tie, no less, and clean-shaven every day) I was obliged to smile obsequiously at everyone, including the stray pig who handed me his shoes to shine and his wife who required someone to "do" her fingernails instantly.

I smiled obsequiously, I rang my little bell, I answered the red telephone as pleasantly as a country pastor. And I brought home the capital sum of 72 dollars per week, a pay cut from my 80 at the bookstore.

Winnie was so glad to be breaking even on daycare costs that for a while she made no references to her Five Year Plan, whereby I would be getting a "real job" if after five years I was not being paid decently as an actor. The terms were elastic (If 72 dollars a week did not qualify as decent pay, what about 144?) but I understood the clock was ticking on my dicey career choice.

One can conceal a lot within the chaos of raising small children. I suppose the checks and balances ensure that middle-class parents raising small children have few issues to conceal. By presumption they are young and in love; not so very long ago they *chose* this course, so (by presumption) they are still playing for the same team. Let the chaos rip, if beneath its wild windblown surface lies the bedrock of love.

Beneath the chaos that enabled Winnie and me to miss connections lay an unseen well of helplessness and sorrow. Whenever I was alone (and too often when I was not), Lara Cleary laid siege to our household. If Winnie called to say she was stuck working late, I was relieved, not disappointed. I hated being relieved, but it meant there would be fewer hours of pretending all was well.

This diverged radically from my state of mind during my prior slip-up, with Sasha Blackburn. I was unworthy of Winnie that month, no question, but at least I loved her without a mote of ambivalence. Loved her more than ever. I was always so glad to get home from those trysts. Talk about abnormality: I would actually fantasize about my wife while in bed with Sasha.

So what was I doing there? My buddy Fitz, in whom I confided, accused me of careerism, of playing *that* game, because everyone believed Sasha was "going places." But he was just hassling me. He knows I don't operate that way. I accused myself of making a mistake and precluded any chance of future favors from Sasha Blackburn by correcting that mistake a bit too bluntly.

If Winnie knew how little that affair meant to me, she might not have minded it that much. Men will be men, her mother liked to say, with pre-feminist resignation, and Winnie had some of that philosophical tolerance in her. There was a line from a song she liked, "I have not always been faithful / But I always have been true." Possibly my dalliance with Sasha could come under that heading.

But the line did not apply to Lara Cleary. With Lara, I had indeed been faithless, and the cost to Winnie was yet to be fully reckoned. The costs to me, so far, were palpable: the overwhelming weight of betrayal, a distraction so constant it was almost comical, and a sadness that really did seem to radiate straight out from my heart.

Then I wrote the stupid letter. Composed it at the HoJo desk, on HoJo stationery. My first attempt was pathetic, endless pages of scrawl and sentimentality. I purged the sentimental stuff ruthlessly, and by the third run-through I had excised every reference to love including the rather mild "I loved that place best."

It hardly mattered which words I put in and which ones I took out, since she would never see the pitiful thing. I honestly believed I was just doing what I always do, refining a voice in my head, getting the character right, even if the character was me. It's funny how some directors will shoot you on sight for changing a single word, while others exclaim over your genius at improvisation.

The version I eventually left for her (alas, she would see the pitiful thing after all) was pared down to a single page. It was still silly, little more than a sort of thank-you note (Thanks for a lovely time!), along with the assurance that this had been no small deal to me and was mighty rough going in the aftermath.

I knew Lara well enough to expect she would be thoroughly annoyed by the letter, yet also pleased. It's nice to be missed, regardless of the circumstances. And what if she was struggling as much as I was? What if the sorrow infecting my happy home had infected hers as well?

What if it had? said Jake, as we drove in silence to Spy Pond with our skates and sticks and a pocketful of pucks. Lara and I had tacitly decided the two critical points: that somehow we "deserved" The Twoweeks and that we deserved nothing more than that. We had chosen to sip from the poisoned chalice. Ian had not. Winnie and the children had not. If we found ourselves sad, or depressed, or obsessed, so what? Jake was right again. Hard cheese, old chap.

Though there were no excuses for delivering that letter (even in its highly sanitized shorthand form), there were reasons. Weakness, self-indulgence, and a complete collapse of discipline don't count as reasons, but maybe the blind hope of relief does? To people who have acted in the classic Greek tragedies, catharsis is real. Catharsis is *supposed* to happen.

Timing was the major factor. At Cronin's, the night before I took the letter to Miller Road, we read the last three acts of *Hamlet*, and I was Hamlet. Oh man, was I ever Hamlet. Talk about inhabiting a character. All his dithering, all that folding in on himself until his mind was hopelessly twisted and constricted? I didn't know a hawk from a handsaw either.

Hamlet's most memorable line was as potent as ever: "To thine own self be true and thou canst not then be false to any man." Like millions before me, I fell under the spell of Shakespeare's words so thoroughly that I nearly called Lara from Cronin's that night to propose a cultural interchange. For here woven together on Shakespeare's loom were our two crafts, the poetry she revered and our lame dramatic presentation of it.

Fortunately, I fathomed how drunk I was, even on the strength of Cronin's watered-down beer. And I understood how easily one could be true to one's "own self," while being false to everyone else—men, women, children. The spell did not last long (spells do not tend to) but it did last the night and before it lifted I had pinned the note on Lara's door.

It met, of course, with a deafening silence. Which was fine, and fully expected. Sober, I only hoped my lapse had not caused her new problems. I rationalized that it might instead have helped Lara, by rallying her together with Ian against a common enemy. Even sober, though, I was not exactly sorry I'd done it. I needed to do it.

And sitting at the HoJo MoHo front desk in my jacket and tie, I could not keep from fantasizing that Lara's would be the next face to emerge from the revolving glass doors. You saw motion, then reflections and a blur of clothing, finally the faces. So the moment of revelation was always suspenseful and we did get the occasional celebrity—Dizzy Gillespie for one, also the writer Bernard Malamud. Maybe she had changed a bit (I was ready for that) but Lara would appear, perhaps on business (to book an upcoming function in our splendidly appointed Blaine Room), with my note showing like a popup handkerchief in her breast pocket.

Or perhaps, I fantasized, we would meet on the icy Weeks Bridge, as we rushed headlong in opposite directions, like two characters in a Dostoevsky novel. The circumstances might be less melodramatic but there was no getting around the law of averages: sooner or later, fantasy might well collide with reality. Apart from our lengthy history of serendipitous encounters, Cambridge is a small city and both of us walked a lot.

Hopelessly restless, I walked even more after leaving the note. One stormy afternoon the kids and I must have logged five miles, to the point where Jake complained he was tired. Whoa, now. Tired? "I'm *not* tired" was my boy's mantra. It was a declaration that escaped his lips with such frequency I could mistake him for a talking doll with its single embedded string-fed phrase.

It was doubtful I'd really worn him down, far more likely I'd pissed him off with too many sidelong glances. Some days I was like the partygoer who chats you up while peering past your ears, scoping the scene for someone more interesting.

"What are you looking for?" Jake said, more than once.

"Early signs of spring. I told you, I can feel spring in the air."

"Papa!" Hetty protested, her arms spread wide in characteristic dismay, her expression poised between the old silly-papa-is-joking-us and a new papa-is-off-his-rocker. "It's *snowing*."

"Hey, if you guys can't handle a few spring snowflakes, we can go home any time," I said, for oh what a rogue and peasant slave was I.

Winnie seemed to suspect nothing. In any event, she said nothing. Never once had she pressed me on where I was during our it's-not-a-separation separation. She merely took my word for it that I felt better. In one way she was offering her jaw for the knockout punch, in another she was making it impossible for any such punch to be thrown. By giving me no grounds for resentment, no context for anger, she disarmed me of everything save my sorrow. And from that she simply averted her gaze.

Then one night she surprised me. Winter was wearing us down, she said. What a shame it was, she said, that we couldn't afford to take a trip. How nice it would be, she said, to escape the cold weather for a few days and travel someplace warm and sunny.

This was something we had never done. We were not like a real grown-up American family of the sort who had money in the bank and took an annual trip to the sun. Occasionally we took a small trip—in the car, no frills. We camped or stayed with friends, counting our quarters at roadside diners. Fancy resorts in Florida were never a consideration.

So I just smiled when she raised this idea. Even when she raised it a second time, I shrugged it off. The weather hadn't been all that bad. Lately, the kids and I had seen some early signs of spring, hadn't we? Things were looking up.

Winnie shifted ground. If we couldn't afford it as a family, maybe I should get away for a few days on my own. Take another break. As brightly and solicitously as she framed it, this was the closest she came to acknowledging the unshakeable malaise I had labored to hide from her. I had been the cheerful caretaker of the children, the willing shopper, the whistling dishwasher. Also the solicitous mate, inquiring after her day at the office, listening to the litanies. Now here she was, undermining my entire masquerade, stoving in the façade.

"No way," I said. "If I go anywhere, we all go. It's only fair."

"Then we all stay," she laughed, more lighthearted than I had heard her in some time. Maybe I had passed another test, because a day later Winnie announced we would be going on a trip after all. A trip we could afford, because it was free.

Unsolicited (or so I was told), Winnie's parents were giving us this present. It was not anyone's birthday, not Christmas, yet they had booked us for a long weekend in the Catskills. "It's almost April," Priscilla chirped over the phone. "We wanted the children to ski at least once before the season ends."

It was true Winnie's folks had done a version of this the previous winter. We stayed with them, however, not at a fancy-dan hotel. And while they did treat us to day passes and schedule a few lessons for Jake and Hetty, it was clear that Priscilla and Johnny were really purchasing three days of grandchildren, not three days of skiing. Hetty skied for about three minutes that first afternoon, reported back that the mountain was *slippery* (who could argue otherwise?) and spent the rest of her time in Priscilla's kitchen.

I was pretty sure this winter's gift had been engineered by Winnie as a replacement for the sunny getaway we could not afford. It may have been a benign conspiracy, but it was a conspiracy nonetheless. Schedules had been coordinated, reservations had been made, the hotel had been paid in advance. We had to accept and go.

The trip was also benign. Transporting the family to a fresh venue gave us a boost, gave me some mental space. In Bearsville, I could focus on what was right in front of me. Winnie was so charming and so pretty (with her green hat and red cheeks, ice chips in her flyaway hair) that I was convinced I could love her. How could anyone not?

And Jake was so consumed with the Olympic competition raging inside his head that he became a child again. Hour after hour I streamed down the hills with him as though the piano, strapped to my back for so long, had finally been delivered. Hour after hour we were pals, not Khrushchev and Kennedy going eyeball to eyeball.

In the restaurants, where all the bills were being siphoned to Johnny, we were under strict instruction to order from the full dinner menu, the impressive wine list, the lavish dessert tray. "None of your usual penny-pinching," Johnny insisted. "If I catch you ordering spaghetti or splitting desserts, there'll be heck to pay." Every aspect of the weekend had to be luxurious.

And so it was. As we sat by the parlor fire with a mug of Irish coffee (the children tucked away in a pine-lined loft so cozy they fell straight asleep), it felt like a honeymoon. There were plenty of actual honeymooners at the inn, and there were all sorts of programs and perks designed just for them. We did not partake of the heart-shaped hot tub or the bizarre frilly nightwear, but we did luxuriate. We did consent to being spoiled.

It felt as though we had broken the back of a tough winter. I was in remission. My blood test showed no trace of Lara Cleary, my brain scan no sign of my maundering obsessive attachment to the idea of her. An obsession, I recalled from Bugsy Brennan's high school psychology class, was rarely founded in reality. It was an emotional glitch, just as cancer was a physiological glitch.

Riding home that Sunday night, we basked in the afterglow of three perfectly self-indulgent days. For the first time in my life, I entertained the notion that maybe the rich really were happier, maybe money really could ease all burdens, cushion all pain. When the license plate game ended and the songs trailed off and the children were finally lulled asleep in the backseat, Winnie reached over and touched my arm in a gesture she has for expressing complete contentment. It had been nine months since my last glimpse of Lara Cleary. Might that be the gestation period of a marital comeback?

At first it was like one of those colds you have trouble shaking; the symptoms seem milder or even gone, then they trickle back. Traversing the slushy streets of Cambridge that week, I felt such a relapse coming on and tried to fight it off. To prevent those streets from organizing themselves into a maze leading to Miller Road, I carved out new circuitous routes around town.

To keep Lara from invading my thoughts, I employed strategies of distraction, tricks really—coping mechanisms roughly equivalent to counting sheep at night. I would present myself such stiff intellectual challenges as reciting the starting lineup of the 1967 Red Sox—or the 1968 Red Sox, a far greater challenge. I would generate lists, propose categories. Who were the ten greatest film actors of the 1940s? Starting with Julie Garfinkle, provide birth name and fake name for ten prominent film actors of the 1950s.

Walking the kids back from school as spring got underway for real, I would identify the birds and blossoms. Hetty listened intently, working to learn them, while Jake was already sufficiently informed to dispute my designations. We could agree about the obvious (Bradford pears with their white cloud of blossoms, forsythia bushes of declarative yellow) but he was having none of my copper beeches and horse chestnuts. Having studied up in a book Winnie gave him, the kid knew more than I did. Copper beech my eye.

Spring gave rise to an idea that got me through a few Sundays. Why not take short, inexpensive trips on the weekends. Day trips. Three gallons of gas would get us to the matchless curve of beach at Ogunquit. For another twenty bucks, we could rent a motel room with two double beds ("Magic Fingers!" Jake exclaimed) plus coffee and doughnuts in the morning. The kids had a blast there and they liked it even better in Mystic Seaport, where they commandeered the penny-squashing machine and got to eat hot dogs for lunch.

After dinner, Jake and I would pore over maps, planning more forays. We were tuned to the siren song of the good old open road, man, and Winnie smiled upon our endeavor. I suppose the program was an attempt to recreate the illusion of safety I had experienced in Bearsville. The problem was that to recreate and perpetuate it, we might need to go on the road for the rest of our lives.

We couldn't do that, but maybe we could move to the Catskills. We *should* move somewhere, I found myself suggesting in bed one night. After ten years in one place you either moved or found yourself mired down. You could wake up decades later and find your entire lives were lived in a place you had come to accidentally, temporarily, for college. Find you had lived out an accidental life.

Winnie disagreed vehemently. Far from being stuck, we were damned fortunate to be in this civilized place, this livable city where the schools were topnotch, the movie houses played Truffaut instead of Dumbo, and no one would have dreamed of voting for Richard Nixon. A city, moreover, where she had a very good job, and where I had more acting opportunities than I could expect to find anywhere except New York.

Did I want to move *there*? To New York *City*?

All lives are accidental, Winnie insisted. Growing up, no one knows where he or she will live, or with whom. No one knows what he or she will do to earn a living. Then the accidents begin to happen, the life begins to unfold. That's just how it is.

All I could do was smile and concede she had made some good points. And that no, I did not wish to relocate to New York City. The song of the open road did not point me toward the Big Apple.

At Cronin's, on the first day of May, we did a reading of Odets' *Golden Boy*. The play is definitely a period piece, 1930s proletarian theater, but Lipsky pushed it as "newly relevant" and chock full of lively language, meaty dialogue. "The waitresses will love us," was his clincher.

When he parceled out the male roles, I was hoping for Joe Bonaparte, the cocky kid. Joe was the Golden Boy and a lot of those good lines were his. Moody, his manager, had some good lines too, but Moody was older, a has-been and a cuckold. None of us was the right age for Moody, but according to Lipsky, I came closest. I was "mature" and had the right voice. Ken Carlisle would read Joe Bonaparte.

Kenny and I were the exact same age, but I didn't make a fuss. I didn't care, really. It was just a Thursday night roundtable at Cronin's, and then I had such a high old time with Moody that I ended up campaigning to stage the silly play, dated or not. Meanwhile, Ken's cocky kid fell flat as the Sahara, mostly because the character was fairly bogus to begin with.

"You did what you could with it," I consoled him.

"Blame Odets," Jennifer seconded the motion. Tradition required we blame the playwright for our bad performances.

After the session, after we closed Cronin's down and departed (a new world-and-Olympic-record *five* sheets to the wind) I took a long route home. Belatedly, I did resent having been cast as a washed-up loser whose life trails behind him like a pathetic footnote. It rankled that Lipsky could see me that way, as someone whose life was a done deal. Whose youthful charm and vitality had dwindled down to a slumped, sad reliability.

It rankled because it was too true, too close to home. Like Moody, I was reliable because I had no choice, no room to maneuver. My once happy home had been remodeled, reduced to a ten-by-ten jail cell with no windows on the world and no chance of parole. All I could do was be a model prisoner; take it like a man. Pace my cell with dignity.

That night, however, in a swirl of sweetened springtime air, I had to bust out. An ill wind got caught up in my five sheets and blew me to Miller Road. Sad reliability my arse.

There was a full moon, directly overhead and so bright it made the leaves black underneath. I could see in clear detail all the small square yards behind the small square houses, the one-time worker's cottages that soldiered down Lara's block. Fresh white paint on a picket fence glowed like phosphorus. This was a surrealist's streetscape, overly luminous and oversimplified, featuring some of the accoutrements of life (bicycles, hibachis) but no living creatures. It looked like a Walt Disney neighborhood the night they dropped the neutron bomb.

Lara's Dart was in its spot. Inside, on the backseat, lay a jacket I recognized and a hat someone had sat on. The floor was cluttered with books and trash, par for the course. As I catalogued the debris, I heard a shade snap up on a second-storey window across the street and saw the silhouette of an overweight man. Standing there in the bright defining moonlight, I sensed the police would shortly be taking a call from an overweight, insomniac, concerned citizen.

Part of me (the part that was five sheets to the breeze) wanted to stay and give them a taste of Estragon as they clapped me in irons. *I was never in the Macon County, I have puked my puke of a life away right here I tell you, here in the Cackon County.*

Or maybe give them Moody. *You can put me in your bug-house right now. Step right up, folks, and wipe your shoes on me—Moody's the name.*

The rest of me (the sober, slumped, sadly reliable portion) gave them back their happy little street and scurried home to my own.

It was a warm June day, though of course we were air-conditioned at the HoJo MoHo. I was at my post (necktie safely loosened because Harry, our beloved day manager, had gone on one of his see-you-later lunches) when a fifty-something couple asked for directions to "the beach." They were from Shipshewana, Indiana, the fellow grinned, "where the ocean is just a notion."

I laughed on cue and told them a truth the Boston Chamber of Commerce withholds, namely that geographical assumptions aside, they were a long way from any ocean beach that might be considered desirable. There was Revere, of course. They could take the train and be there in half an hour. "So we'll go to Revere," said the gent, interrupting before I got to the less desirable aspects. I felt compelled to make mention of "items" washing up on the strand, of "things" floating in the surf. Of gravel where they might expect sand.

In the end, he tipped me two bucks and they went to walk around Castle Island. All they really wanted was the smell of salt water, the long horizon, and a bucket of fried clams. I watched them go with a twinge of envy, which at first I misinterpreted, presuming it was about their day at the beach versus mine at a carpeted hotel lobby.

Then it smacked me square in the face: Revere Beach, on a summer day. I glanced at the date on today's paper and saw it was the literal anniversary. One year ago precisely, The Twoweeks had commenced. An entire bloody *year* had passed.

I should have seen it coming, but then again, why assign special meaning to 365 days? It was one more than 364, one less than 366. Missing Lara (and missing was a word that dramatically understated the difficulty of being apart from her) was by now a given, a constant, that might well go on for 10,000 days. That it was the "anniversary" should not have mattered. The fortune cookies tell it true: today is always the first day of the rest of your life.

That fine June day, though, as shirtless scullers glided past us on the glistening surface of the river, it mattered. Truisms notwithstanding, it made itself felt. Not so much the first-day part as the rest-of-your-life part. Cut off from those sun-drunken boats, imprisoned behind my wall of plate glass, I realized that for the first time in conscious memory I could not describe myself as a happy man. The rest-of-my-life seemed a longer darker prospect than it ever had before.

"Big fucking deal," I could hear my pal Fitz say, for such was his unvarying assessment of all developments, large or small. My perennially impassive pal, to whom such darkness was axiomatic and for whom any relief from it intermittent at best, drug-induced whenever possible. What saved Fitz wasn't drugs, though, it was humor. What had saved me thus far was dumb luck.

Winnifred was right when she claimed that life is largely accidental. She and I had met by chance. As definite as she seemed, Hetty had been the product of pure chance, a happy "accident." Really, though, everyone's birth, each specific existence, is fraught with a million variables large and small. The dance of sperm and egg alone—this one or that—can tip you toward Aunt Sophie with polio or Uncle Jack who swam the Bosporus at sixty.

Lara Cleary had come into our lives (first Winnie's, then mine) via a hundred uncharted variables, a sequence of one chance after another. And The Twoweeks? The dice had taken some mighty crazy bounces for that one to be dreamed, much less broached. So it should not have been surprising when, by chance, Lara and I finally did cross paths.

I was coming downhill from the Delmar Street playground (the one where she had found me and spoken The Sentence) and she was coming uphill from Mass Ave. It seems we had each wandered those quiet leafy side streets with some frequency through the late winter and early spring, and now there we were. There she was. Wearing a dress, for some reason I didn't think to ask. I did notice the color (pale blue, radically faded) and that the dress was sleeveless, with a plain white tee-shirt underneath. I took in the outfit. I was almost afraid to look up and take in her face.

One misremembers details. Lara seemed smaller than I recalled. She had been five foot six (and no doubt was still five foot six), but she struck me as shorter than that and more vulnerable, her face surprisingly delicate. Fragile. Lara's natural expression was one of an illusory sorrow, flowing from the liquidity of her eyes and the Renaissance Madonna conformation of her facial structure, the classical triangulation from cheekbones to chin. The tension between that visual suggestion of mournfulness and her actual joyous demeanor was a large part of Lara's allure, in the same way the tension between a horn player's serene countenance and the wild flight of notes is a large part of his cool.

"You're still here," I said. "I didn't know."

"Didn't you?"

"Well, not really. I mean, I hadn't seen you, or heard, you know—that you were at this party or that concert—"

"I knew you were still here," she said, in a tone that pointed unambiguously to my all-but-forgotten lapse, the stupid note.

"I shouldn't have written that note. I was just having a hard time."

"Were you?" she said, with hefty irony.

"I am, I should have said. Am having a hard time."

Then, shifting gears abruptly, she stepped out from under an invisible cloud of anger and asked after Jake and Hetty? "How are they doing?"

I told her about Jake's hound dog instincts and his relentless unspoken disapproval. Though it had happened a year ago, I told about Hetty's brief rebellion at Morning Glory, when she pretended I was not her father.

"What did you do? When she said that."

"That's not the point."

"I know. I'm just curious how you got out of it."

"I had them vet me by calling—"

"Your wife," she supplied, as my hesitation to speak Winnie's name stretched out.

"Yes, Winnifred was willing to vouch for me."

"That was good of her," she said, ducking back under the darker cloud.

Though Lara had me on the spit and kept poking me with the fork, I was adjusting to the fact she was standing there. I was becoming glad she was standing there and also aware it was happening, or had already happened: the quickening, the jump to a higher level of being alive. We had always been drawn together like atomic particles with no plan of their own, no powers of intention, and clearly we still were.

"It's a little strange not to be holding you. Now that here we are, I mean."

"That's the deal, though," she shrugged. "Whether here we are or not."

"It just feels a little strange."

"Life is strange."

"Love is strange," I corrected her. "That's the song you probably have in mind. But we could remedy the not-holding part, I should think."

"Should you? Because we're friends, and friends hug hello?"

"That would work. Or we could take a huge gamble that the FBI are all watching somebody else at this precise moment. Is Richard Kimble still on the lam?"

The hug was more a clutch of relief, like the full-body lock a parent puts on a child safely returned from danger. The kiss we slipped into might have lasted ten minutes, though. I suppose we must have breathed at some point.

"I might have two hours," said Lara, pulling back to assess me with a half-smile that said she might be joking and she might not. Holding my eyes, daring me to laugh or cry, say yes or say no. (Or to guess what she really meant, if she even knew . . .)

"That would set me back another year."

"So you don't have two hours?"

"That's not what I said."

We did not take the fastest route to the nearest bed. This wasn't a movie and, short of checking into a room at the HoJo, there was no bed we could readily access. Sex was present (even our ears were erogenous zones) but we both got that this was not about sex. Unfortunately, it was about something far more serious and frightening.

We did not take the fast route to anywhere. Absently, we made our way to the river. Still dazed, we sat on the grass, not far from the Weeks Bridge. Though our hands were laced together, our attention was turned outward. Toward the boys flipping a Frisbee and boisterously running it down, two girls basting themselves in new bikinis, bikers and hikers streaming along the footpath. The whole familiar riverbank scene was an upbeat flashback, a reminder that Cambridge was still there, that life could still be fun. There were still carefree people loose upon the land.

"So do you think we've successfully melted into the crowd?" Lara asked.

"I honestly don't care," I said.

"What if I care, though?"

"In that case I will too. I can be flexible."

"You?" But she was smiling, and leaning against me. We both knew it was her line, not mine.

Lara told me that the instant she saw me she had flashed on an image of two cats lying in the road, a snapshot that had stayed with her. She and a friend were driving a lakeside road in Scotland when they spotted the cats.

"Dogs in the road, absolutely. Black labs, yellow labs, always. But I couldn't remember ever seeing a cat lying in the road before. They didn't move, either. We blew the horn forever."

"Maybe they had made a suicide pact," I said, more caught up on the part where she and a friend were driving in Scotland than on the cats.

"There's always that. Would you want to do that?"

"Suicide for two? Lie down in the road together and wait for death?"

"Want to?"

"What did you call the poem, Lara? 'Cats in the Road'?"

"No poem yet. It's just how I measure surprise now. The millisecond I saw you, I thought of those two cats."

"I didn't think a goddamn thing. When I saw you. Just went blank."

"What do you think now?"

"Not a goddamn thing. I don't think thinking would be a help right now."

She put her hands around my neck and strangled me gently. I gave her a few playful puff-punches in the belly. After all the time and energy we had devoted to daydreaming one another, neither of us was remotely prepared for the reality.

"If this hadn't happened?" I said. "If it never happened? Might we have gone through life without ever speaking again? Do you suppose?"

"Hard to say."

It was hard to say much of anything, really. There was the "what to leave in/what to leave out" aspect, for starters. And though our hands were behaving badly, we understood our basic situation was unchanged. It was no less impossible than it had been an hour earlier or, for that matter, over a year ago, when we parted. The question remained: if we had not met by accident, would we ever have met by design?

Nevertheless, this chance meeting had a force or logic of its own. And while it could not change our situation, it definitely messed with the program. There was still no way to reconcile the principles threatened on both sides, hers or mine, hence no way to express the unspoken conviction that this time we were not going to let go cleanly.

So we worked without words. The topics and the emotions we had stored up were too large to fit into a small borrowed space anyway, much less into sentences. The whirling carnival of runners, dog-walkers, cyclists, and sun-worshippers seemed to speak for us, as shoulder to shoulder, temple to temple, hand in hand, we absorbed the faintly salted breeze blowing off the tidal river.

I know what was going through Lara's mind only because she revealed it to me a week later, when we took our next two hours. She was acknowledging to herself, after long resistance, that she was angry with me. I had not called, not begged or come crawling back to her, and I should have.

At the same time she was acknowledging (to herself, after long resistance) that she was not angry I left the note. She was glad about that. It had been a struggle, apparently, coming to these truths—or to these lies she had been telling herself. That she wasn't angry at me when in fact she was; that she was angry at me when in fact she wasn't.

"*This is all so screwed-up,*" she would say, strangling me gently again, for such was her truest formulation. But surely now (and *now* encompassed that first two hours and the next and the next) was the time for complete honesty. After a year spent incommunicado, nothing else made any sense.

I felt pressured to supply a parallel narrative, to offer some truth about my own state of mind: where I stood, once divested of lies and disguises. I had become so habituated to disguise, though, that I hardly knew how to step out of character, out of costume. I had lost the ability to follow ideas in a straight line, to a sound conclusion. Even when I tried to convey them to myself in the night silence, I tangled them in knots. Tangled them up with God, of all people.

I did not dismiss or ridicule the notion of "true love." Of love not as a means of selling magazines or Valentine cards, nor as an immature state of mind or a passing fancy. I did not discount the possibility that love could be akin to silver or tin, something hard and deeply embedded, so that when you mined it out it could not be reduced or dissolved. It was not a gas or a liquid, it was a solid.

That was a fairly straight line: love was the gold standard and I loved Lara Cleary. Yet even setting my feelings for Winnie aside, there was no question I loved Jake and Hetty. That much was bedrock. If there were different kinds of love, which kind should take precedence? Which love was greater in God's eyes?

Oh yes, after decades of disdain, I found myself involving Him. Churches were fine by me. They were community centers, where goodhearted people came together over coffee and crullers on Sundays. God, however, was obviously a wishful construct, a desperate metaphor—the outward expression of a universal need that nevertheless went unattended century after century. Pray for peace or justice? For man's humanity to man? Get out your very best prayer rug and give it a try.

Such was my belief system: no belief. To believe in God (or in a benign God) you had to make a leap of faith far beyond the objective and observable. Beyond silver and tin, beyond the trees He supposedly made, or the houses we made from them. God was no different to me than the Tooth Fairy or Santa Claus. To conclude otherwise was to blink away 100% of what you knew. It took a fool.

Now, for the first time since I was eight years old, I was that fool. God had lost me when I found out He once required Abraham to sacrifice Isaac—to kill his own son—as a sign of respect. I had no grasp of the War or Hiroshima or the Holocaust, each of which my own father took as proofs that God must have died, a popular strophe at the time. I only knew that God had told a father to kill his son for no reason.

Now I saw a different lesson in that Old Testament parable. Clearly God had made this demand the definitive test, the hardest choice. No greater sacrifice could be asked because nothing could be stronger or more important than a father's love for his son. Face it, God did not say to Abraham, "Bring Sarah, bring your wife." It was the sacrifice of Isaac that would prove the man's faith.

To sacrifice a child, or two children, so you could go to bed with someone other than their mother? Go to Revere Beach, or to a Conway Twitty concert? It was absurd to believe God was ambiguous on the matter.

I could hardly communicate this tangled "truth" to Lara. I couldn't begin to summarize my three A.M. debates with God, with my parents, and with good old Father McGowan. Whether it was useful or not, the truth I had to offer was simple: I did love her. I needed her as much as she needed me and I could offer myself, my physical and emotional presence, in whatever creative way she could devise. After all, she had come up with The Twoweeks.

But I could not sacrifice my children.

Lara had never been willing to have an affair. That was why The Twoweeks had to end after two weeks. To her this was a matter of principle, not of mere semantics, and I respected her position completely. Yet now in our time of truth-telling (or blood-letting) she felt obliged to speak of casual affairs undertaken last autumn, in Europe. For Lara had gone abroad on her own; Ian had not gone with her.

I was obliged to listen. I was expected (since these affairs were "casual" and also "useful" for clarifying her state of mind) to remain emotionally neutral as I listened. In effect, Lara's honesty required me to be dishonest. If I rolled over on my back and started kicking my feet in the air in jealous protest, the conversation could not have continued.

At some juncture in a succession (she tossed the word off so lightly, a succession) of arbitrary "liaisons" (another casual usage, equally fraught with referred pain), she had begun asking herself this question: if she was signing on for ill-considered, self-destructive relationships, why not ours?

One answer she provided herself was control. She had invented those relationships. She had drawn up the terms. They could not harm her the way ours could, and they could not harm my children. Plus it seems that Ian had condoned them.

Then there was her fear that an open-ended connection ("a skulking back-alley affair," as she invariably called it) would risk losing everything that had impelled us together in the first place. This one made my head spin. Hadn't that been her precise goal in The Twoweeks? To lose everything that impelled us together? Now she was torn between destroying our bond and preserving it! It was "worth something" even if we couldn't have it.

So for both of us, this was a time for tortured logic. As each new two hours drew to a close, we would arrange for "one more rendezvous to sort things out," whatever that meant. To me, it likely meant backsliding into carnal sin; to Lara it meant continuing (or concluding) the conversation. On her way home, in any case, she would regain her senses, revisit first principles, and decide to cancel the sorting-out.

The first time this happened, she had an opportunity to convey the decision almost immediately, when by truly perverse chance we both found ourselves at the Turtle Café for dinner. Lara with Ian, and I with Winnifred.

Lara's balmy father saved our bacon that time. Only small talk was made, and all that small talk was deflected toward and filtered through Francis Xavier Cleary. It even helped that he was hard of hearing, as each harmless remark needed repeating. But as the restroom relay began, Lara managed a whispered aside: "Cal, we can't. I can't, anymore. Okay?"

I'm sure I was white as an albino coming back to the dessert and coffee after that little zinger. It felt like a version of the Cosa Nostra kiss: the embrace and the muffled shot to the gut.

At the slid-together tables, Ian, in bizarrely high spirits, was not only offering Winnie a taste of his flan but actually feeding it to her. He asked Lara's dad to pass the cream, got no response, and with hearty familial cheer promised to buy him an ear trumpet next Christmas. He even had a line for me: "You look relieved, Cal."

I had relieved myself—that was the joke, of course—but I am sure he could see I was the opposite of relieved, *burdened*, I suppose. Gutshot, by his damned wife.


That would turn out to be the first, not the last, of Lara's pained resolutions. There would be more meetings and more partings, and she would be proven right about losing the magic we had. Even when it was rousing between the sheets, we did not laugh a lot. The buoyancy of the past had been displaced by a leaden acquiescence. Our drive to meet derived less from the benefits of being together than from the deficits of being apart.

"Nothing has changed, Cal," she would remind me. "You know that, right? We have no reason to be here."

Did Lara want things to change, though? Did she want me to ditch Winnie and the kids? Was it even certain she would ditch Ian? These were the seismic questions we shied from even asking; this was where the honesty stopped. If we were going to take up such inquiries, we had better be ready to act on our conclusions and I don't think we were.

I know that both of us hated the aspect of melodrama that had entered our lives. Among other things, The Twoweeks had been a brilliant counterpoint to melodrama. It had been proposed as one part frivolous lark, two parts cold business arrangement.

Lara liked to describe herself as a realist. Even professionally. Though they all wrote prose, not poetry, she revered Tolstoy and Flaubert above all others, honored Chekhov and Maupassant. These were the writers who seemed able to transfer life directly onto the page unaltered. As we fell into a scattered pattern of assignations (as it began to be an affair, albeit unapproved and undefined as any such thing), Lara undertook to reread those master realists and soon discovered that Realism was a little scary.

"This is too obvious," she said, in a conversation that for us at that time passed for humor, "but I had kind of forgotten that both Emma Bovary and Anna Karenina kill themselves in the end."

"Remember, though: they never really lived," I comforted her, adding that we would be extremely odd twentieth-century American citizens if we allowed characters in nineteenth-century European literature any voice in our decisions.

Decisions, though? We were on our own there, and for my part I was still as incapacitated as Hamlet. I could make the hard choices, I just couldn't make them the same way two days running or, accordingly, act on them. I was like the cigarette smoker who has quit a hundred times—one step forward, one step back.

Lara never pushed. If she wanted me to be free for her, she would no sooner demand it than she would ask Abraham to sacrifice Isaac. She would simply remind me there was no upper case Us, and then pronounce the lower case us kaput, yet again.

I ransacked the text of the play for clues. Did Shakespeare see Hamlet as a pathetic man of weak character, or as a man facing an insoluble problem? What could Hamlet have done to avoid the orgy of madness and death to which the tragedy descends? What had he *missed*? What was I missing?

I never brought these maunderings of mine to Lara. *Hamlet* was arguably the greatest tragedy ever written and we were just modern people with a made-for-TV conflict. I did waste a few brain cells on Lipsky's theory that if television had existed in 1600, Shakespeare would have been writing for the networks. Who knows, maybe Shakespeare would have elevated our made-for-TV problem to something grander.

Obviously, I needed to set aside idle thinking and come clean with my wife, but that was another hard choice I made too many times. One night I was literally forming the first sentence of my confession when Winnie woke up shaking from a bad dream. Lost inside my own waking reverie, I was surprised to discover she had been asleep. Holding her as she subsided, I lost all momentum, lost conviction, never said a word.

Winnie herself might be the one to set things in motion. Indeed, that was part of the case for telling her: this was her life too. Infuriated, she might kick me out unceremoniously. Injured, she might insist I end all contact with Lara and commit to our marriage—or *else* be kicked out unceremoniously. Unfortunately, these outcomes boiled down to the same two I already had in my power. To shift the burden onto Winnie seemed worse than weak, it seemed cowardly. To tell or not to tell, cowardly either way.

Thus Lara and I stumbled along without definition. It was never every other Monday, or every third Wednesday, because it was *not* an affair. Nothing could be assumed, much less taken for granted. Lara might say, as we were parting, "I don't want to make a plan, let's just let it go for now."

Did this refer to the relationship as a whole, or merely to the specifics of a future rendezvous? Lara did not clarify and I did not seek clarification. Then after we had met again (and had done so because I dropped a note on the seat of the Dart) she would say, "Don't leave me any more notes, Cal. Just stay the hell off my street."

I would comply, and withdraw for a week, two weeks, or more, at which point she would put on her sunglasses and hat and come strolling up to the HoJo MoHo desk. Because by now, of course, we did know how to find one another.

# 8

# Boxing Day

(DECEMBER 26, 2008)

"Fairlee's next," said Jake, in his comic train-conductor voice. "All out for Fairlee."

"We can't stop, Jake," said his sister Hetty. "We do not have time to stop."

"I know I know, but we have to stop anyway. I can't see out the back window."

"Fine, scrape the window. But we can't go in and eat anything. We're only an hour away."

"True, but if we went in and ate just pie?—then we'd be an hour-and-a-half away!"

"I want cherry," said Al, from the way-back.

"No, baby," said his mother Cicely.

"Maybe baby," sang Jake, a snatch of the old Buddy Holly song.

"I wouldn't entirely mind a pit stop," said Iris. "But any pie had better be secret. Dad's making the banana cream especially for someone."

"Secret pie sounds good to me," said Jake.

"I want *cherry*," reiterated Al.

"That's cool, bud, they'll have that too. What do you say, Cissy? Just pie, no ice cream, and only for those who want it."

"That's so considerate of you, dear. We're not *required* to eat a piece of pie?"

"All's fair at the Fairlee Diner."

They were the only patrons. Late on a Friday afternoon, snow falling. The waitress (Connie, embroidered in script on the pocket of her dress) said they had just been debating whether to close early.

"We'll be quick," Cicely assured her.

"No problem, honey," said Connie. "You take your time."

"We'd like to try the secret pie," said Jake, with a wink for his son (no worries, cherry pie would be forthcoming) "but I'm not sure how many. Show of hands?"

Five hands went up, Cicely abstaining. All the secret pies would be cherry, Jake specified, and only his would require a scoop of ice cream. "Chocolate or vanilla?" said Connie, in a slightly weary just-the-facts tone.

Out the front windows, on the Route 5 side of the diner, eighteen-wheelers would occasionally obliterate the prospect and shake the glassware in passing. In back, at the base of a steep declivity, the ice-fringed Connecticut River made its way between snowy fields that were taxed in Vermont and snowy fields that were taxed in New Hampshire.

Hetty, always fascinated by the arbitrary nature of borders, wondered aloud who paid higher taxes and whether they complained about it constantly. Iris (soon to be a doctor *without* borders) shrugged and rubbed her eyes.

"You feeling okay, I.?" Jake asked her.

"Just tired. I was on nights this week and we were busy nonstop. Three A.M., four A.M. . . ."

"Why don't you snoozle for an hour? When we get back on the road."

"Yeah, right. With Al and Lorna on a sugar high?"

"Sit up front with me."

"In the death seat?"

"We can talk."

"And this would be while I'm snoozing?"

"Four A.M. on a weekday?" said Cicely. "I would have guessed everyone was sleeping."

"Teenagers don't sleep. They stay out late crashing cars. They also drink and drug and get sick a lot. The flu has started. There was a heart attack—a real one. We get ten false alarms for every real heart attack."

"Heart attacks that turn out to be indigestion, you mean."

"Or anxiety. I used to hate false alarms, sort of like who needs *this*, but I've learned to be grateful for them. You get to send everyone home happy."

"Iris, you are going to just *love* it in Uganda," said Hetty.

"Not a help."

"Sorry. I'm just feeling for you in advance."

"Do you remember the time we took you to the emergency room in the middle of the night, I.?" said Jake, though of course they all remembered. It had been designated a Family Event.

"I fell out of bed and busted my chin open. Graceful, as always."

"Ten stitches," said Jake. "I watched the guy do it. It may have been the inspiration for your career, but it was when I knew for certain I could never be a doctor."

"That happened the week you turned five," said Hetty, who then referenced another Family Event: "The Chuck E. Cheese birthday."

"Yuck E. Cheese, you guys called it."

"You insisted on a normal party. You wanted whatever Heidi had, or Heather, and they actually complied. They bent their value system for you."

"Anything for Baby I.," Jake ribbed her.

"Come on. Like they didn't do what you wanted on your birthdays?"

"I didn't want anything," said Jake.

"I wanted presents," said Hetty. "No parties. I hate birthday parties to this day, don't I, Lorna?"

Her daughter shrugged. Busy playing handsies with her cousin Al while they waited for their pie, she had not been listening to the grown-ups' talk, barely heard her name mentioned.

"There's a snapshot from that party," said Jake, "with Dad staring at the Chuck E. Cheese clown like he was one big contagious germ. You know the picture?"

"I do," said Hetty. "I also remember something really mean you said."

"Jake's never mean," said Iris.

"To Pop he was. He said if Pop didn't like the way the clown was acting, why didn't he apply for the job himself."

"Because Dad always thought he could do it better."

"Maybe he could," said Iris.

"Oh he could," said Jake. "That wasn't the point."

"What was the point."

"He always put people down for those gigs. Clowns and mascots at games, ads on TV—*commercial* work was the buzzword. Except when it was him doing it. Then it was always 'elevated to new heights.'"

"He was joking."

"Sort of. How many times has he told people he 'starred' in the last Brylcreem ad ever made?"

"He's joking when he says that too, stupid."

"Then how come he has the tape of it? How come he showed it to Cissy the first time I brought her home?"

"He did do that," said Cicely. "I assumed it was a joke too, though you can't always tell with your parents. The strangest part was his hair, all that dark hair. I didn't entirely believe it was him."

"His hair was dark then," said Hetty. "That's probably why they chose him."

"Come on," said Iris. "I mean, there were probably a million actors with dark hair."

"She's right, Hetto. Dad was just perfect for the role."

"Meanie."

"It's so funny you guys knew him with dark hair," said Cicely. "To me he's this distinguished looking silver-haired man, who must have always been that way."

"You and I watched that TV show, Cissy," said Hetty. "Where they dyed his hair red and pinned a red beard on him."

"That was weird too," said Cicely, laughing.

"That was his swan song," said Jake, because Cal had called it that, saying he would do nothing but Shakespeare from then on. "A principle," Jake pointed out, "he violates only when someone offers him work."

"Come on, cut him a little slack," said Iris. "It's what he does."

"Someone tell *him* that, is all I'm saying."

"Plus he is your father."

"No kidding. Hetto. Remember how we pretended it wasn't him on *Path of Gold*? Rick and Ginny would say I saw your dad, and that their mom watched it every day while he was on, yada yada, and we would say it's not really him—even though his name was right there on the credits."

"I don't get why you guys were embarrassed," said Iris. "It's not like that stuff was all he was doing. I saw him in lots of good plays. Or serious plays, anyway. I never actually liked any of them."

"We never got to go to plays. They would always say it was too late at night."

"That was just Mom," said Jake.

"Why do you say that?"

"Obvious. If Iris got to go and we didn't, then Lara must have said okay and Mom must have said no. Dad was the low common denominator."

"Low?"

"You know what I mean. The common denominator."

"Some of them my mom said no to," said Iris.

"Our mom said no to all of them."

"That's just your theory," said Hetty. "Maybe the plays were different a few years later. Less sex or violence, or whatever."

"We can ask them tonight," said Jake. "After we finish reading *Under Milk Wood* for the nineteenth time."

"Is your mom coming up?" said Iris.

"Saturday, I think. They're all coming," said Hetty, raising her eyebrows slightly. "Mom, Big Bob, and Little Bob."

"Last time I saw him, Little Bob was like six feet tall," said Iris.

"He's eight feet tall now," said Hetty, "Taller than Big Bob ever was."

"Anyway," said Jake, "we can ask Mom and Lara what the rules were and who laid them down. Then Hetty and I will know who to thank."

"You know what, Hetty, he *is* mean. I never knew he was so mean."

"You stop agreeing with her, Baby I., or I won't pay for your pie."

"Know something else, Jake?" said Cicely. "I believe I am seeing a few of those silvery hairs on *your* head. Check this out, you guys."

"Get away from my head," said Jake.

"She's right, bro. There's half a dozen on this side."

"So you see, honey, by the time Al brings his first gal home to meet us, that gal will not believe *you* once had dark hair on your ornery head."

"Unless I dye it."

"Not a choice," said Iris.

"You think your brother is mature enough to meet reality head-on?" said Cicely.

"He'll curse the gray hair," said Hetty, "but he'd never color it."

"Enough of this good clean fun," said Jake, standing. "Time to get back on the road. Hey, bud, get over here and get your coat on."

Al and Lorna had moved to the counter, to work the stools. Now Al spun his stool toward Jake, laughed at the coat idea, and kept spinning. Jake got there, applied the hand brakes, and spun him back the opposite way. "Take it easy, bud, you don't want to upchuck that gooey pie now."

"No *way*," said Al, and then—slightly concerned over the prospect—"Stop spinning me, Daddy."

They struggled back into their winter armor and stepped into the storm, their six heads angled away from a biting north wind. The highway lanes were covered with rutted slush, while curling waves of whiter uncompressed snow flowed down to the bottomland.

"Thank you, Jake," said Iris.

"My pleasure, Baby I. You know how I like to grab the really small checks."

"How much was it?" said Hetty, in her role as the detail person. She didn't care, she simply wanted to know. Everything.

"Thirty."

"Thirty bucks for pie?"

"Well, half of that was the tip."

"Oh, okay. I get it."

"We all do that, don't we," said Iris. "It's not normal, you know. My friends laugh at me."

"That one is on Dad," said Jake. "The common denominator."

"But my mom and your mom are both really generous people. Maybe all of them are big tippers."

"That's what I think," said Hetty. "Common denominators be damned."

"What about Bob?" said Iris. Because he only occasionally joined in when the "extended family" gathered, Iris did not know Winnie's husband nearly as well as she knew Winnie. "Is Big Bob a big tipper?"

"He just does the math. Fifteen percent, on the dot."

"So I guess not all of them are excessive," said Jake.

"All the ones who are our DNA parents, is what I meant," said Iris. "The ones who made us tip ridiculous amounts, like say one hundred percent?"

"It was the right tip."

"I don't disagree. I'm just saying."

"And I'm just hearing, Baby I. Basically, we all want Connie to be happy, right?"

The car had gone cold while they sat inside the diner and for a few minutes they hunched against the chill. Soon, though, the car became so warm that the unreeling wintry landscape seemed unreal, a sort of exaggeration.

Jake was about to do his standard "Cell phones . . . off!" routine when Hetty's phone beat him to the punch, forcing him to switch riffs: "Carlos calling," he said, "come in, Carlos."

"Answer, answer," said Lorna, though it would turn out to be her grandfather, not her father, on the line.

"Hi Pop," said Hetty. "We're getting there. Departed Fairlee at 1600 hours."

"I'm just calling to remind you about Al and Lorna."

"What about them?"

"You should go back and get them at the diner."

"You're guessing."

"About the diner? I know you stopped at the diner. I am guessing about whether you remembered the children this time."

"Pop, we only forgot them once, and they were hiding. Besides, Al is old enough now, he remembers anything we forget."

"So do I!" protested Lorna.

"Let me have a word with Al. Is he available?"

"Hi, Grandpa," said Al, wrestling the phone away from his aunt. She had tried to keep a hand on it.

"Hi, Aloysius. I hear you are getting old. Like me."

"Not like *you*, Grandpa."

"No white hairs yet?"

"Silly Grandpa. I'm just a kid!"

"Glad to hear it. Your Aunt Hetty had me worried. Now if you will be so kind, let me have a word with Lorna."

"She's asleep," Al whispered.

"I am not," said Lorna, grabbing at the phone. The two children fussed over it and suddenly their voices filled the car as though a flock of birds had gotten in.

"All right," said Jake, "Repo that sucker and shut it off. Tell Dad we'll be there in forty-four minutes."

"Passumpsic or Bust," said Iris, pumping a fist in self-mocking exuberance before she finally closed eyes and stopped trying to stay awake. Jake reached over and stroked her temple, brushing back the loose-falling hair.

The snow had been coming down for hours, blowing and swirling in the open fields where the wind had carved soft channels like sled runs. But it was tapering off as they came through the town of Wells River (the dark river, which they crossed just north of the village, absorbed each large flake as it fell) and by Ryegate Corners it had stopped. They had emerged on the other side of the storm.

This was unexpected, and cause for suspicion, yet proved to be true. To the west they saw pale blue sky and the implied light of the sun behind the tree line. Then in Passumpsic, where it "always" snowed, the moon had started up (an orange globe, a perfect circle, in perfect focus) so the fresh twilight was composed in equal parts of sunlight, moonlight, snowlight, and finally just the headlights of the car on the barn door, where they saw Cal and Lara crouched low, restraining the eager, excited dogs.